Moving Forward

SHELLEY
SHEPARD GRAY

BERKLEY ROMANCE
New York

BERKLEY ROMANCE
Published by Berkley
An imprint of Penguin Random House LLC
penguinrandomhouse.com

Copyright © 2023 by Shelley Shepard Gray
Penguin Random House supports copyright. Copyright fuels creativity, encourages
diverse voices, promotes free speech, and creates a vibrant culture. Thank you for buying
an authorized edition of this book and for complying with copyright laws by not
reproducing, scanning, or distributing any part of it in any form without permission.
You are supporting writers and allowing Penguin Random House to continue to
publish books for every reader.

BERKLEY and the BERKLEY & B colophon are registered trademarks of
Penguin Random House LLC.

ISBN: 9780593438107

First Edition: August 2023

Printed in the United States of America
1   3   5   7   9   10   8   6   4   2

Book design by George Towne

For Jeane, someone who knows a lot about moving forward with style and grace.

You can clutch the past so tightly to your chest that it leaves your arms too full to embrace the present.

—JAN GLIDEWELL

You don't have to see the whole staircase, just take the first step.

—MARTIN LUTHER KING JR.

Chapter 1

JUNE

*G*reg pressed a hand against the cool metal wall of the fire engine as Chip veered right. Through the window, he saw two pickup trucks hastily pull over to the side of the road as Chip, the fire truck's engineer and driver, picked up speed. "Whoa, cowboy," he teased. "The goal is to make it to the fire in one piece, right?"

"Stop worrying, Tebo. I got this. I mean, I do, as long as all these folks stop sipping their morning coffee and get it through their heads that pulling over for us isn't going to make them late for work." Chip blared the horn at a stubborn driver, then gunned the gas. After a second's pause, the fire engine lurched forward like it was in a Formula 1 race.

When Chip blared the horn as he sped through another intersection, Greg took care not to look out for oncoming traffic. Every once in a while, all the lights and horns played with his head—a gift that kept giving from Afghanistan. This was one of those mornings.

He breathed deeply and attempted to center himself by

silently counting backward from twenty—no small feat while traveling inside a speeding fire truck.

"Idiot," Chip muttered as he blared the horn again.

Feeling his vision swim, Greg started over again. *Twenty. Nineteen. Eighteen. Seven—*

"Greg, what's up with you?"

"Huh?" With effort, he pushed aside his numbered lifeline and turned to the person in the jump seat next to him.

Samantha Carter, a firefighter about his age, grinned at him. "You okay, T? You're looking a little uptight. What's up?"

He wasn't surprised she'd noticed, but he did wish he'd been able to hide his discomfort better. "Nothing."

She arched a brow. "Want to try that again?"

Irritation surged forward as Chip weaved through more traffic. Just in time, Greg bit back an impatient reply. The truth was that it wasn't just the sirens that had been giving him fits today. He'd been a little short-tempered during the entire forty-eight-hour shift. He'd hoped it was because it had been slower than usual.

Too much time on his hands was dangerous for him. Too much time meant he spent hours staring into space instead of actually sleeping. Too much time to think about how he hadn't gone back home to West Virginia to see his mother in far too long. Time to feel guilty for not being around for his youngest brother, Copeland, when he was growing up. Time to wonder if he'd chosen the right profession after the army.

Of course, none of that could be shared—especially not while Chip was driving hell-for-leather through the streets of Woodland Park.

He shrugged. "Don't worry about me, Cat," he murmured, using his pet name for her. "I'm good. Just glad this shift is almost over."

Sympathy filled her gaze just as Chip slammed on the brakes—before gunning the accelerator again. "I'm with you. I hate boring shifts."

"Four minutes," the captain said through their radios. "Fire looks to be contained, but be ready for anything. This is a garden center. Lots of flammable substances on the premises."

"Roger that, Cap," Greg said as he started fastening the buckles on his turnout coat.

Next to him, Samantha did the same. "Does that ever catch you off guard, Greg?"

He glanced her way. "What?"

"You know, calling another person captain when you were one?"

It took him a second to figure out what she was talking about. His former life. For a dozen years, he'd been an officer in the army; the last six, a captain. Back then, he'd had an answer for everything and was comfortable barking orders, certain that he was always right, too.

All that changed when one of his orders had cost a private his life. Though his actions and orders had been deemed necessary by his superiors, the boy's death lay heavy on his heart.

A couple of months after, plagued by a mixture of insomnia and nightmares, he knew it was time to get out.

Realizing Sam was still waiting for an answer, Greg shook his head. "To be honest, I never even think about how I used to be an officer." He grinned, just in case he sounded a little melancholy. "Heck, most days I'm positive that I don't want to be in charge ever again. Too much paperwork and red tape, you know."

Samantha looked confused but nodded. "Yeah, I guess so."

Obviously, she thought his reply was pretty worthless. If she did, that made two of them.

Chip screeched to a stop. Just in the nick of time.

Glad to end the heart-to-heart, Greg stepped out of the truck, Samantha on his heels. In front of them, a pretty good fire was burning, but as the captain had reported, it didn't look to be out of control. Apparently, lightning had struck an old scrub oak that should've been cut down years ago. Though the fire had reached the surrounding area, the spread was slow, mainly due to the storm that had just passed through—and the fact that next to the pasture was a field of plants and shrubs that the nursery owner was growing.

As he alighted and began pulling out the hoses to hook up to the hydrant, Greg spared a glance toward Anderson and Dave Oringer, who were in full gear but had unloaded a stretcher. Belatedly, he remembered that the dispatcher had said the nursery owner had a heart condition and might need help.

When he heard a loud pop followed by a curse, followed immediately with an intense string of orders from the captain, Greg focused on the fire that had just found more fuel. It was a blessing that it was too early for the shop to be open—or for any other employees to be on-site.

"Here we go," Sam muttered as she headed toward the flames.

At the captain's direction, Greg took a position about four feet from her and braced himself as the water surged forward from his hose. But still the fire blazed.

Within five minutes, another truck arrived, along with the big Mack tanker truck. Sirens filled the air as more orders rang out and more firefighters joined him and Samantha.

Spying a new band, he moved farther to his left and attacked the new flames. The noise from the fire was deafening, and even through his helmet, face shield, and turnout gear, he could feel the intense heat.

He was glad of his earpiece. Greg widened his stance and emptied his awareness but for the only thing that mattered: doing his job.

Thirty minutes later, the last of the flames were extinguished. Only smoke remained.

Greg breathed a sigh of relief and couldn't help but

reflect on how intense the moment had been—and how it had been quickly replaced by a feeling of satisfaction.

It was always like that. An adrenaline rush in the midst of extreme focus, the slight edge of panic without which he wouldn't perform to the best of his ability, followed by the sense of satisfaction that came from seeing only smoking embers.

And the all-encompassing relief that his PTSD hadn't kicked in and made things worse instead of better.

He stayed in position, waiting for directions.

"Sam, you stay on-site. Tebo, go assist Doc with the owner," Captain DeWitt ordered.

"On it." He dragged the hose to the truck, where Chip would unfasten it from the valve and secure it back into place. Less than a minute later, he strode through the open door of the garden center and up a short flight of stairs to assist their paramedic Anderson Kelly, known to most everyone as Doc. Doc had ridden to the scene in an SUV outfitted to act as an ambulance.

But instead of treating a gray-haired old woman on a stretcher, Greg found Anderson crouched next to a young woman with bright-blue eyes and a mass of strawberry-blonde hair. She was a little thing, though not skin and bones, her shoulders were lightly tanned, she had full cheeks . . . Pretty much everything about her screamed girl next door.

Except for the fact that she was agitated and holding an oxygen mask to her face with one hand. Anderson was checking her other wrist for her pulse.

When the woman appeared to tense the moment she saw him approach, Greg lifted his breathing apparatus from his face. Some victims were so shook up that being surrounded by firefighters with their faces covered up was difficult.

Of course, he was as sweaty as all get-out, so she was probably going to wish he'd kept his mask on. At least he'd just buzzed all his hair off. Otherwise it would be sticking to his forehead like gnats on a screen door.

"How can I help, Doc?" he asked.

Their usually calm and collected paramedic looked annoyed. "Glad you're here, T. Stay put, if you would." Anderson stood and held up a phone that must have been resting by his side. "I'm on the line with the hospital and the new guy in receiving is acting like I've got nothing better to do than hang on hold."

Greg chuckled. "No prob."

"Keep an eye on her vitals, yeah?"

"Yeah, sure." Looking down at the woman, he made sure to project ease and calm. Chances were good that she was scared and shaken. Lowering to a crouch, he said, "Hey. My name's Greg. I'm going to sit with you for a bit. All right?"

When she nodded, he smiled, just like they were at a bar or in line at the grocery or something. "What's your name?"

"Kristen."

"It's real nice to meet you, Kristen. Sorry it's under these circumstances, though."

"Me, too." When she attempted a small smile under the mask, he relaxed slightly. Kristen appeared to be coherent.

"So, how are you doing?" Some victims needed a gentler hand than others. To a lot of his coworkers' surprise, he always seemed to have patience to spare for their victims, even when they behaved erratically or angrily. It was only when things slowed down and he had too much time to think that he became terse and impatient.

"I've been better," she said in a weak voice. "Were you out fighting the fire?" A second later, she closed her eyes. "Sorry, that was a dumb question."

It wasn't exactly dumb, but the answer was pretty obvious, given that he was in his turnout gear and likely smelled like a chimney. What mattered, though, was that the question signaled that Kristen was more affected by the fire than she was letting on. "I did help out with the fire." Leaning forward a bit, he looked directly in her pretty blue eyes. "It's completely out, darlin'. You're not in any danger now."

She let out a deep breath. "I'm so grateful. If y'all hadn't arrived so quickly, I would've lost everything."

"I'm glad you didn't."

"Me, too."

Noticing that her pulse was starting to accelerate again, he reached for her wrist. "This plant shop is great. I've driven by here before but never came in. Is it your family's place?"

Some of the warmth in her eyes cooled. "No, it's my garden center. I own it."

"Sorry if calling it a plant shop was rude." He smiled at her. "Blame it on me being a small-town hick from West Virginia. I call everything by the wrong names."

"You're far from home, too. I'm from Houston."

"I heard that *y'all*." He allowed his accent to thicken a little bit. "It's real good to meet a fellow southerner. We're both a long way from home, aren't we?"

She nodded.

As he checked her pupils, he said, "When you're better, I'll have to stop by and get some gardening tips. I can't keep a thing growing out here. I swear, it's like even the flowers consider the air around here too thin."

"It is thin, but there's a whole lot more rain out east."

"That's a fact." Pulling out his best good ol' boy charm, he added, "And that, ma'am, is why I hope you'll be able to help me out some."

"I'll be glad to. Helping gardeners is my job."

He was about to ask her how a Texas city girl came to be living in the foothills of Pikes Peak when Anderson joined them again. Greg said, "Look, here's Doc. I bet he's gonna have some answers for you."

Her eyes darted to Anderson, but instead of looking pleased, she seemed stressed again. "Hey."

Anderson appeared just as serious. "I talked to your cardiologist, Kristen. You need to head to the hospital with us. We'll load you in the ambulance in no time."

She looked crestfallen. "Dr. Gonzales really said that?"

"He really did." When Chip and Sam approached with the stretcher, he said, "Here we go."

"I don't want y'all to have to lug me around." Kristen looked at Anderson like he'd just asked her to pick up a toad with her bare hands. "Can't I at least walk out of here?"

Anderson didn't give her question even a moment's consideration. "No, ma'am. It's medical protocol. There's still danger of fire, too." His tone turned even firmer. "It's better to be safe, right?"

But instead of agreeing, she frowned. "Listen, I know my heart and I know when I'm in trouble. I'm okay."

Greg realized Anderson was just about out of patience. What a surprise. Anderson didn't get flustered about much.

It was time to do an intervention before either Doc or Kristen started trading barbs. "How about you give Anderson a break, Kristen?" Greg interjected smoothly. "We're all just trying to do our jobs here, right?"

She turned to him, looking contrite. "I'm sorry. I'm really not trying to be difficult. It's just that I need to be here. My employees are going to arrive soon. They're going to wonder what's going on. Like I said, this is my business. Practically my whole world is in here."

"In that case, we need to get a move on, right?" Greg asked. "After all, the sooner we get out of here, the sooner you can come back."

When she still hesitated, Anderson spoke. "Please, ma'am. There really is no other option. Let me do my job."

"I'm sorry. All right. Fine."

"Thank you."

Then, like she was an accomplished liar, the fool woman surged to her feet, and immediately paled.

Anderson cursed. "Miss—"

Those pretty baby blues rolled back in her head. Greg

reached for her just as she fainted. Picking her up in his arms, he took care to arrange her on the stretcher. "She's a pistol, huh?"

"She's stubborn, that's what she is," Anderson muttered as he started checking her vital signs again.

Greg couldn't deny his buddy's assessment, though there was a part of him that sympathized with the woman's wishes. She was obviously concerned about her business, and who could blame her?

Seeing that she was already coming around, he smiled at her when her eyes fluttered open. "You okay?"

She blinked. "Did I just faint?"

"Yep."

"Your doctor's waiting, Miss Werner," Anderson said. "We need to leave."

"All right. Of course. I'm sorry for all the trouble." She barely moved a muscle as they carted her out and helped her get situated in the waiting ambulance.

Crawling in after her, Anderson waved Greg off. "Thanks for your help. I owe you," he added as the door closed and they sped away.

Greg stayed where he was for a moment, wondering why someone so young had a cardiologist on call.

"Cap is going to stay at the scene and wait for the fire inspector." Chuckling, Sam added, "He even told the owner that he'd inform the employees that the place was closed today."

He grinned at her. "She'll be pleased about that."

"So . . . you ready, Tebo?"

"Hmm? Oh sure, Sam. Thanks."

None of them said much on the way back to the station. It was just as well. They were sweaty, in need of showers, and they had to wash the engine before leaving. It was standard procedure never to leave work for the next crew on a forty-eight-hour shift.

After Chip parked in the bay, the three of them began a methodical inspection of the truck, hoses, and other equipment. Dave, who'd stayed at the station, came out to help.

"More hands and all that," he joked.

"Thanks."

An hour later, Greg was getting in his own vehicle—a sweet charcoal-gray Ford F-150 Lariat with matching leather interior—and heading home.

As he drove, he thought about Kristen again. He wondered how she was doing. Thought about how she hadn't asked them to call her husband or boyfriend. Remembered that she hadn't been wearing a wedding ring.

Caught off guard by the direction his thoughts had gone, Greg shook his head. He never thought about the victims they'd rescued. Obviously he was overtired.

It was time to eat, shower, and collapse. He had three days off and he intended to spend the majority of his time with his eyes closed.

Chapter 2

The hospital in Woodland Park was a good one. It was small, but super clean and well run, and the staff was kind and caring. Most of them were smiling and it was obvious they shared a great camaraderie.

All of which almost made Kristen feel bad about how much she hated being there. *Almost.*

She couldn't help how she felt, though. She'd spent far too many days and nights in hospital rooms—most of them carbon copies of the one she was in now. When she was younger, she'd done her best to be good. She sat in the uncomfortable overlarge beds, watched television shows that she didn't care about, played games on her computer, and read mountains of books. She'd been taught to not complain or put up a fight about needles or being woken up all the time or even about awful hospital food.

She was so over being a good girl.

While Dr. Gonzales continued to talk, Kristen pushed her bed's remote control. She needed to be sitting up as straight as possible for the conversation they were about to have.

At last he paused for breath. "Do you understand, Kristen?"

"What I understand is that I need to get out of here. Please sign the release forms."

Dr. Gonzales was her favorite physician and one of the best cardiologists in the state of Colorado. It was her good luck that he'd bought a house in the woods just outside the area and saw patients once or twice a month at the Pikes Peak hospital in Woodland Park. The rest of the time he saw patients at his office in Denver.

His credentials were so good, in fact, that she'd actually moved to Woodland Park for him; his opinion was one of the few her parents would listen to without question.

Since she had previously been treated at the famed MD Anderson medical center in Houston, that said a lot about Dr. Gonzales's reputation. Few other doctors had inspired such a vote of confidence from her overprotective parents.

The reality was as good as his reputation, Kristen had to agree.

Dr. Gonzales was brilliant, had received numerous awards and honors, and knew her heart and its faults like the back of his hand. He always found the time to call her back if she had questions and never kept patients waiting more than twenty minutes past their scheduled appointment time. That alone was something to be grateful for.

However, what was most important to Kristen was that the doctor was one of her favorite people in the world. He was easy to talk to, had a good sense of humor, and never talked down to her. She'd often joked that she wished they were neighbors instead of doctor and patient. He was the kind of man she'd want to share a beer or go for a hike or sit and watch a baseball game with.

Unfortunately, he was extremely difficult to boss around. Which was why she was still dressed in a hospital gown and tethered to three cords and monitors instead of sitting in the chair by the door and wearing tennis shoes and jeans.

"You had a pretty bad scare, young lady," he said with hardly a moment's hesitation. "Don't pretend you're not aware of that."

"I'm not." Feeling his continued stare, she added, "I know that I had a bit of a scare, but I'm also aware of the fact that I can rest just as easily at home." Yes, her tone was just a touch on the whiny side.

"My dear," he began as he sat down in the chair beside the bed, "do you really think I believe you'll have no problem lying in your bed bingeing Netflix instead of going at your usual speed? Especially when a portion of your garden center recently went up in flames?"

She couldn't stop the burst of heat that was fanning her cheeks. "I could promise not to work—"

"Sorry, but I know you better than that. A promise not to work is a pretty empty one coming from you."

"That's not very nice."

"Neither is ignoring my advice, but we know you've done that more than once." His voice had turned clipped.

She averted her eyes. She hated seeing that combination of disappointment and exasperation on his face. It was also pretty embarrassing that they'd played this game before. More than once, actually. "I am sorry."

"You should be. Now stop fussing so much. My mother would say that you sound like a broken record."

Kristen opened her mouth but closed it fast. She'd been about to apologize a third time. She really needed to get it together. "I'm afraid I'm not much of a bingeing type of gal, Doctor." She could say that she'd had to sit quietly in bed for far too many days to ever do it again willingly. But really, she felt that being busy was simply in her makeup.

"That's not a bad thing, but you're going to stay here and rest for the next twenty-four hours." He waved a finger at her like she was a naughty four-year-old. "And you know what I'm talking about, Kristen. Do crossword puzzles, talk on the phone, read a book. But whatever you decide to do, make sure your body does nothing but concentrate on getting better." Staring at her intently, he added, "Do you understand?"

Feeling cowed, she nodded. "Yes, Dr. Gonzales. I promise I'll be good."

Looking pleased, he inclined his head. "Those words are music to my ears. I can't wait to tell Ginger what you said."

Ginger was his nurse, and she was as chilly as Dr. Gonzales was warm and friendly. "There's no need to get Ginger involved," Kristen murmured. She'd put Kristen in her place with a pointed look that conveyed how she felt about Kristen wasting the respected doctor's time by not being a well-behaved patient.

"I promise, Ginger's bark really is worse than her bite."

Since Kristen had received more than a few biting remarks from the nurse over the years, she privately disagreed.

After checking his watch, he got to his feet. "Your test results should be in later this afternoon."

"And then?"

"And then . . . if your numbers have improved, I'll schedule your discharge for tomorrow afternoon." He stared intently at her over the rims of his glasses. "If the papers aren't in today, Dr. Jensen will have to make the call. Don't give her a hard time."

"I won't." Dr. Jensen was about five years younger than Dr. Gonzales, and a whole lot tougher. She always made Kristen feel kind of like a wimp for complaining so much.

He raised his eyebrows at her easy agreement but nodded. "She'll be delighted to hear that. Now, I must go. I promised Daniel that we'd go hiking after dinner."

"Thank you for taking the time to see me, Dr. Gonzales."

"I always have time for you, my dear. Now, be good and get better."

When the door closed behind Dr. Gonzales, Kristen at

last let down her guard. She leaned back against her pillows, pressed her palms to her eyes, and tried not to cry. She really hated crying in front of other people. She didn't like anyone to see her being weak—plus, she wasn't a pretty crier; within seconds, the skin around her eyes got blotchy. Her friend Chelsea always said Kristen looked like she'd gotten stung by a bee (or a swarm of bees) after a crying jag.

She sniffed and blinked furiously. Practically willed her eyes to stay dry. It was a silly concern, but there was something about being in a hospital gown and looking her worst that really got to her.

Lying in a hospital bed epitomized everything that she hated about her condition, pulmonary arterial hypertension, or PAH for short. She'd been born with a heart defect, a small hole in her left ventricle. She'd had surgery, but there were still a number of lasting effects that she'd carry with her the rest of her life.

Living with her condition meant that she had frequent checkups. Kristen had been poked, prodded, scanned, and x-rayed more times than she could remember.

She'd also been hospitalized several times over the years, leading her to feel like an expert on hospital rooms, food, and even personnel.

Woodland Park was just fine, as was most of the staff. But there was something about today's head floor nurse, Paige. In short, she and Paige did not get along. And it wasn't just because Kristen knew she was a handful for the staff. It was because Paige was always gossiping to her about a patient or a nurse or one of the doctors. Kristen didn't like the idea that she could be fodder for Paige's daily gossip rundown.

Oh well. Just one more day of sitting in this darn bed. Just one more day of hoping and praying that her latest test results were good. Then she could go home and attempt to repair all the damage the fire had done.

"Knock, knock," Paige said as she opened the door without waiting for a response. "Are you resting or are you up for visitors?"

"Who is it?"

"Would that be a yes or a no?"

And that was why Paige drove her crazy. She never even attempted to be helpful. Instead, she was always pulling some power play that drove Kristen crazy. Figuring that her guest was likely Jen or Alan, who had been working at the nursery yesterday, she nodded. "It's a yes. Thanks."

Paige looked her over, kind of smirked, and flipped her perfect hair. "All right. I'll let him know."

Him? Glad that she was wearing a zip-up hoodie over her hospital gown, Kristen pressed the remote on her bed to help her sit up a bit.

She heard heavy footsteps and put a smile on her face for Alan.

But the man who entered was a stranger. He had really, really short dark hair, light-brown eyes, and had to be at least six foot five. He also had impressive biceps and a scruffy beard. He was gorgeous. Period. Which meant she didn't exactly feel bad for taking a moment to check him out before sending him on his way. "I'm sorry, I think you're in the wrong room."

He paused in midstep. "Oh. Sorry." Looking a little taken aback, he looked down at his feet for a second. Ran a hand over his scruff. "I'm not in the wrong room, but I don't know what I was thinking. I should've realized you wouldn't remember me."

Once more giving thanks that she was more or less covered up, Kristen said, "Have we met?"

"Yeah. About twenty-four hours ago, give or take. I was one of the firemen who was at your nursery."

She had a spark of memory. Of this guy in a full fireman's uniform crouching next to her, of telling him that she didn't need to go to the hospital . . . right before she fainted.

She smiled. "I do remember you. I'm so sorry. I should've recognized you right away."

"No, I know better. Being in full uniform does cover up most of my best features."

She laughed. "Not your smile. I think that's the same."

His smile widened. "I was just here checking on the mom of one of my friends when I heard you were still here. I thought I'd stop by to say hello."

"I'm glad you did. Thanks for saying hi. Now, may I say thank you for saving my business? And for helping me when I was being stubborn with the paramedic? I shouldn't have been such a pill."

He laughed. "I'll consider myself thanked. And you're welcome, Kristen. I could say it's my job, but I'm also glad it gave us a chance to meet."

"I feel the same way."

Pointing to the chair, he said, "Mind if I stay a couple of minutes?"

She couldn't figure out why he'd want to, but she wasn't about to turn him away. "Of course not."

He sat down in the small chair like it was the most comfortable thing in the world. "So, how are you feeling?"

"Okay."

His expression was sympathetic. "Sorry, that's a silly question to ask someone who's sitting in a hospital bed."

"I don't know if it is or not. All things considered, I really am feeling okay. I hate being in here, but I'm grateful to have so many people looking out for me."

"Where's your family?"

"My parents are back in Houston."

"Are they flying in soon?"

"No."

He looked caught off guard by her terse answer. "I see. Well now, that's too bad."

"This probably won't come out the right way, but I'm glad they aren't headed here. I *asked* them not to come."

"I see."

She doubted it. "My parents are wonderful people, but they have a habit of overreacting a little bit." It was actually a lot, but what could she do? "Besides, I'm going to be released soon. I don't want them to go to the expense of flying out for no reason."

"When are you getting sprung?"

"Hopefully tomorrow." Unable to help herself, she added, "That is, I'll get released if I'm a good girl and my tests come back all right."

Amusement lit his eyes. "Is that part of the discharge form now? Patients must be good boys and girls?"

"It's a joke between me and my cardiologist. I'm afraid I have a pretty bad track record when it comes to following doctor's orders."

"Sounds like this isn't your first time in the hospital."

"It isn't. I was born with a small heart defect. It's all healed and doing its thing now, but every once in a while it acts up."

"You're the first person I've met who's admitted to having a heart defect but brushed it off like it's no big thing."

She did sound ridiculous. "And *that* is probably why I have to be given warnings to be on good behavior." Tired of talking about her medical history, she said, "How are *you*, Greg?"

"I'm good. I have another forty-eight hours off before I go back on shift." He stretched his powerful-looking arms. "I plan on spending most of the day tomorrow sitting on my deck and being lazy."

"That sounds like heaven. It's sunny but only in the mid-seventies. Practically perfect weather for sitting outside."

"A little different from the weather in Houston, right?"

"For sure. I really meant what I said. I am grateful for your service. Thank you for saving my business and myself."

His expression softened, showing that he appreciated

her words, but he shrugged, too. "You're welcome, but it's all in a day's work. Now, how about we talk about something else? How does a nice girl like you get into the lawn and garden business?"

"I have two parents who love to garden, fuss with the yard, and buy things to help them garden and fuss with the yard. It would've been hard *not* to do something with plants," she said with a smile.

"I'm jealous. I can't grow a thing."

"One day you'll have to come by the shop. I'll set you up with a couple of pepper plants. Next thing you know, you'll be eating your own jalapeños."

"I might take you up on that."

"I hope you will. Anytime."

"Thanks."

"T, you ready?" a petite brunette poked her head in the room.

"Yeah." He beckoned her. "Sam, come on in and meet Kristen . . . what is your last name?"

"Werner."

Greg grinned. "Kristen Werner. Kristen, this is Samantha Carter. She's one of the firefighters at our station."

The athletic-looking woman strode forward with a smile. "Hey, you're looking better. It's nice to meet you. Sorry you're in here."

"Thank you and it's nice to meet you, too. Thanks for everything."

"It's what we're here for. Don't make a habit of it, though." She winked. "There's better ways of making friends."

"Don't worry. I don't plan on being in this situation ever again."

"Good to hear." Turning to Greg, Sam said, "I'll be out in the hall."

"Give me five."

After Samantha waved good-bye and walked down the

hall, Greg stuffed his hands in his pockets. "I guess that's my signal to get out of here."

"I guess so." Kristen was sorry to see him go, but she figured she really couldn't ask for much more. It was already beyond what she'd ever expected, for him to make an effort to come see her . . . hmm, unless he did hospital visits like this all the time.

"Hey, Kristen?"

"Yes?"

"Any chance I could have your number?"

"Why?"

He looked taken aback. "Uh, so I can give you a call? Is that okay? Or are you seeing someone?"

"I'm not seeing anyone," she said quickly. "I was just surprised. Yes, you can have my number."

He pulled out his cell phone. "Ready when you are."

After she gave him her phone number, he texted her so she'd have his, too. "Save it, all right?"

"I will. Thanks again for coming by."

"I'm glad I did. And, uh, do me a favor and try not to give the staff here too much trouble. I'm glad they're looking out for you."

"I promise, even though I wish I wasn't here, I'm grateful for them. Enjoy the rest of your time off."

"Always." With another of his charming smiles, he exited her room.

When the door closed again, she couldn't help but grin. Greg was a hunk and he'd asked if she was seeing anyone! Even after she'd been honest about her heart condition.

If she was inclined to look for a silver lining in a bad situation, this was surely one.

Chapter 3

*T*wo days later, Kristen was home at last. Even though her apartment above the store smelled a bit smoky and she was constantly reminded of all the work and repairs she needed to do, it was still more relaxing than her hospital room.

The last twenty-four hours had felt like an eternity. Just when she'd thought she was about to be discharged, Dr. Jensen had come back in with a grim expression. One of her stress tests had generated some elevated numbers. They wanted to give her another round of meds and monitor her progress.

She'd spent most of the day looking at her phone. Telling herself to get ideas for a new garden display and to make a list of items she wanted to order.

Of course, what she was really doing was waiting for a text from Greg. She knew he might have been blowing smoke. A lot of guys said stuff but never followed through. She'd been hoping he would be different, though.

No, she'd been sure he was.

But, as each hour passed and she didn't hear anything,

she started thinking that Greg had changed his mind about wanting to see her again.

And with that, some of her confidence dwindled. She started remembering all the things Clark used to tell her. Things like how demanding she was, how she expected too much from him and not enough from herself. *Or that she was damaged.*

It took time, but she finally came to believe he was wrong about that. Wrong about a lot of things, actually. But maybe he'd been right after all. She *was* difficult. Stubborn. Simply too hard to love.

Or at least too much trouble for a handsome guy like Greg to put up with. He could have anyone he wanted. Why would he want a woman whom he'd seen be only either sick or difficult?

In the middle of all this self-recrimination, her parents called. They were in a tizzy about her being in the hospital, which meant she had to spend a full thirty minutes talking her mother off the cliff.

The moment she hung up, she took a long, hot shower and did her best to get a new attitude. For the first time she'd been up-front about her health history, which was a plus. Ever since Clark had broken their engagement over it, she'd run the gamut of denial, anger, and acceptance—with a good dose of tears mixed in. On more than one occasion, she'd gone on first and even second dates without offering a single hint about either her illness or her past. Then when she did share the information, the men were shocked—and more than a little annoyed.

Since it was the end of June, the weather in Woodland Park was absolutely perfect. Not too hot, no humidity in the air, and all her customers were eager to plant gardens and display flowerpots.

Jen and Alan had hung a tarp over the damaged section of the store. It wasn't ideal, but Alan had told her that the customers didn't seem to care.

It was difficult not to run downstairs and help out, but she was going to honor her promise to Dr. Gonzales. Tomorrow would be soon enough to jump back in.

When her phone buzzed, Kristen smiled in relief. Maybe Greg wasn't blowing her off after all.

Or . . . maybe he was, since the text was from Jen, announcing that she was standing outside her door.

Swallowing down her disappointment, Kristen let her in.

The seventeen-year-old hovered in the doorway. "Hi. I didn't wake you up or anything, did I? Emme said you might be sleeping."

And just like that, a little bit of her good mood returned. Jen had that way about her. She was a very bubbly recent high school graduate, and one of the best employees Kristen had ever had. She was also extremely close to her older siblings, Emme and Bill, and talked about them all the time.

She never mentioned her mother, though. Kristen figured there was a story there, but never wanted to pry into the girl's homelife. Every time she asked a question Jen deftly changed the topic.

Standing up a little bit straighter, Kristen said, "I wasn't sleeping at all. Actually, I've been trying my best not to look out the window and spy on y'all."

The girl flopped down on the couch. "I wish you would have. Guess what just happened!"

Kristen smiled. Jen could be referring to anything from a grumpy customer to a new shipment of garden hoses to a freak accident. "I've no idea."

"Ryan Halstead was here with his dad." Jen gave Kristen a pointed look.

Maybe she was still in a brain fog from all the medications she'd received at the hospital, but for the life of her, Kristen could not understand what that was supposed to mean. "I'm sorry, I have no clue who that is."

"Oh my gosh, Kristen! Ryan was our team's receiver."

Receiver. Ryan. Jen's giddiness . . . at last it all made sense. "So, he played football at Woodland Park High School?"

"Uh, *yeah*." Tucking a lock of her chin-length hair behind her ear, Jen added, "I can't believe you don't know who he is. He's been in the papers a ton. He's kind of a big deal."

"I'm sure he was a big deal around campus."

"He's a big deal around the *whole city*." When Kristen raised her eyebrows, Jen looked even more incredulous. "Don't you read the papers?"

It was obviously not the time to point out that neither their town nor the local paper was all that big. "Ah, no. I mean I haven't looked at the Woodland Park paper lately. I usually only pick it up when I've placed an ad. Are you saying that you do?"

"Kind of. Since my brother used to be such a big shot years ago, I still look at the sports section."

Jen's brother Bill used to be a star athlete. He'd played football in college and now worked for an accounting firm. Jen adored him.

"Now that I've put it all together, why is it a good thing that Ryan and his dad are here? Did they buy a thousand dollars' worth of mulch and plants?" Because that *would* be a big deal. Insurance could cover only so much of the damage from the fire.

"No, ma'am. It's better than that. They came here looking for trees!"

Kristen was still trying to figure out why Ryan's visit was so noteworthy. "And . . . did they buy one?"

"They did, but here's the best part. Mr. Halstead asked Ryan to come back on Monday to pick up some flowers and a whole bunch of other stuff." She took a deep breath and kept going at an ever-faster clip. "And then Ryan asked if I'd be working on Monday." She beamed. "And I said *yes*, of course, and *then* Ryan said, 'I guess I'll see you around.'"

As meet-cutes went, it didn't sound all that promising to her ears, but Kristen figured that she was probably too scarred by her bad relationships to recognize a good thing anyway. "That's great," she said at last. "I'm happy for you."

Jen nodded just before her expression fell. "That's why I came up here to talk to you. See, I've got a problem."

"What's wrong?"

"I'm not scheduled to work on Monday."

The girl was staring at her like she'd just announced that she was going to have a tooth pulled. "Boy, Jennifer, that's really too bad," she teased.

"Kristen, please? If I'm not here Ryan might think I blew him off."

Or . . . that she had the day off?

Deciding to put the girl out of her misery, she grinned. "Sure, honey. I was going to ask if you'd work some extra hours the next two weeks anyway. Between the fire and my hospital stay, I've missed a lot. We're behind."

Looking all sunshine and roses again, Jen popped up out of the sofa, a bright smile on her face. "I'll see you Monday."

Glancing at her calendar lying open on the coffee table, Kristen said, "What about Tuesday? Do you want to work then as well?"

"I think it's okay, but I have to ask my mom." She waved happily as she bounced out the door.

Kristen was still smiling about the girl's exuberance when her phone dinged again. Figuring it was either her mom or Jen, it took her a moment to realize Greg had followed through after all.

Hey Kristen, it's Greg. Sorry I didn't reach out yesterday— I ended up helping a buddy move. How are you?

I'm home from the hospital and sitting on the couch :)

Feeling better?

Much.

I go back on shift tomorrow. Do you have dinner plans tonight? I could bring you something.

He was practically asking her out to dinner. Looking around her small apartment, she winced. Everything was dusty and now that she thought about it, it smelled like smoke. And oh, she looked even worse than her apartment! Besides, what could possibly happen between them? She pictured women throwing themselves at him at all times of day. And at least one of them *wasn't* still recovering from being publicly jilted by a fiancé.

As much as it might pinch, she needed to stop things before they even began.

I'm sor . . .

Darn it, this was hard. Okay, she needed to do it. Now. Like ripping off a Band-Aid.

She forced herself to continue.

I'm sorry but I don't think I'm up for company.

I wouldn't have to stay.

That's real nice of you but maybe another time.

She paused before sending. Was she making a big mistake? Was she pushing Greg away because she was afraid of hurting him—or getting hurt?

Maybe she needed to push herself a bit. Dip a toe in the water, or whatever other stupid cliché she could come up with.

But as the seconds passed, Kristen decided that the "real" reason she was putting Greg off didn't matter. She wasn't ready to see him. Not yet.

She pushed send.

And then, like the fool she was, she stared at the screen, silently willing him to try again to convince her.

Several seconds passed before he replied.

Gotcha. I'll let you go. Feel better soon.

Well, there it was. She'd gotten her way. So how come it felt like she'd just lost? Hating the mind games she'd been playing with herself, she typed again. He deserved a polite response.

Thank you. Good luck at work.

She pressed send and then grimaced. Telling a fire-fighter good luck sounded pretty bad. Quickly, she typed,

I meant please stay safe.

This time, his text appeared right away.

Will do.

She gazed at her phone another moment, waiting to see if he was going to add anything. He didn't.

Which meant that she was getting the silence she'd implicitly asked for.

Too bad it also made her feel empty inside.

Chapter 4

*G*reg had spent far too much time wondering why Kristen had turned him down last night. Had he come on too strong? After reviewing his texts, he knew that wasn't the case. All he'd done was reach out to make sure she was doing all right and then offered to bring food by.

And she'd had every right to turn him down.

So, why was he feeling rejected?

That made no sense. They didn't know each other well. He'd briefly spoken to her at the scene and then spent a half hour with her at the hospital.

While he didn't often reach out to people he'd helped rescue, he had popped in on some of them in the hospital before. So, while his attention to her was unusual, it wasn't completely out of the ordinary.

But his attraction to her sure was.

He wasn't sure if it was her girl-next-door looks or the way her slight accent reminded him of home, or the fact that she was busy covering up her vulnerabilities the same way he was used to doing.

Whatever the reason, he couldn't stop thinking about her.

And it was obvious that she didn't feel the same way.

Rejection sucked.

Greg was still stewing on that when he returned from a quick grocery run. It was his turn to cook and he hoped it would pull him out of his funk.

Though some of the crew dreaded kitchen duty, he didn't mind it. KP was easy enough, and his momma had made sure he'd left West Virginia with a couple of basic recipes under his belt. Plus, it was an easy job when the weather was either blowing snow or blazing hot. Their calling meant they spent the majority of their shifts outside in the elements. Any time indoors wasn't a bad thing.

Unless he was on duty with a bunch of slobs.

He'd gone out with Sam on an early-morning call for a cat rescue. After retrieving the feline from the top of the owner's roof, he took a two-hour nap back at the firehouse. Then he headed to the kitchen to do some quick food prep . . . and was brought up short.

The area was a mess. There were dishes in the sink, cups and glasses on the counter, and even the remains of a sandwich on the table.

Then there was the refrigerator. It was packed to the gills yet again. Why didn't anyone other than him ever clean it out?

Greg slammed one of the cabinet doors shut. A little too hard. The clap rang out through the dining area and into the rec room area where the other guys were playing cards.

They all stopped and stared at him.

"You all right in there, Greg?" Anderson called out.

"Not really. *Someone* left a mess in here and now *I've* got to clean it up so I can make dinner."

Chip laughed. "You sound like my wife."

That was the wrong thing to say. First of all, he was no one's wife. Secondly, his mother would have his hide if he ever talked so disrespectfully about her—or about his future wife.

"Are you trying to tell me that you're the one who left your dishes in the sink, Chip? Or the plate on the table?"

"I don't know," he replied. "I don't think so."

"Really? Well, someone better have the guts to admit it." Scanning the room, he zeroed in on Anderson. "Was it you, Doc?"

"No, Greg, it was not."

Anderson had spoken to him the way he used to when they were in the service. Back when he was a captain and most everyone tacked a *sir* onto their replies. That tone was a sure sign that Greg was overreacting.

Unfortunately, he couldn't seem to stop himself.

Still playing detective, he folded his arms across his chest. "I'm still waiting. Who did this?"

The other guys looked at one another. Some looked away, others smirked right in his face. "You guys aren't taking this seriously! This is a real problem!"

Finally, Anderson came to his side. "What's going on?" he asked in a low voice. "I know the mess is aggravating, but it's not *that* that's bothering you."

"No, it is. Everyone's a bunch of pigs in here. I'm sick of it."

"Sorry, but I don't think you care all that much about the dishes." Not waiting for a reply, Anderson opened up the grocery bag on the counter and pulled out two cooked rotisserie chickens. "What are you making?"

"Chicken and pasta."

"I'll help."

"You don't need to help me cook. Just do your part around here."

Everything in Anderson's body language signaled that Greg had just crossed the line from irritating to flat-out rude. He dropped the chicken on the countertop like it had burned his hands. "It's all yours, buddy."

Watching him turn to walk away, Greg inwardly winced. He felt like a jerk. "I'm sorry. I didn't mean to sound like that," he blurted. "I've got something on my mind that I can't shake. I'll get over it."

"Listen, if you don't want to talk about it, that's fine, but you've got to get your act together. We're going to be living here for the next forty-four hours."

Looking over at the guys, Greg saw that all of them were listening and not even attempting to pretend that they weren't, either. He didn't blame them; he would've acted the same way. "Sorry, everyone. I was out of line. I don't know what's eating me, but I'll snap out of it."

Dave brushed off his apology with a wave of his hand. "No worries."

Feeling more at ease, Greg found the bacon he'd bought and started frying five strips in a cast-iron skillet. He was making pasta carbonara, his go-to dish for the crew on duty. It was easy to make, filling, and full of carbs. It was also his mother's recipe, which meant it was pasta carbonara, mountaineer-style. In addition to the rotisserie chicken, he used frozen peas, canned mushrooms, and a carton of fake eggs—all stuff that his last girlfriend would have turned up her nose at, given that not much of it was fresh, organic, or keto-friendly.

As he fried bacon, he grabbed a trash bag and cleaned out the fridge himself, feeling good about every square inch he was uncovering as he worked.

While he did that, Greg also did some soul-searching. It didn't take him too long to realize what had gotten stuck in his craw. Kristen Werner had rejected him.

Okay, she hadn't actually *rejected* him as much as she'd given him a line. He knew all about letting someone down easy—he'd done it lots of times over the years.

Though Kristen hadn't been playing him, he still felt like he'd been brushed off. Oh, she'd been sweet and kind about it. As sweet and kind as one could be while saying no thanks. And to please leave her alone.

But it stung, all the same.

He cut up most of the chickens and placed the carcasses in a ziplock bag. He'd take those home and make soup.

Grabbing a pair of tongs, he fished out the cooked bacon and set it on paper towels, then put chopped onion and the canned mushrooms to cook in the grease. The smell hit him in his gut, bringing forth a multitude of memories of his mother. She seemed to be always smiling, always praying, and never complaining. Not even when his dad died and she was raising seven kids on her own.

He stirred the mushrooms and onions a couple of times, added the chicken, and let it get good and hot and seasoned for a few minutes.

At last, he added the eggs, cream, and a bunch of noodles, finally crumbling up the bacon and adding it and the peas to the mix, too.

Turning the flame down low, he stirred and thought some more. And realized that his ego had gotten inflated. That was why he was so off-kilter. He wasn't used to getting blown off.

The fact of the matter was that he was a fairly good-looking guy. He was also a confident one. Add that he'd been an army officer and he had garnered more than a little female attention. He was used to women acting pleased by his interest—not like he was annoying them. Feeling his cheeks heat, he grunted. His sisters would be giving him grief coming and going if they ever heard him so full of himself.

They'd be right to do it, too.

Now he was upset with himself for becoming that guy. The guy who'd strayed so far from the man his mother had raised him and his brothers to be.

Maybe what he needed was to go home. Mom still lived in the modest house they all grew up in. His brother Drew lived just down the street and Rachel, Quinn, Stacey, and Copeland all lived within five miles. Only he and Hope— the baby of the family—lived outside West Virginia.

Yeah, next vacation was going to be heading back to

Beckley instead of skiing or to the beach. He needed to be around home and memories and learn to relax again. His family would put him back on track within a quick ten minutes.

"When you gonna stop stirring and let us eat, Tebo?" Mark asked.

"Hmm? Sorry." Greg put down the spoon and stepped away. "It's all done, help yourselves."

Samantha picked up a pasta bowl and grabbed the tongs he'd left on the counter. "I tell you what, Greg, this stuff is amazing. It's so good I don't even care that it's got about a thousand calories."

"My sisters used to say the same thing."

She smiled at him. "I'm picturing you with a couple of sisters. Did you boss them around all the time when y'all were little?"

He laughed at the image. "Ah, not even a little bit. I'm the middle kid out of seven. I got it from all sides growing up."

"Seven? Your mother was obviously a saint." She raised an eyebrow. "Either that or tough as nails."

"She *was* tough, but sweet as could be. We all adored her. My dad especially." His father always said that their mother was right even when she wasn't. "Back home, everyone would say my momma raised me right."

Dave grinned. "I bet your dad has his hands full, now that they're empty nesters."

"He never seemed to mind my mother's drill sergeant ways." Greg shrugged. "He died when I was in the army. Cancer."

"Sorry to hear that."

"Thank you. My father was a good man and my mother is special. I don't know why, but I was just thinking about home," he said slowly. "Shoot, it's probably guilt. It's been too long since I've spent time with my mother. I need to go see her soon."

Anderson nodded. "I think you should. You can't get time back."

When the bells rang out, it was almost a relief. "Car accident on the pass again," the captain said over the speaker. "Tebo, Sam, Doc, you go."

Samantha took another big bite before heading down the stairs.

Realizing he was leaving a mess for someone else to clean up—doing the very same thing for which he'd been faulting everyone else—Greg sighed as he trotted down the stairs. *You need to get your head back on straight*, he thought. They encountered enough crises throughout each shift. He didn't need to start adding things that didn't matter.

Chapter 5

Ryan Halstead came back to the garden center, just like he'd promised. That was the good part. As far as Jen Ferguson was concerned, everything else was all bad.

He'd been at the shop for twenty minutes but hadn't looked at her once. No, that wasn't true. He'd given her a stupid chin lift when he entered the store. It had been awkward, too. Because she'd been standing at the front of Werner's Garden Center like a greeter at the supercenter. Obviously looking for him.

But then, he'd walked on by like she might as well have been a complete stranger, half glancing at his phone as he mumbled something to his mother.

That was the extent of their interaction.

She'd even passed up a shopping trip to the outlets in Castle Rock for this. She was such an idiot.

Thank the Lord she hadn't told her girlfriends the real reason she couldn't make it. All she'd said was that her boss needed her to work. It was kind of the truth, though Kristen wouldn't have asked her to give up her day off. She was cool like that.

"Jen, there's a lady over there who needs some help. Go see what she wants," Alan said.

And . . . everything had just gotten worse. Of course Alan would send her to the one set of customers she really didn't feel like helping.

"Okay." But then she didn't move. Oh, she was going to go help Mrs. Halstead. She just needed a second. Maybe two.

Alan raised his eyebrows. "Anytime now."

"Sorry." Feeling a ball of dread, she summoned up a smile as she walked over to Ryan's mom. "Did you need some help, Mrs. Halstead?"

Ryan's mom shot her a surprised smile. "Do we know each other?"

Glad that Ryan wasn't standing there smirking, she said, "Kind of. I went to school with Ryan. I think you helped me once when our class went on a field trip in fifth grade."

The lady smiled. "What's your name?"

"I'm sorry, it's Jen Ferguson."

"Oh. Of course." She nodded like she was reuniting with one of her son's long-lost friends. "Ryan's mentioned you before. How are you, dear?"

"I'm fine, thank you."

"This seems like a lovely place to work. Are you enjoying it?"

"I am. Kristen is really nice."

"Where are you headed to school?"

Jen smiled tightly. "I'm planning to take some classes at Pikes Peak Community College."

"Ah. I see. Are you going down to the Springs? I've always liked that campus."

"No. I'm, uh, going to stay here in Woodland Park."

Mrs. Halstead's eyes flickered as she processed that piece of information. Jen didn't blame her for needing a moment to do that. About half the kids in her graduating class entered the military after high school while the other half went to college. A small number of kids simply went to work . . . and an even smaller number stayed home and took classes at the local community college.

People would wonder why a girl like her was one of those—a girl who lived in a big house and supposedly came from money.

Mrs. Halstead kindly nodded. "I bet your mother is going to enjoy having you close."

Jen nodded. Maybe her mother would, if she thought about things like that. Mostly her mom just drank and cried over Jen's father dying. That took up most of her days.

When Mrs. Halstead just kept smiling at her like Jen's appearance had made her day, Jen cleared her throat. "Alan said you needed some help?"

"Hmm? Oh yes. Ryan went to go grab some bags of potting soil, but I wanted to get one of these hummingbird feeders." She pointed to the most expensive kind they carried. Ironically, even though it was the most expensive, they were the most popular. There was only one left.

"I'll be happy to get it for you. I'll be right back."

"Oh, but it's on the very top shelf . . ."

"I've worked here for almost two years. I get things from up there all the time." Just down the aisle was one of the three movable ladders that Kristen had bought for the store. They were easy to carry and super sturdy.

She carried it over and locked the mechanism to keep it in place. "I'll be right down, Mrs. Halstead."

"I'll be right here, dear."

Jen had climbed three steps when Ryan appeared. "Mom, here's the five bags of potting soil you wanted."

"Thanks, honey. We'll go as soon as Jen gets that feeder for me."

Jen could practically feel Ryan's gaze on her, but she pretended not to notice. "I'll have it down in a second."

"Mom, I would've gotten it for you."

"There was no need. Jen said she climbs up there all the time."

Jen rolled her eyes. She might be a few feet off the ground, but she could hear them. She climbed one more step and paused to catch her balance. She had climbed the ladders a lot, but never as high as she was now.

"Hey, Jen, you want me to do that?" Ryan called.

Even though she had a death grip on the ladder, she smiled down at him. "Thanks, but I've got it."

"Are you sure?"

"Positive." Jen reached for the hummer box, but it was still about three inches out of reach. Great. Now she was going to have to go all the way to the top step.

Reaching for the edge of the metal shelf to hold on to, she took one more step up. Her body was shaking now. Gingerly, she grabbed the box and placed it one shelf down, where it would be easy to pick up as she climbed down again.

So that would be a piece of cake . . . if she could figure out how to climb down. When she made the mistake of looking at the ground, a wave of dizziness rushed in.

Boy, she shouldn't have done that.

"Hey, uh, Jen . . . are you stuck?" Ryan's voice was a whole lot softer. Maybe even tentative, like he was afraid he'd spook her if he said too much.

Which, of course, made things worse. Jen groaned inwardly. This was mortifying. Why did she have to go to work today? Realizing that she needed to answer, she tried to sound chipper. "No, no. I'm just . . ."

"Stuck," he finished. "Would you like me to help you get down?"

"No." Her voice quavered, so the word had three syllables. "Thank you."

Now all she had to do was move her feet. If only Ryan and his mother weren't staring at her, maybe it wouldn't feel so daunting.

"I'm so sorry," Mrs. Halstead said. "I don't know what possessed me to have to have that particular bird feeder."

"This is the most popular one. Everyone loves it." And . . . she was really being stupid now. She needed to get down the ladder and hand the customer her item. "I'll be right there," she added.

"Ryan, maybe you should help her," Mrs. Halstead whispered.

"Yeah, I'm on it."

Before Jen could inform him that only employees were allowed on the ladder, Ryan was halfway up and had his hands on her waist.

This was absolutely *not* how she'd ever imagined Ryan touching her! But the way he somehow made her feel secure and not self-conscious, she was having a hard time deciding whether to close her eyes and commit the moment to memory . . . or die of embarrassment.

Oh, he smelled so good, too. Like expensive soap and shampoo, and . . . Ryan. It was a perfect combination.

"What are you doing?" she asked the second she found her voice.

"Sorry, but I thought it would be better to grab you here than a lot of other places," he murmured. "You don't mind, do you?"

"No." No, she did not mind. Not at all.

"Take a step down. I've got you."

She was still holding on to the shelf with a death grip, but she somehow managed to glance briefly down at him. "I don't want to step on you."

"Don't worry about me. I'm good."

She nodded. At the last minute, she grabbed the box with one hand and placed it on the next lower shelf. Then took a big breath and stepped down.

If she was honest, concentrating on the fact that Ryan was gripping her waist did make it easier to descend the ladder. Of course, she was probably bright red—and she was still thinking about how *Ryan Halstead was touching her*—but she managed one more step down. When she reached for the hummingbird feeder again, Ryan lifted an arm, grabbed it with one hand, and set it on the ground.

Both of her hands were now on the ladder and her whole body wasn't shaking as badly.

So that was all a plus.

The minus, of course, was that now they'd always have this awkward, embarrassing memory. He was probably thinking it was too bad she wasn't skinnier. You know, in case she slipped or something and fell on top of him.

"You okay?" he said.

"Oh yeah. I mean, I'm good. Thanks for helping me down."

"No problem." Both of his hands had returned to her waist.

And she still hadn't moved away. Honestly, she could have probably remained where she was for another couple of minutes. An hour, even.

But she needed to get a grip on herself. "Hey, I'm okay now. You don't have to keep holding on to me."

"Huh? Oh! Yeah. Sorry." He let go of her waist like he'd just realized he was touching her.

She would've closed her eyes if she weren't suspended on the ladder. This was really horrifying.

"Well, now," Mrs. Halstead began in a bright tone. "I really am sorry for making so much work for such a little thing. But I guess the hummingbirds will be thankful for their new feeder. Thank you, dear, for climbing up there."

"No problem," Jen said as she reached the ground. "I'm glad I was able to help." She could barely look at either Ryan or his mom. "I'll, uh, go put this back." Grabbing hold of the ladder, she started pushing it down the aisle.

"Wait a sec, Jen," Ryan said. Before she had time to turn to see what he wanted, he was already at her side. "I'll help you push the ladder. It looks pretty heavy."

"Thanks, but you can't. This is my job."

"You're like five foot three. There's no way I'm going to

stand around and watch you maneuver that thing around the store."

She knew he was being considerate, but unfortunately, all she felt was embarrassed. "I need to do this, it's part of my job responsibilities. Plus, my boss isn't much bigger. She wouldn't take it well if she saw me acting helpless."

"Fine. I'll walk with you."

"I promise, I've got it."

He let out a low groan. "Boy, you sure are making it hard for a guy to talk to you."

She stopped so abruptly, Ryan had to reach out with one arm to prevent the ladder from continuing to roll down the aisle. "You want to talk to me?"

"Well, yeah. Obviously."

Jen was pretty sure she was gaping at him. Oh well. She was about five steps past acting cool around him. "Why? What do you need?"

"Uh, to talk to you?" His lips twitched, like he was trying really hard not to laugh.

"Okay."

Ryan suddenly smiled. "You're not playing a game, are you?"

Her cheeks heated. "I don't know what you're talking about."

"Other girls—like Gretchen—always expect me to chase them. You know, cajole, make up reasons to talk to them. But you're not playing a game, are you?"

Jen shook her head. She knew who Gretchen was, and the girl was not nice. Jen assumed she was nice to Ryan, though.

"You don't have to play a game or help me move a ladder if you want to talk to me."

"What do I have to do?"

She smiled. "Just send me a text or something?"

He stared at her for a few seconds. "Want to go to the movies on Friday night?"

"Okay."

He pulled out his cell. "Give me your number."

She watched him add her number to his contacts, then smiled as he texted her. "There. Now you'll know my number."

Mrs. Halstead's voice rang out. "Ryan?"

"Sorry, but I've got to go. I'll text you later."

"Bye." She went to the counter, where she realized Kristen was staring at her with a big grin on her face.

Great. She'd had a witness. And now that witness was going to tease her about this for days.

Jen figured she couldn't blame her. But she also didn't regret a single second of what had just happened, either. It had been awkward and magical and sweet and painful. It was the best moment of her summer.

Maybe even her life.

Chapter 6

$\mathcal{K}$ risten had joined Jen and Alan in the showroom right after lunch. She'd gotten a lot of sleep the night before and was feeling a little better. Well enough to finally assess the damage that the fire had done and to get a feel for how things were going at the store.

Tamera, her mentor back in Houston, had told her that customers could be superstitious. One robbery, accident, scandal, or fire would send customers fleeing to other stores. Kristen had always thought Tamera was exaggerating a bit . . . but now she wasn't so sure. There seemed to be fewer cars in the parking lot than normal.

After helping Marty clean up the last of the debris in the cordoned-off section, she saw Jen staring at her crush.

The last thing she'd wanted to do was embarrass the girl, but Kristen hadn't been able to not watch the interaction between Jen, Ryan, and the boy's mother. Of course, she should've told Jen not to climb so high on the ladder and absolutely not to let Ryan climb it to "rescue" her . . . but Kristen just couldn't do it.

It had been obvious that Ryan was just as taken with Jen as she was with him.

Now that it was all over and the guy and his mother were gone, Kristen could admit the truth to herself: She was officially jealous of a seventeen-year-old and her magic moment.

Oh sure. That might be putting things a bit too strongly, but that was how it seemed to her. Everything had to work together to make what had just happened happen. First his mother needed that particular bird feeder. Then of course Jen had to climb up to get it. Then that boy had to hold her so she didn't fall. Then he asked her out.

It was adorable to watch.

"I happened to see the whole ladder incident."

"Are you mad I climbed up there?"

"I should be. You know I would've rather you asked Marty or Alan. But . . . then I saw how intent you were on being independent."

"Even though I was scared."

"Even though you were scared," she echoed. "Actually, I was very touched. You went above and beyond to help that woman."

"That was Mrs. Halstead. But I didn't do anything special, Kristen." Jen sighed. "And I had to be rescued."

"That is true. But don't forget, you went out of your way to help a customer. I think that is special."

"Thanks, but I didn't just do it to help Mrs. Halstead. It was to impress Ryan, too."

"Ah. So, how did it go? Was he dazzled?"

She snorted. "I don't think he was dazzled at all. Actually, the whole thing could have blown up in my face. Instead of looking brave, I froze when I got to the very top."

"Oh no."

"It was awful. There was the box right in front of my face and I was almost too scared to let go of the ladder to get it. Then I didn't know how I was going to get down."

There were a lot of things Kristen wanted to say—

starting and ending with the fact that Jen shouldn't have been on the ladder in the first place—but she held her tongue. Instead, she looked at her sympathetically. "Uh-oh," she said.

"Uh-oh is right. Ryan probably thought I was going to break my neck!"

"I did come onto the floor in time to see him help you down."

Looking even more embarrassed, Jen nodded. "It was awful and crazy and kind of awesome, all at the same time. I mean, I've tried for years to get him to notice me. For him to see that I'm more than just one of the band kids." She lowered her voice. "Or the nerdy girl who sat two seats behind him in chemistry."

"I bet he'll notice you now."

"I think he will . . . because he asked me out! I couldn't believe it!"

"Jen! That's fantastic." Kristen wouldn't let on she'd overheard everything.

Jen nodded. "I know, but now I'm starting to wonder how I should act when we go out. What do I even say?"

It was so sweet that the girl trusted her enough to ask. Thinking of her ex again, Kristen shrugged. "I think I'm probably the last person to give you advice about that."

"Why? Because you're so old?"

Ouch! "I am a lot older than you, but I was thinking it's mainly because I haven't dated in quite a while."

"How come?"

"There're a lot of reasons," she hedged.

"Like what?"

"Well, I was engaged. But he ended up breaking the engagement."

Jen gasped. "That's awful. Were you surprised?"

"You know what? I was. Thinking back, I now realize that I should've been a lot smarter. The signs were there but I didn't want to see them. Now I'm glad I didn't end up marrying Clark. Letting everyone know that the wedding was off wasn't easy, though."

Jen wrinkled her nose. "That sounds like something out of a book."

"It felt like it—except that there wasn't a happy ending." She frowned. "I guess it left me gun-shy."

"If our situations were reversed, you'd be telling me to stop worrying and do something."

Kristen smiled. "You're probably right. And I will, one day. But until then, I think you need to take some chances and go on fun dates. You can tell me how they go."

"Deal."

The door opened again, and in walked Greg Tebo. He was in a pair of faded jeans that clung in all the right places, a snug, gray T-shirt with the word ARMY across the front, and flip-flops. In short, he looked like a model in an athletic catalog.

"Whoa," Jen said.

"Yeah," Kristen muttered under her breath.

Greg stood in the doorway, pretty much looking like he owned the place, and then focused on her. "Hey, Kristen, I was hoping you'd be here."

"Oh my gosh," Jen whispered.

Greg really did appear larger than life, with his model-worthy looks and intense gaze. So, she couldn't fault her employee for looking starstruck. She, on the other hand, was older and wiser. That should mean something.

Belatedly pulling herself together, she walked out from behind the counter. "What's going on? Are you having trouble with some plants?" Yes, that was apparently the best she could do conversationally.

Greg raised his eyebrows. "Uh, no. I was actually looking for you."

She could practically feel little Jen staring at them. "Jen, I'm going to take Greg back to my office. Let me know if you need anything."

"All right." Jen sat down on the white stool behind the counter but smiled at Greg.

He smiled back. "I won't keep her too long."

Kristen chuckled as they walked down the short hallway. "Does this happen wherever you go?" she teased once they were out of earshot.

"You've lost me. What are you talking about?"

To her embarrassment, she realized that he really didn't know.

"Jen seemed a little starstruck."

When he still looked blank, Kristen felt even more flustered. Now she'd gone and made a big deal of his looks— and if she tried to explain herself further it would make their conversation even more awkward.

"You know what? It was nothing." She opened the door to her office and gestured to one of the chairs near her desk. "Have a seat. I think I have a couple of bottles of water in the fridge, if you're thirsty. Would you like one?"

Greg didn't sit down and he didn't look too interested in water, either. "Thanks, but I'm good."

She'd been leaning on her desk, hoping she would look at least semicasual, but at his tone, she stood straight again. Greg really did have something on his mind. "What did you need, Greg?"

"Sorry to corner you at work, but I didn't want to do this on the phone."

"Oh? What's wrong?" She racked her brain but couldn't think of a single thing that would necessitate his seeing her in person.

"I'm not sure. Kristen, I'm just going to ask this. Did I scare you away?"

She was really starting to feel like they were having two separate conversations. Did he scare her away from what? "I'm confused."

He ran a hand across his features. "You know what? Don't answer that. I think I better say my piece first."

Greg, all six feet five inches of muscle and good looks, seemed both frustrated and upset. With her. Realizing that she was not only clueless about what was on his mind but at a complete disadvantage, she swallowed hard. "Greg, you're so much taller than me, it's a little hard to look you in the eye. Are you sure you don't want to sit down?" Because not only would she not have to crane her neck, she could try to conduct an actual conversation.

"Fine." He sat.

She sat next to him. Pretended she was a whole lot more at ease, and neatly folded her hands on her lap. "So, um, you were saying?"

"Kristen, if you aren't interested in dating, that's fine, I get it. I just need to know for sure."

It took her a minute to make sure she understood what he was saying. "Greg, are you referring to . . . is this about me saying I wasn't up for company?"

He nodded. "Was it too much? Did I come on too strong? If I did, I can scale it back." He leaned forward slightly. "I'd say I learned to be so assertive in the army, but I can't even blame it on that. The truth is that I've always been a little bit of a lot to deal with." He rolled his eyes. "My older sister Rachel likes to say I'm a bulldozer."

Kristen was taken aback. He was so different from Clark. Clark considered himself perfect and wanted her to be perfect, too. Greg, on the other hand, seemed to think he was the one with all the faults. It was really endearing.

"Greg, I don't want you to change."

"I mean, we can do anything," he said, obviously still in his apology zone. "Would you rather we go to coffee or something? You know, meet in public? Someplace you'd feel safe? Because we can do that."

She felt terrible. She'd allowed all her fears based on a bunch of what-ifs to push him away. "I promise, me saying no wasn't because of anything you did. I just wasn't up for anything. I'd just gotten out of the hospital—"

"I know. And I would've totally understood if you hadn't been feeling well."

"Then . . . ?"

He opened his mouth to speak, then grimaced. He ran a hand through his hair in an impatient way. "Boy, am I making a mess of this." He sighed. "Sorry, but see, I've let women down before with lame excuses that were obviously made up."

"So, that's what you thought I was doing. You thought I was giving you the equivalent of *I had to wash my hair*?"

"Pretty much." Greg met her eyes before quickly looking away.

Even though she was feeling that same knot in her stomach she'd experienced when they'd been texting, Kristen tried to think of the right thing to say. She was tired of hurting and tired of being scared.

But how could she explain her insecurities without sounding like she didn't have an ounce of self-esteem? Because she did. Just not around him.

After staring at her another few seconds, Greg got to his feet. "I can tell that I just managed to make a bad thing worse. I'm really sorry. I promise I won't bother you again."

She was being a fool and he was going to leave.

Greg was not only the most attractive man she'd ever met, but he was nice, too. And she was just about to let him think that he was a jerk. She could either let him leave and feel safe—or be as willing as he was to be honest and open.

"I was scared," she blurted.

"Of what? Of me?" A horrified expression crossed his features. "Oh man. Did I really mess everything up?" He lowered his voice. "Kristen, no matter what you think of me, please know that I would never hurt you. That's not me. That's not ever me."

"Of course it isn't." She motioned him back with her hand. "Please sit back down." When he gingerly sat, she knew it was time to stop guarding her heart.

"It wasn't you, it was me." She grimaced. "And I know that sounds like a line, but it isn't. The truth is that I haven't dated in a while. The last person I dated was my fiancé." And now she felt like a total loser.

"What happened?" A second later, he blurted, "Did he die or something?"

"No." She couldn't believe she was smiling. "As far as I know, Clark is alive and well. He just broke up with me."

A line formed between his eyebrows. "Clark, like Clark Kent?"

"Definitely Clark, like Clark Kent. He liked to say I had my own superhero."

Greg rolled his eyes. "I bet you didn't like him telling you that."

"At first I thought it was kind of cute, but he ended up being far from heroic."

"He sounds like a jerk."

"I thought he was."

"I'm sure he was if he took off on you."

She liked how he said that. Like she was worth sticking around for. She smiled. "Even though you don't really know me, thanks for saying that."

"My momma would say you're better off without him."

"Mine did say that." Feeling the need to add something of substance to the conversation—or at least make it not sound like she was difficult to be around—Kristen said, "He found out about my heart condition."

"And . . . ?"

"And he wanted a wife who—well, wasn't broken." She stopped there. No way was she ready to tell Greg the whole truth.

"Do you actually believe that you're broken?"

This was hitting a little too close to home. "I didn't say that."

"I didn't say it, either, Kristen. That's why I think you should say yes to a date."

Oh, this was hard. His eyes were dreamy and his smile was perfect. Worse, he made her think of all kinds of things she'd firmly pushed out of her mind. Things like love and romance and passion. Things like being a little reckless and pushing her boundaries.

Things like really living.

But what would happen when her body told her to slow down? Would the change be difficult for him to accept? Would Greg begin to realize that a lifetime with her just wasn't worth it?

"Thanks, but I don't think I'm ready." At least that sounded better than everything she was thinking.

"Maybe you are, Kristen. Maybe you are ready and you just haven't let yourself believe it."

She *wanted* to believe it . . . but realized that she wasn't ready to get emotionally involved again. It was better to head things off now, before her heart became even more attached.

Standing up, Kristen said, "Look, this is all flattering, but I'm not ready for a new relationship."

He stared at her a long moment. "Okay . . . how about this? Say that we can be friends."

"We can be friends," she dutifully repeated. Even though she felt deflated, she smiled again. "I'm glad you understand."

"I do." He shifted. "So, six o'clock on Friday night?"

"Greg, I just told you no."

He had the gall to look affronted. "I'm not asking you out on a date, Kristen. I'm asking you to come to a party—as a friend."

"Wait, what kind of party?"

"It's an engagement party for a buddy of mine at work."

"I don't know . . . won't everyone else there be coupled up?"

"Oh no. Everyone at the firehouse is buddies. Nobody's matchmaking there."

Greg sounded a little too glib . . . so why did it also sound like fun? "Are you sure you want me to go as a friend?"

"Well, yeah." Stuffing his hands in the front pockets of his jeans, he nodded. "Like I said, it's a party. Everyone's going to be relaxed and having fun. Plus, we're already friends. Right?"

She raised an eyebrow, just to let him know that she didn't completely believe his spiel.

He folded his arms over his well-muscled chest. "Come on. It'll be fun. Plus, you already know some of the other women going, right? Chelsea, Anderson's wife, for one."

"You're right. I do know Chelsea."

"So, Friday?"

"Fine. Yes."

His grin was almost blinding. "Great. I'll pick you up at six." After giving her a little salute, he strode out the door.

Only when he left did she smile right back. She was going out with Greg Tebo. He was gorgeous, fun to be around, and made her feel like she was the only person in the room whenever they talked.

Yes, she was scared. If she started imagining life as his girlfriend . . . and then he broke her heart . . . it was going to hurt something awful. She really didn't want to get hurt again.

But suddenly she realized something else. If she continued to push him away and he ended up dating another woman, that was going to hurt, too.

If that was how it was going to be, at least she'd have some good memories if she went out with him.

"Hey, Kristen?" Jen called out. "Can you help me?"

She got to her feet with a sigh of relief. Work, she knew how to do.

Chapter 7

*G*reg knew he should be ashamed. For most of his life, he'd used his smile, his looks, and his well-practiced charm to get what he wanted.

As a teenager, he'd been all about instant gratification. He'd been blessed with an outgoing personality and a way with people. He could talk his way into just about anything. On the downside, he'd suffered the consequences of getting his way relatively easily. Some things just weren't meant to be obtained without work, perseverance, and prayer.

His siblings had learned from an early age to egg him on. When his eldest brother, Drew, had a job delivering papers, he convinced Greg it was the best job in the world. Even though his mother said Greg was too young for so much responsibility, Greg had cajoled his way into sharing the job. Next thing Greg knew, he was getting up at four thirty to fold and prep the papers. Then Drew delivered them, and received all the tips.

His sisters loved egging him on to tattle on the boys. That would lead to stirring speeches to their parents about the latest sin or injustice, only to be scolded for his pettiness.

Over and over, Mom and Dad would sit him down and tell him to stop trying to talk his way into whatever shiny new thing he had his eye on. After each lecture, he promised he would try. And then he would go back on his word a couple of hours later, his promise already forgotten.

Greg talked his way into accelerated classes that he wasn't quite ready for, pushed to start on the football team when he should've been second string. He'd even wheedled his way into Officer Candidate School instead of just enlisting.

And now he'd talked his way into a date with Kristen and she didn't even realize it was a date.

All because he couldn't stand the idea of not seeing her again.

"You were right, Dad," he whispered to the empty interior of his truck. "My mouth has gotten me into trouble again. Then, there I'll be, embarrassed and regretful, but still pining for her something awful."

His phone rang, giving him chills when he saw who it was. Obviously, his father up in heaven had heard him whining and sent help.

"Hey, Momma."

"Hey, honey. What's going on?"

"Nothing. I'm just driving home. Is everything okay?"

"Of course. I . . . well, for some reason I just had a feeling it was time for the two of us to catch up."

He was selfish in a lot of ways, but he was going to give credit where it was due. "I know what happened. I was just sitting here talking to Dad."

"I'm sorry, what did you say?"

She sounded rattled. He didn't blame her, but he had to admit the truth. "I was just sitting here talking to Dad up in heaven while I was driving. I think he had something to do with you giving me a call."

After a pause, his mother murmured, "Do you do this often, Greg?"

"Talk to Dad?"

"Yes."

"Not so much. Just when I miss him, you know?"

She chuckled under her breath. "Yes, honey. I surely do know. So, what were you chatting with him about? Do I even want to know?"

He grinned as he stopped at a red light. "Probably. I was talking to Dad about how the two of you always said that my mouth was going to get me into trouble. Y'all were right."

"Uh-oh. What happened this time? Did you say too much at work?"

"No, ma'am." After debating a second about whether to share more, he added, "I said too much to a girl."

"A girl, hmm? Now, isn't that something?"

He could feel his neck heat up. "Yes."

"I didn't know you were serious about someone. How long have you and this woman been dating?"

"Not long. As in not at all."

His mother's laughter wasn't unfamiliar, but it wasn't exactly a welcome sound, either. "I know," he mumbled, hoping to prevent a lecture. "You don't have to say anything."

"There's no way I'm going to stay silent. No wonder you were talking to Dad. He was so proud of you, son. You did well in school, did your chores without complaining, and looked out for your sisters. You tried to get along with everyone. You might have tried to wheedle your way into things, but you weren't a bully." Her voice lightened. "Plus, you never got into fights like Copeland."

His younger brother had practically been born a felon. "How is he not in prison, Momma?"

"Hush now. What I was getting to is that your father knew you had so many wonderful gifts, but he was constantly trying to think of a way to get you to shut up and listen more."

Taking a right turn, he grinned. "We weren't supposed to say shut up, remember?"

"That doesn't mean we didn't think it, son. Now, you want to tell me what you did wrong? After raising seven kids, I'm pretty good at thinking of ways to smooth things over."

"This girl, this woman I met, Kristen, is pretty special, but she's got some issues and a jerk of an ex-fiancé. She told me flat out that she wasn't ready to date but I didn't listen."

"Honey, *that's* what you're upset about?"

"No, ma'am. It's that I told her we could just be friends." He sighed. "So we're going out on Friday night as friends."

"I'm sorry, but I'm still confused. What is it that you're so fired up about?"

Continuing his impromptu confessional, he kept talking. "First off, I lied to her. I don't want to just be friends. I only said that because I wanted to spend time with her."

"I could be wrong, but I have a feeling she knows that."

"Really?"

"I'm sure she's a smart young woman, Gregory."

Kristen was that . . . but . . . "When we go out I'm afraid I'm going to do or say something that will make her realize I was full of it and that I don't want to be just friends at all." He turned left onto his street. "Then she won't trust me, and I'll have ruined everything." When his mother didn't say anything right away, Greg added, "Do you understand what I mean? I don't want to ruin everything with her before I even get a chance to start something up."

"Well, I understand why you were talking to your father. He really was better at this sort of stuff."

"Actually, you're not doing too bad of a job."

"Thank you so much." She chuckled. "Here's my two cents. I think you're jumping ahead of yourself. See, I don't think she trusts you yet. So, you don't have to worry about losing her trust because you don't have it."

"Really?" This was a new spin.

"If she trusted you, she would've said yes to dating you. Trust takes time."

"You sound real sure of it."

"Dad and I raised three girls, son. As much as you seemed to think I was oblivious, I did have an inkling about what was going on with each of you. When girls like boys—and trust them—they say yes."

"So my no means . . ."

"Exactly what you don't want to hear, Gregory. You need to be patient. And stay in the friend zone."

"I know. I just . . ." His voice trailed off, unable to say that he might have learned to control his runaway mouth at work but not with women.

"Don't say you can't handle that," she interrupted in a firm tone. "You will."

"Yes, ma'am."

"I mean it, Greg. You were mouthy when you were eight, but you learned to keep your mouth shut in that fifth-grade science class."

He had learned . . . after he had to stay after school and help clean the rats' cages.

"And then you learned all over again, when you made the football team."

He had . . . after the coach made him run extra laps after practice three days in a row.

"Of course, we can't forget about how your sergeant didn't put up with your foolishness when you went into the ROTC, can we?"

"Yes . . . I mean, no, ma'am."

Sounding pleased that he was listening, her voice softened. "You were an officer, dear. No one would've promoted you if you hadn't learned impulse control. At last."

"You have a point." Of course, in the army he'd taken his responsibilities so seriously, he'd always been careful to weigh his words.

"I think if you handled that, then you can handle this lady, too. If Kristen is worth it, you'll figure out how to be the man she needs."

"She's worth it."

"That's settled, then."

"You sure know how to make a good argument."

"Where do you think you got your glib tongue from?"

Greg laughed. "I guess you have a point." Since he was almost home, he said, "How are you, Mom? Is anything new with you?"

"Not really. Sometimes I think it's a full-time job keeping up with all of you kids."

"There's a lot of us, especially considering that you have grandchildren now, too."

"That's a fact." A new tone entered her voice. "That's why I started to think I could use a vacation. That maybe I would go on a cruise, in fact."

He parked in his driveway. "What? Who with?"

"A bunch of people I met in my seniors group."

His mother had joined a seniors group? "Is this a new thing?"

"Kind of. They keep me busy and they like to travel, which is why I'm thinking about the cruise." Her voice brightened. "I'm looking forward to it."

"Momma, you're not a real senior. You're barely even sixty. And you don't like cruises."

"No, that's not true. I always wanted to go on one. It was your father who didn't."

"You're not just considering it, are you? You're really going to go." Just the thought of his pretty mother on some sort of Love Boat gave him the willies. Randy men were probably going to be following her around nonstop. And his mother was so sweet, one of them would likely get his hooks in her before he or any of his brothers and sisters figured out what was going on. "Mother, I think you need to think things through a little bit more."

"Greg, I mean this in the best way, so don't take it wrong, okay?"

"Take what wrong?"

"Your father died and I miss him something awful. I loved him very much. I didn't even mind staying home all the time because being home meant being with him. But no matter how hard I wish otherwise, your father is not coming back. No matter how much I pray or talk to the ceiling, it's not happening." She sighed. "So I decided I had a choice, right?"

Greg swallowed the lump in his throat. "Stay the same or move forward."

"That's right. I can either spend the rest of my days sitting home alone and missing your father . . . or I can live a little bit." Her voice turned husky. "Sitting by myself isn't all that great, Greg."

Greg felt like his father had just leaned down from heaven and given him a hard verbal shove on his shoulder. Putting him in his place again. "I understand," he said at last.

"I sure hope so."

"How did everyone else take the news?"

She laughed softly. "I haven't told anyone else. You're the first."

"Well, good luck with that." He could already imagine how Drew and Stacey were going to take this cruise news. Not all that well. Actually, not well at all.

"What do you think about breaking the news for me?"

There was so much hope in his mother's voice, Greg knew he was going to have to call up his siblings. "You know I don't love the idea. They're gonna wig out."

"You could put all your silver-tongued wheedling skills to good use for a change."

Oh brother. "Sure, Momma. I'll be glad to." He was going to get an earful from every one of them, but better him than her.

"Really? Thank you. I know it's not right, but I don't even want to think about sharing my cruise news six more times. They'd wear me out."

"How about this? I'll call and text everyone, then you can tell us all about your big plans at our next Sunday supper." They'd started meeting for supper once a month, FaceTiming anyone who couldn't be there.

"That sounds good. But you're not going to turn the tables on me and side with them, are you?"

"No, ma'am."

"All right, then. It's . . . it's appreciated, Greg."

"I love you, Momma."

"I love you, too." Sounding almost chipper, she added, "Good luck with Kristen. Bye now."

"Bye. See you next Sunday."

When she hung up, Greg finally got out of his truck and walked to the front door of his two-bedroom condo.

As he pulled out his keys, he realized that his conversation with his mother had reminded him that they all had important things to get through. Very few things in life were easy. Not things that mattered, at least.

All kinds of things were possible, though. All you had to do was take one step at a time—and maybe call for help, occasionally.

Chapter 8

*R*ing!
    The loud, jarring noise that invaded every inch of the firehouse had never sounded so good. Greg didn't actually want anyone in Woodland Park to be hurt, but it had been a really quiet shift. When there was too much time on everyone's hands, tempers started to fray.

"Thank the Lord," Chip said as he trotted to his turnout gear. "I cannot inspect hoses for one more hour. I was starting to feel like pulling out my nails."

Greg nodded as he adjusted the straps of his breathing apparatus. "Cap was on a mission. It was like he was sure that we'd never rolled the hoses properly in our lives." Now that he had his turnout gear on, he adjusted his radio just as Dave started the main fire engine.

Anderson was getting into the driver's seat of the SUV that he and Dave took on their calls. The specially outfitted SUV was able to navigate the hills and snow better than a traditional ambulance.

The captain's voice came over the radio again.

"Listen up, everyone. House fire. Two-story home. Mom and two kids. No confirmation yet on who was inside."

As the dispatcher patched in and relayed the address one more time, Chip turned on the lights and sirens and pulled out. With expert care, he slowly increased their speed as they headed toward the house.

As expected, there was a new seriousness in the air. Not that they took any emergency lightly—but when there were kids involved? That was everyone's worst nightmare.

Chip, who'd only recently gotten his license to drive the rig, looked so tense he could crack. Greg had heard he'd asked to drive the rig because he felt more sure of himself behind the wheel than when fighting fires. Greg had supervised Chip a lot during firefighter training, so he knew that Chip was more than capable as a firefighter, he just needed to build up his confidence. That said, he understood the feeling. Machines could weather mistakes—and were easier to control than a cagey fire.

Greg had seen all kinds of reactions from their victims. Some seemed to have shut down and were barely responsive, others were so frightened they fought the firefighters, and still others were frantic to save every piece of memorabilia in their house. Yep, if there was one thing they could all count on, it was that everyone reacted differently to a blaze. Quickly judging their victims' state of mind and getting them to safety as fast as possible was a skill that no amount of book learning could teach; you had to learn on the job. It was nerve-racking for recent graduates. Chip didn't have that much experience yet, and he was still dealing with losing a victim in a house fire last month.

They were only about thirty seconds away. When Chip blared the horn and shot the truck through the intersection before swerving to the right, Greg knew it was on him to say something encouraging. Captain DeWitt was with them, but he'd been on the radio with the chief and the dispatchers almost the whole time.

"You trained for this, Chip," he called out. "Keep your head out of the past and focus on the present."

"I will."

Remembering some of the tools for PTSD his counselor had taught him, Greg added, "Take it one step at a time, and rely on your training."

"I know, Tebo."

"If you know, get your game face on. You look like you're gonna lose it."

"Kids freak me out. Plus, I lost that lady . . ."

"That's always rough, Chip, but we did everything possible for her, yeah? The coroner said she was too badly burned. You've got this. I promise."

Just as he screeched to a stop, Chip muttered, "I sure hope you're telling me the same thing when we pull out of here."

The house was older, made of wood. The grass was freshly cut, which was good. Unfortunately, there was a thicket of overgrown brush in the back, which had probably ignited in seconds and fueled the fire like it was made of gasoline.

Greg got out, latched his coat, and pulled on his oxygen mask. Today, his brain seemed to be working fine and his PTSD was staying firmly at bay. He faced Captain DeWitt. "Sir?"

"Tebo, come with me. Neighbor reports that a six- and seven-year-old are home."

Greg fell in step beside DeWitt. "Parents?"

"Just a mom, apparently not home."

Greg cursed. "Any idea about the names of the kids?" Firefighters looked so scary with their masks on, Greg always looked for help to coax kids to climb into his arms.

"We got names yet, Sandy?" Captain asked the dispatcher.

After a second, he said, "Mandy and Kit."

"Roger that." Mandy and Kit, Greg repeated to himself. Mandy and Kit.

With an ax, the captain broke the locked front door. Immediately they were enveloped by smoke. Though it was the middle of the day, the heavy smoke made the house hazy and dark.

"Mandy! Kit!" Greg called out. "Mandy, Kit, where you at?"

They didn't hear anything but that didn't mean much. The fire was loud and kids were less likely to respond than adults. Greg had seen children determined to hide, sure they were going to get in trouble for something that wasn't their fault.

He looked to the captain for directions. Cap motioned Greg toward the right while he himself ascended the stairs.

Greg went into the living room. An old recliner had caught fire and was burning steadily, but the flames hadn't spread to the walls yet. The tile floor also seemed to be a good barrier. Greg was so glad that the floor wasn't wood. When he was still a probie, he'd watched a rotten floor burn like oiled pine. He'd never forgotten the sight of the victim staring at them from the other side of a blazing living room with a look of pure fear. Knowing that another firefighter was just steps behind him and would douse the recliner, Greg concentrated on finding those kids and getting them to safety.

Pulling down his mask, he bellowed, "Mandy! Kit!" After a second passed, he deepened his voice. "Girls, I'm a firefighter. I've come to help but you gotta answer me!" Scanning the area, he felt his heart start to beat faster. Panic was on the verge of settling in. He could not lose those girls. Not on his watch. "Mandy! Kit!"

Just as he pulled up his mask, he heard a cry.

"Help! We're here!"

"Cap, downstairs," he said into his radio. "I heard them."

"Roger that. Take care, Greg."

After taking another deep breath, he pulled down his apparatus again. "Girls, my name is Greg. I'm a firefighter and I came to get you out of here, okay?" It was hard to sound approachable when he was in full gear and had most of his face covered up. Sometimes it was the little things that mattered when trying to establish trust, especially with kids. "Yell for me again, 'kay?"

"Here!"

Thank you, Jesus. Whatever he'd said worked. It felt like his heart had just started beating again. "Keep it up! Keep yelling, okay?! I'm gonna find you!"

"We're here! Hurry!" Their shouts eventually led him to a small metal table next to the kitchen. The girls were hiding underneath, their arms around each other.

"Kitchen!" he radioed to the captain.

When he got closer, he saw that while they looked relatively unharmed, they were absolutely scared to death. He removed his mask again. "Hey," he said, "I'm Greg. Are y'all Mandy and Kit?" When they nodded, he felt a burst of relief. "I'm so glad I found you. Either of you hurt?"

"Kit hurt her hand but I'm okay."

"Kit, when we get outside, I'll take you to my friend who patches people up all the time, 'kay?" When she nodded, he smiled. "Good job. Now, first things first, is there anyone else here?"

"It's just us."

"Okay, then let's get you two out of here."

"We can't," Mandy said. "Momma said we aren't supposed to leave the house."

Hearing that made him sick, but he neatly pocketed those dark thoughts. He hated thinking about parents not looking out for their children. "I promise that your momma wants you to get out of here, honey."

The girls exchanged glances but otherwise didn't move.

The captain came up behind Greg. "Girls, I'm Captain DeWitt. Listen up, now. I've spoken to your momma. She wants you to come outside right away."

"She does?" Kit asked. "Are you sure?"

"Positive. Now come on. We don't have time to chat."

The younger girl, Kit, held out her hands to the captain. He covered her up with both a fireproof blanket and part of his jacket and immediately started carrying her out.

"Now you, Mandy," Greg said.

She stood frozen. "I'm scared."

"I know you are, and that's good."

Her eyes were wide with fright, but she was still holding it together. "It is?"

"Yep. It means you're being smart. People who aren't ever afraid are stupid in my book. But the captain was right. We need to get you safe. Now, come on."

She gingerly stepped toward him but froze again, giving him no choice but to pick her up in his arms and hold her tight.

As expected, she burst into tears. "Hold on. Close your eyes if you want, Mandy. We're getting on out of here."

He turned and went the way the captain had. But in the interim, flames were flowing across the tile. Reminding himself that he'd already made sure she was covered, he said, "You cling to me like a vine, honey." Then he raced through the flames, not pausing until he was outside.

Immediately Dave rushed to his side and pulled the little girl from Greg's arms. He felt her absence just as the adrenaline rush subsided.

Turning, he immediately went to Mark, who was holding a hose and spraying the flames on the second floor. "What's going on?"

"Ask Cap," replied Mark, "but I think I'm good here. Guessing it's seventy percent out."

"Tebo, take over for Oldum. Mark, come help me over here," Captain called out.

Greg took over the hose and focused on the job at hand for the next fifteen minutes. And then it was out, nothing but smoke and ashes left.

Forty minutes after that, the girls had been taken to the

hospital to be checked out, while their mother had been taken in for questioning since it was apparent she'd left them alone for several hours. And it wasn't the first time, either.

Returning to the truck, Greg leaned back as Chip drove to the station.

Greg noticed that the lines of worry around Chip's mouth had eased. "Did you do okay?"

"Yeah. One step at a time."

"Good. Glad to hear it."

"Cap said you did a good job with those girls. Took some coaxing, huh?"

"They were scared." He shuddered, thinking of how they were determined to mind their mother no matter the circumstances. "I'm glad they're all right."

"Me, too."

When they were almost back at the station, Chip said, "Fighting fires feels different than I thought it would."

"How so?"

Slowing down so he could make the turn, Chip glanced his way. "It's better, because I love actually helping our community. But it's worse, too, you know? Sometimes I just feel so helpless."

Greg knew exactly what Chip was saying.

"I was just thinking the same thing." Giving it some more thought, he added, "But today was a good day. We saved two little girls, yeah?"

"Yeah." Chip smiled for the first time. "Thanks for your help earlier."

Greg nodded, but he couldn't help feeling he should be thanking Chip for the very same thing.

Chapter 9

$\mathcal{K}$risten was really starting to wish she hadn't agreed to go shopping with Chelsea. They'd met at their friend Kaylee's bowling party for her twenty-fifth birthday. They'd ended up on the same team and by the time they came in second place, they'd become fast friends.

Now she was even happier she knew Chels since she was one of the reasons she'd said yes to Greg about attending the party. After she'd started second-guessing herself, she made the mistake of calling Chelsea to discuss what she was going to wear.

That had turned into a discussion about clothes, which had led Chelsea to do a thorough inspection of Kristen's closet, which led to Kristen's realization that 90 percent of her clothes were for working at the garden center—or for actual gardening. Her most recent cute outfit had been bought two years ago.

After Kristen admitted that she had nothing to wear to the party, Chelsea happily suggested they go shopping together.

Now they were in Home Town Closet, Chelsea's favorite

boutique on Main Street. Kristen had driven by it lots of times but had never gone in.

It had taken only ten minutes to wish that she'd stayed away. All the outfits seemed to be girly and formfitting. Kristen was normally at peace with her figure, but the clingy dresses seemed to accentuate every unwanted bulge. Unfortunately, Chelsea, who was slimmer and far more petite, looked great in everything.

Feeling more uncomfortable by the minute, Kristen started thinking of excuses to leave.

"I should get on back to the store. Marty is there alone. There's no telling what trouble has found him."

"You have your phone, right?"

"Right."

"Then I bet he'll call if he's really in a bind."

What could she say to that? "I suppose."

"Come on, stop worrying about work." Chelsea held up a navy sweater with bows holding the shoulders and sleeves together. "What do you think?"

"That I'd be in real trouble if one of those ties came undone."

Chelsea chuckled. "Oh, stop. I bet this is real cute on. It would be great on you, since you've got that light tan and your arms are so toned."

"You think so?" It still looked awfully delicate.

"I know so." Handing the hanger to Kristen, Chelsea smiled. "You should try it on."

Kristen held it up in front of her. "The V-neck is kind of low, don't you think?"

"Uh, no. It's not scandalous or anything. Besides, you've got enough going on to fill it out."

She supposed she did, but that wasn't the problem. The problem was that, with that neckline, the top of her surgical scar would probably be visible.

She put it back on the rack. "I don't think so."

Chelsea frowned. "Really?"

Desperate, Kristen pulled out a pink crew neck cotton-and-silk sweater. It looked boxy and loose. "This might be better."

"Yeah, if you were doing sorority rush in winter. Don't you think it's a little prim for women our age? And, sorry, but I didn't think you wore pink much because of your strawberry-blonde hair. Or do I have that all wrong?"

"You don't. I forgot about my hair." Placing the sweater back on the rack, Kristen said, "Maybe we should just forget this. I've got plenty of clothes at home. I can probably make my usual jeans and T-shirts look okay."

Chelsea looked concerned. "We can do what you want, but I don't get why you're hesitating so much. What's going on?"

"It's complicated."

"I know you're still gun-shy, but Greg is a good guy. Anderson's shared a lot of stories about him. Greg might seem like a player, but I feel certain that he's not going to push you to do anything you don't want."

"I'm not worried about that. I think he's great. Besides, we've decided to just be friends."

"Then what *are* you worried about?"

That she was going to want to be more than just friends. That eventually he'd discover just how flawed she was and want to break things off. And that if he did, her heart would be broken.

But to admit any of that was embarrassing. "I don't know."

"Come on. You do. We might as well talk about it." When Kristen hesitated, Chelsea asked, "Does Greg not know about your heart surgeries?"

"He knows. But I have a pretty significant scar on my chest. I don't want it to be so noticeable."

"I can understand that." Chelsea nodded, then looked down at the rack again. "Oh! Look. How about this?" She held up a silk blouse. It was black and at first glance looked deceptively staid. But, while the front neckline was modest, the back draped far lower. The silk was also woven in such a way that all her curves were going to be on display.

Before she could help herself, Kristen reached for the hanger. "This is gorgeous."

"I think it would be perfect for you. At first glance it looks low-key and simple. And then, pow!"

Kristen laughed. "I kind of like that."

"You're going to look stunning." Eyeing Kristen critically, she added, "You can wear a pair of skinny jeans and some sandals or even heels."

Kristen held it up to the mirror and blinked. It was sexy and pretty but not too froufrou. She felt prettier just holding it up to her collarbones. "You really think this is me?"

"Well, yeah!"

After wincing at the price tag, Kristen started thinking of what she could wear with it. The answer, of course, was everything. Tonight, she'd wear her good jeans, black low-heeled boots, and silver hoops. If she had a dressier occasion, she could pair it with slacks or a skirt. She could even wear a blazer over it. "Fine. What about you?" When Chelsea hesitated, Kristen added, "Please don't say nothing."

"If you don't mind, I'm going to get that navy sweater with the bows on the sleeves."

"I don't mind it at all. Anderson is going to love it."

A dreamy look floated over Chelsea's face. "Yeah, he is."

Kristen smiled, but inside, it was hard not to be jealous of Chelsea's good fortune. She and Anderson had been high school sweethearts, broke up for a decade, reconnected, and were now married. It hadn't come easy for them, but their closeness was a thing of beauty. No matter where they were, they could barely take their eyes off each other.

Anderson was always touching his wife, too. Playing with the ends of her golden hair, pressing his hand to the middle of her back, reaching for her fingers, pressing kisses to her temple. Which meant, of course, that Chelsea's soon-to-be-almost-bare arms weren't going to be left alone all evening.

"You're going to look beautiful. I can't wait to see you in it."

"You, too." She smiled sweetly. "Kristen, I'm looking forward to seeing you all dressed up!"

"It's been a while. I hope I remember how to put on eyeliner," she teased.

"Want to get ready together? You're welcome to come over. Jack has a sleepover tonight."

"Thanks, but I've got a couple of things to do at the shop first, so I'll get ready at home."

"Okay. But if you change your mind . . ."

"If I change my mind, I'll give you a call."

"Fine." Looking at the price tag on the sweater, Chelsea squared her shoulders. "Let's check out before I decide I should be spending my money on Jack."

Kristen smiled. There was no better mom than Chelsea. "Deal."

_H_ey, how are you?" Greg said as he took the empty space next to her on the couch in Chip's apartment.

Kristen chuckled. "You asked me that half an hour ago."

"It was over an hour ago."

"What?" She couldn't believe so much time had passed.

"Not only that," Greg replied, "but I've been trying to get this seat next to you for the last fifteen minutes. I finally had to bribe Anderson to pull Chelsea away so I could claim a spot."

"I have no idea what you mean. What's wrong?"

"Nothing. I'm just trying to spend some time with you."

"Ah."

"Yeah. Ah." He draped a hand over the back of the couch. The position brought him closer . . . and also treated her to a whiff of his cologne—and the reminder that she wasn't nearly as immune to him as she was trying to pretend.

The truth was that Greg was everything she'd ever wanted in a man. He was attentive, funny, and just cocky enough to give off a sheen of confidence. He also spoke his mind, which she found incredibly attractive. A man who didn't play games? That was amazing.

For her, there was nothing worse than a guy who was so closed off she was left in the dark about what he wanted— or who was so focused on getting her to go out with him again that he acted as if everything she said was interesting or witty.

Greg, on the other hand, had been easygoing and relaxed. They'd found a lot of things to talk about, none of it too serious. Maybe they really could be good friends.

After they ate, Greg started talking shop with his coworkers, leaving her the perfect opportunity to sit next to Chelsea and meet a few other people.

So, things had gone far better than she'd expected, and time had flown by.

"My gosh, Greg, every time I looked your way, you seemed happy to be hanging out with the guys."

"And you seemed happy to be hanging with all the women. I was trying to let you do that." He cracked a couple of his knuckles. "Sorry. I'm trying not to sound like a jealous fool, but you're gorgeous and that silky top you're wearing is dangerously sexy. I've been half-afraid that some guy was going to catch your notice and you'd change your mind about not wanting to date anyone seriously."

"I wasn't teasing, Greg. I'm really not ready to date anyone right now."

"Sorry." He lowered his voice. "I like you, and even though we're doing this friend thing, I still feel like you're putting up defenses. Then, a couple of minutes ago, I noticed a couple of the guys act like maybe they had a chance. And maybe they do—it's not like you don't have a choice. It's just that that would really suck for me, you know?"

That had been a heck of a speech. She wasn't sure what

to tackle first, but she decided to start at the end. "First of all, I'm not available. I told you, I don't want to date. So, if somebody did put some moves on me—which would be really rude, by the way—I wouldn't have any trouble shutting them down."

"I didn't mean to suggest that you couldn't take care of yourself."

"Also, Greg, if you really did want to spend more time with me, all you had to do was ask."

"Without coming across as possessive and needy?"

She chuckled. "Not at all."

"Well, at least there's that."

"I'm really glad we're friends, Greg."

His expression shuttered. "Yeah. I am, too. Sorry for getting weird. I guess I had too many fries or something."

As excuses went, that one was pretty bad. "Greg, is something going on that I'm not catching? Because I'm starting to get confused. I mean, I thought I was honest with you."

"No, there's nothing going on at all." He closed his eyes for a second in a grimace. "I mean, nothing that you want to hear."

"Are you sure about that?" She had really thought he was okay with the two of them keeping things platonic. But if he wasn't, she needed to know. She hated surprises, and she sure didn't want him to be upset with her.

"Yes. Positive." He looked around the room. "What do you say about us getting out of here?"

"Are you sure you want to? These are all your good friends."

"I'm sure. Things are going to be winding down pretty soon anyway. Look at Chip and Jackie."

Kristen turned toward the newly engaged couple. Chip had his arms around Jackie's waist, hers were around his neck, and they seemed to be dancing, although the music from the speakers was barely audible.

They looked completely oblivious to everyone else in the room. No, it was more than that. They looked like everyone else was ruining their evening. They didn't need another soul.

A lump formed in her throat as she realized that Clark had never looked at her like that. Not even the night they'd announced their engagement. Clark had acted pleased, and she remembered feeling relieved because the decision had been made. But had they felt euphoric, like no one else in the room existed?

No, she was sure they had not. She'd certainly never felt like that. Not even for a moment.

Feeling blue all of a sudden, she cleared her throat. "You're right. It is probably time for everybody to take off."

He stood up and held out a hand. "Ready, then?"

After the conversation they'd just had, she felt awkward even holding his hand. Withdrawing hers, she stepped toward the kitchen. "Let me go help with some of the cleanup first."

"Kristen, I was just in the kitchen. Everyone's got a good handle on it."

"I know, but it seems rude not to." She smiled and took another step away. Firmly out of his reach and the temptation to grasp his hand again. "Give me twenty minutes?"

"Fine. Let's go clean up Chip's kitchen."

"You don't need to come with me. I'll find you when I'm done."

"I'm going with you, Kristen."

She realized that she'd inadvertently solved the problem. She'd just firmly put him in the friend zone . . . or maybe in the she's-not-worth-it zone?

Everything about his demeanor was different now. It was cooler. More distant. His hand was no longer resting on the small of her back—instead he was walking slightly ahead of her. Almost as if he was walking away from her.

Chapter 10

"Jennifer!"

Her mother's voice cut through the drone of the television, stopping Jen in her tracks. Turning around, she walked back into the living room. "Yes, Mom?"

"Tell me again. Who are you going to the movies with?"

Her mom sat in her dad's old easy chair most of every day, half watching television, sometimes looking at Facebook, but mostly lost in her memories. A plastic cup of vodka and soda was her usual companion.

By nine or ten at night she'd be asleep. On better nights, she made it up to bed. On worse nights, she'd dissolve into tears before passing out on the couch.

At first, when relatives and neighbors came by, her mom tried hard to shower and put herself together. As the months passed and the rest of the world moved on, her fragile grasp on herself seemed to slip. Things got worse when Jen's brother, Bill, had left for college.

Now her mom only went through the motions of parenting.

Focusing back on the present, Jen answered her mother's

question. "I'm going to the movies with a friend from school, Mom."

"Who?"

"Ryan." She folded her hands in front of her. "Don't you remember?" Jen did her best to look innocent, though she knew she should be looking guilty. Of course she hadn't told her mother about Ryan.

"I don't remember you mentioning him before." Mom leaned back on the couch and peered at her over a pair of readers. "Or have you told me all about him and I forgot?"

Her mother looked sober. She even looked like she was attempting to give Jen her undivided attention. Taken aback, Jen sat down on the couch. "I thought I mentioned him, but maybe I just meant to." Doing her best to act like Ryan meant nothing to her, she shrugged. "Ryan's just a guy I know. Sorry."

Her mother continued to study her. "You went to high school with him?"

"Yes. We were in a couple of classes together." That was a stretch, since she was pretty sure they'd been in only chemistry together. Feeling like she needed to add a bit more, Jen added, "You know how busy I was with marching band. All I ever did was talk about that."

Mom blinked, like she was trying to remember the past year. "You were busy with the band. What did Ryan do? Was he in the band as well?"

"No. He played football."

"Oh." She blinked again. "How come you're going out now?"

No way did Jen want to recount how they'd met at Werner's Garden Center. "I don't know. I guess we've been enjoying spending more time together now that we've graduated."

"Is he going to college?"

"Yes."

"Where?"

"Down in Pueblo. There's a Colorado State campus down there." When her mother continued to stare, she added, "I heard he's thinking about walking on the football team there."

"I see."

Her mother didn't "see" anything at all. But, based on the fact that Mom was still staring at her, Jen realized she'd just made a tactical error.

She'd revealed too much.

"If you know about his plans for the future, you two know each other well. Maybe better than you're letting on?"

"Everyone knows about his plans, Mom. Ryan really likes to play football." Even though she yearned to stand up, Jen forced herself to cross her legs and act like she was having fun. Like she was used to her mother being interested in her social life.

"Well, I think this is great. I'm glad you have plans tonight. I'll look forward to meeting him."

There was no way that could happen. Her mother might be coherent, but the house was dark and a mess. It practically reeked of old alcohol and disuse. "I don't think he's coming in, Mom."

"Why not? Do boys not do that anymore?"

Guilt mixed with preservation in a huge knot in her chest, causing her anxiety to kick in. Before she could stop herself, she started talking fast. "Tonight is no big deal. Ryan and I are just friends, nothing more. Plus, all we're doing is going to the movies and maybe we'll go out with a bunch of kids for ice cream afterward. So, it's not like we're on a date or anything."

"That's what you two are going to do? Go to the movies and eat ice cream?"

"Yep." Holding her breath, she shrugged . . . hoping Ryan would never find out that she had cribbed the description of their date from the diary of a seventh-grade girl. Her sister, Emme!

"Oh. Okay." After a pause, the familiar, distracted expression appeared on Mom's face again. "Have fun."

She exhaled. "Thanks. I will."

She wasn't sure if her mother heard her, though, because after she'd taken a fortifying sip of her drink, she turned back around and was once again staring at the television screen.

Pleased to have finished the conversation, Jen looked down at her phone and realized that Ryan could show up within minutes.

Afraid to go all the way up to her room, she darted into the light-blue powder room near the front door. Closing the door for privacy, she inspected her reflection for the fourth or fifth time since getting ready.

She thought her hair looked okay. Being out in the sun so much at the garden center had brought out a bunch of highlights, making her usual dark-blonde bob look almost golden. She'd put on a blue sweater that brought out the color of her eyes. She knew her jeans looked good and the Tory Burch flats she was wearing were awesome.

Figuring she looked like her regular self but a little bit better, Jen grabbed her purse and peeked out the front door. She wanted to catch Ryan before he did something awful—like rang the doorbell.

Jen shivered. That would be such a huge mistake. Not only would he see the state of the living room, but her mother would either ramble on about nothing or be so oblivious to them both that Ryan would realize there was something really wrong with her mother.

And, if that happened, well, he'd probably never want to see her again. Nobody wanted to date a girl with such a messed-up homelife.

Two minutes later, Ryan pulled up in his tricked-out black Explorer. She opened the door. Though it was tempting to simply slink out, she made herself do the right thing.

"Bye, Mom," she called out in her most cheerful voice. "I'll be home by curfew."

"Hmm? Okay, sure."

She closed the door, pulled out her key, and locked it. At least her mom would be safe.

She gave a little wave as she went down the stone walkway that led from the front door to the driveway. "Hi," she said with a big smile.

He'd just gotten out of his SUV. "Hey. You didn't have to come out. I was going to come to the door to get you."

"I know. I thought I'd save you the trouble."

Glancing at her front door, he said, "Your mom doesn't want to meet me or anything? I don't mind."

Ryan was perfect. That's all there was to it. "No."

He frowned. "Really?"

Realizing that she didn't sound very nice—and worried that he might think she was embarrassed by him—she forced herself to explain a little bit. "Sorry, that came out wrong. What I meant was that my mom's, um, fine and all, but she's not great around people she doesn't know. So she's usually okay with not meeting my dates." She was now officially mortified. Why couldn't she have kept her mouth closed? He hadn't asked her about any of that.

And what was she doing talking like she had tons of dates?

His hand on the passenger door handle froze. "I just realized I probably sounded like a jerk. I know your dad died. I shouldn't have acted like she should want to meet me." Still looking regretful, he added, "I don't know why I made a big deal about it."

She knew why. Because she didn't talk about either of her parents if she could help it. She especially didn't talk about her mother's descent into addiction with anyone she didn't know well. She smiled. "It's okay. My father died two years ago. It's been a while."

He relaxed. He opened her door before walking around to his side of the car. "Still, that does suck about your dad."

As she put on her seat belt, she took in his jeans, leather Adidas, and long-sleeved North Face T-shirt. He was definitely dressed more casually than she was, but more dressed up than most kids their age. She knew he didn't have a ton of money like her mother did, but each item was nice.

As he backed down her driveway, then pulled out onto the street, he said, "You sure live in a fancy neighborhood. All the houses are awesome."

"Thanks."

"Who else lives around here?"

"What do you mean?"

"Like, who else from our school? I'm only asking because I don't remember ever driving around here before."

"Oh yeah. You used to drive around half the football team, right?" It had been a common sight, especially her senior year: Ryan and his Explorer, packed with guys.

"I just had a car and a lot of the younger guys didn't. It helped everyone if no one was worrying about how to get a ride to practice." He grimaced. "Coach gave us all major crap if just one guy was late. So I wasn't being so nice, just, you know, worried about myself."

"I didn't know things like that happened."

He grinned. "That's because you weren't subject to the wrath of Coach Holst." He said it in a funny, scary voice.

Jen giggled and said, "Are you going to try to walk on when you're in Pueblo?"

"I'd like to. I was a pretty good receiver. Not good enough for a big school like CU, but I might have a chance at an NCAA D2 school."

"Do your parents care about your continuing to play?"

"Nah. All they cared about was that I got scholarships. I got some money for my grades, the science club, and being on student council. The Rotary Club came through, too." He paused as he stopped at a light. "I like football a lot, but I realized a while back that I was never going to be big enough to get an athletic scholarship. I mainly played for fun, plus stuff like that helps on the college applications. Anyway, the scholarships, plus the money I make this summer, will be enough to get me through freshman year."

All of which made her feel completely inept. She'd been very much a B student. Plus, when her dad died and with her mom falling apart, she hadn't been able to do much besides just get through each day. *Stop*, she ordered herself. *Don't go thinking about how things would've been different if Dad hadn't died.* "I forgot you did so much with the science club."

He looked embarrassed. "Don't know why you would've thought about it. It's not that interesting."

"Didn't you get an award or something?"

"The whole team did."

It was pretty much a known fact that Ryan did just about everything really well. "You're the only guy I know who doesn't live to talk about himself," she teased. That was the truth, too. Most guys she knew talked only about what they were interested in.

But instead of grinning, he said, "I could say the same about you. You're like a sealed vault."

That was news. It wasn't all that flattering, either. "Oh, come on, what does that mean?"

"Come on, Jen. You never talk about yourself."

"I . . . well, I guess I've never thought there was much to brag about."

"Uh-huh."

"I'm serious. I was in band, that's it. I was good, but I wasn't great. I wasn't a football star or anything." She also had a lot of other things going on that she'd never wanted anyone to know about.

"Hey, it's not like I'm saying that being private is a bad thing. It's not." He turned left when the light turned green.

"A couple of the guys always thought you were stuck-up. When I moved here, I thought the same thing, but then I realized you were just quiet."

"Okay." Tucking a strand behind her ear, she looked out the window.

"Jen, I mean it. I mean, look how much time you spent with Crystal Beur. You wouldn't have given her the time of day if you were stuck-up."

The home ec teacher had paired them up and they'd hit it off. "Crystal is nice. She can't help it if her family doesn't have any money."

"I know. All I'm saying is that when I saw the two of you together at lunch, I knew all the stuff I'd heard about you being stuck-up was wrong."

She felt relieved, but also a little surprised. Had people actually thought she hung out with Crystal because she felt sorry for her? She *liked* Crystal! Then she thought of something else surprising: Ryan had noticed whom she ate lunch with.

Jen felt her cheeks heat. "Oh my gosh. I'm so glad I graduated. I couldn't take another year of the rumor mill."

"I felt the same way. College is going to be better." Pulling into the parking lot of the movie theater, he said, "Are you ready to see *Doomed*?"

"I am. I just hope it's not too scary."

He chuckled. "If it is, you can grab hold of me."

She rolled her eyes but inside, she was doing cartwheels. "Get ready, I might do that."

"Good."

Getting out of his vehicle, it was all she could do not to start grinning like an idiot.

As they neared the theater entrance, she was shocked at how many people she recognized congregating in the lobby. It seemed as if half the high school was there—and every one of them was watching her walk in by Ryan's side. If he hadn't been so popular and she so less-than-that, Jen figured being watched wouldn't have bothered her. But she couldn't change the fact that they were an unlikely match.

When one of the girls looked at her like she couldn't believe her eyes, Jen felt like staring right back. But instead, she pretended no one was looking.

"Halstead, hey!" Calder Bradberry called out.

"Hey," Ryan said as they walked by him.

Jen didn't know if she was glad about that or not. On one hand, she had no desire to talk to a guy who'd pretty much ignored her for the last four years.

On the other hand, she couldn't help but wonder why Ryan wasn't stopping. Was he really not interested in talking to Calder—or did he feel embarrassed to be seen with her?

Chapter 11

The lobby was packed and it seemed as if he knew most everyone there. Half the football team, a handful of JV and varsity cheerleaders, even most of the kids he'd been on student council with.

Not to mention the band kids, drama kids—every clique seemed to be well represented.

They were also all staring at him and Jen.

It was awkward.

Especially because Ryan could practically feel Jen tensing up beside him. He really hated that. It felt like he'd just finally gotten her to relax around him.

The sad thing was that Ryan had only himself to blame. This was their first official date and they were on display. The more he'd gotten to know Jen, the more he realized they'd lived pretty separate lives while they were in high school. He'd been on one end of the spectrum, she on the other. He'd been really social, both because it was his nature and because he'd felt the need to do everything he could to get scholarships for college.

Jen, on the other hand, had kept to herself. She had lived

in Woodland Park her whole life but seemed quiet and shy. While he talked to just about everyone, she'd hung out with her small group of friends.

Of course, she'd also been mourning her father and dealing with her mom's grief, too.

Every little bit of herself she'd shared with him had felt special, especially since he had a feeling she didn't tell all that many people much about herself. For some reason, she'd decided to trust him enough to share some of her circumstances. But, instead of protecting that gift, he'd brought her right into the center of the high school rumor mill.

Ryan glanced her way. Jen's posture was stiff and the muscles in her face looked tense.

He should've taken her someplace else. He'd asked her to the movies because it had always been his go-to first date. They could talk, but if things got weird then they could just stare at the screen.

Obviously, he should've thought things through. He pressed his hand in the middle of her back. He wanted to reassure her—and maybe show everyone that he was proud to be with her. He leaned toward her and said quietly, "We can go somewhere else if you'd like."

"Ryan, it's too late to do that. You already bought the tickets."

"I don't care about the tickets."

"I do."

"Jen, really." He lowered his voice. "I promise, I didn't realize so many people were going to be here."

"Of course not, how could you?" She shook her head. "If we leave now, it's going to send the wrong message to everyone. They're going to assume I made you leave. I don't really care what they think, but I don't want them to get upset with you."

"They won't." Honestly, she was right. A couple of people would get pissed off, but who even cared? Not him. Not anymore.

"Sure they will. I don't want to spend the rest of my life having to avoid half of our graduating class. Plus . . ." Her voice trailed off.

Ryan was just about to tease her for worrying so much . . . until he realized what she was looking at. His stomach sank.

"Hey Ryan," Campbell said as she sauntered closer. She flipped a lock of her long blonde hair over one shoulder. "This is a great surprise, right? I didn't know you were going to be here."

"I didn't know you were going to be here, either. I thought you were out of town." He'd thought she would be in Vail for the summer and was glad. They had dated for only a few weeks, but it was long enough for him to learn she was borderline crazy.

Campbell needed a lot of attention, which was the opposite of Jen in every single way. Jen worked all the time while Campbell didn't work at all. Jen cared about everyone. Campbell, on the other hand, didn't seem to care about anyone but herself. Jen was sweet to him. She was encouraging and positive. Campbell expected him to lift her up. Jen didn't need to be part of a crowd, Campbell craved being in the center of everything. When they were alone, they hadn't had anything to say.

Going to the movies was perfect for him and Campbell. They would be seen, surrounded by other people he liked better, and didn't have to talk to each other too much.

Campbell frowned. "I decided to bail. Everything there is really expensive and my parents hardly gave me any money. I was bummed, but now I think it's a good thing." She smiled. "We'll have to do something since I'm back."

"Yeah, I don't think so." Realizing they were standing alone, Ryan looked around for Jen. He found her standing a couple of feet away, talking to some girls from band.

Relieved that she didn't look upset that he was talking to his ex-girlfriend, Ryan relaxed slightly.

Campbell, on the other hand, was eyeing Jen with a look of distaste. "Are you going out with Jen Ferguson?"

"Obviously."

She sniffed. "I didn't think you two even knew each other." Her smile turned smug. "Or did you two hang out without me knowing?"

There was no way he was going to give Campbell any information to use against Jen.

"Nope. See you, Campbell."

She put a hand on her hip. "Wait. That's it?"

"Uh, yeah. We broke up, right?"

"Yes, but—"

"It really is over, Cam. Deal with it or don't, I don't care. But if you make a scene here, I'll see you regret it."

Ignoring Campbell's shocked expression, Ryan moved to Jen's side. "Hey. Sorry about that." He reached for her hand. After a second, she threaded her fingers through his. "Don't worry about it. I was fine."

"I'm glad." Turning to her friends, he said, "Hey, Kris. And . . . Amanda, right?"

"Yeah. Hi," said Amanda.

"How are you, Ryan?" Kris asked.

"Okay. How are you? Are you still working at Jo's Kolaches?"

"Yep."

Jen looked surprised. "I didn't know you two knew each other."

"We were in science club together," Kris explained.

Ryan smiled at her. "Did you get into University of Denver?"

"Yep." She grinned. "They gave me a great scholarship."

"That's awesome. Congrats."

"Thanks. What about you?"

"Colorado State–Pueblo."

"I'm glad. Hey, I can't believe you got Jen to see *Doomed.*"

The amusement in her voice made him pause. "Why is that?"

"Uh, because Jennifer Ferguson hates scary movies," Amanda supplied.

Ignoring the way Jen was pulling on his hand, Ryan said, "Really? Jen told me it was fine."

Amanda grinned. "She lied."

Their date was going from bad to worse. "Jen, do you want to see something else?"

"No."

"Are you sure?"

Looking perturbed, she shook her head. "My friends are just giving me a hard time. I'll be fine. And we should go in or we're not going to be able to find good seats."

"Are you two going in now, too?" asked Ryan. "You can sit with us if you'd like."

"Thanks, but we're gonna go see the new John Green tearjerker."

"You couldn't pay me to see that," Ryan said with a grimace.

Jen smiled at him. "Which is why I said yes to *Doomed*. I knew you wouldn't be up for that."

"Oh, but, I mean, I would've gone if *you* wanted to," he backpedaled.

"I know. And you would've also been miserable. I wasn't going to do that to you." She held up the hand that he wasn't clasping and waved to her friends. "See you later."

"Call me, Jen," Kris said.

"I will."

Now that Campbell was out of the way, it seemed like everyone who had been actively watching them had calmed down. Ryan was relieved. Jen was still holding his hand, so he figured she wasn't too upset by all that had happened. Maybe this date wasn't going to be a catastrophe after all.

After waiting in line for a couple of minutes, he paid for two Cokes and a large popcorn. "I'm so glad you wanted popcorn," he said. "I was afraid you wouldn't." Most girls he knew refused to eat much when they went out, as though guys would be shocked that they also consumed food.

She smiled shyly at him. "I love movie popcorn. I don't know why."

"Because it's freaking delicious." When she laughed, he squeezed her hand. "Do you really hate scary movies?"

"Kind of, but I need to get over it."

He didn't ask what she meant by that. After handing over their tickets, they walked into their theater at last. It was already dark and the previews were on. When they found their places, he took a chance and lifted the divider between his seat and Jen's. When she scooted a little closer to him, he knew it was the right move. Surrounded by the dark, Ryan felt truly comfortable for the first time all evening. At last he wasn't worried about his friends or if he was saying the right thing. Jen was relaxed, and their hands kept brushing against each other's every time they reached into the popcorn container. It really was like being in their own private little space.

When the first notes of *Doomed*'s opening theme played, he reached for her hand. "Squeeze my hand every time you get afraid," he whispered.

She smiled. "Okay, but you might regret it."

"I won't." If a scary movie was what it took to get her to hold his hand the entire time, then he'd take her to nothing but.

Three hours later, they were sitting at a table in the back of Granger's and Jen was still beet red.

"I'm so sorry," she said for about the fifth time. "I hope you won't have a scar or anything."

When the serial killer found the heroine, she'd squealed and dug her nails into his hand. The sting of pain caught him off guard, though by then he'd realized that Kris hadn't been exaggerating even a little bit. Jen didn't just dislike scary movies, she hated them.

Because they petrified her.

Looking down at the tiny cut that one of her nails had made on his knuckle, he rolled his eyes. "This little mark is nothing. I got hurt a whole lot worse every day at practice."

"It's more than just a little mark, Ryan." Neither of them had noticed the little half-moon of dried blood until they'd sat down at their table. And once they'd figured out that it came from her nail, she'd looked like she'd been about to cry.

After he returned from washing his hands—and showing her that you couldn't even tell it was there—she'd started apologizing again.

"Some date I am. You take me to the movies and I repay you by drawing blood." She held up a hand. He didn't even try to stop himself from smiling. Every time the killer was on the hunt, she'd leaned closer and closer to him. By the time he attacked, she was almost sitting in his lap. He'd loved the excuse to keep his arms around her.

She sighed. "I guess I'm being ridiculous."

"It's not ridiculous, it's cute."

Their server's approach cut off any further discussion about it. "What would you like?"

Ryan gestured to her. "Jen, you go first."

"I'll have the soup-and-sandwich combo."

"Got it," the server said. "And for you?"

"A burger and fries."

"Which one, hon?" the server asked.

"A Granger with cheddar cheese."

She scribbled on her notepad. "Y'all want anything to drink?"

Noticing she still seemed reluctant to go first, Ryan prompted her again. "Jen, what do you want?"

"Just water, thanks."

"I'll take a Coke," Ryan said.

The server winked at him. "You've got yourself a good one there, honey. Good for you."

After the server walked away, Jen chuckled. "That was kind of odd, right? I have no idea what she was talking about."

He knew. He'd taken Campbell to Granger's a couple of times and she'd been so difficult, he was pretty sure the waitstaff drew straws to see who would have to put up with her. "She was talking about you not ordering anything expensive. Some dates take advantage."

"Oh."

She wasn't looking at him, which made him wonder if maybe Jen was only thinking of the price of everything. "Hey, you know this meal is my treat, right?" He was worried she hadn't ordered a drink because she was trying to economize.

"No way, Ryan. I can pay for my meal."

"That's not the point."

"Maybe it isn't. But I didn't come out with you to get a free meal."

"I never thought that."

"Okay. I'm just saying that you don't have to pay all the time."

"You are full of surprises," he said.

"Why is that?"

"You live in this really fancy house, but you never dress like you're rich."

"Ah, that's because I'm not rich."

"You order the cheapest thing on the menu even though I was paying."

"The soup tonight is broccoli cheese. It's my favorite."

"Okay . . ."

"I'm serious!"

"I get it!" He laughed to cover his realization he was sounding like a jerk. "Sorry, I'm not trying to make a big deal out of nothing. It's just that I'm used to something different."

"You're used to Campbell."

"Maybe I am, but I hope not. We didn't date all that long."

"Not as long as you dated Allie, I guess."

Surprised again, he blurted, "You've kept track of who I've gone out with?"

"I promise, I haven't been stalking you. It was just kind of common knowledge."

"Common knowledge?"

"Pretty much everyone knew who you were going out with."

"Yeah, right."

She raised her eyebrows. "Come on. You aren't surprised, are you? You were a pretty big deal. Plus, it wasn't like you were trying to keep it under wraps. Allie and Campbell sure weren't. They were pretty proud to have snagged you."

"I hate that word."

"Sorry, but that's the one they used."

Ryan drank about half his glass of water. "The truth is that I've dated a lot of girls who were into showing off. Not like you."

"What do you mean?"

"I mean, I have no idea who you dated last year."

She chuckled. "That's because I didn't date anyone."

"Not at all?"

She shook her head as she shifted with obvious discomfort. "And now I feel even more like you're out of my league."

"What are you talking about?"

She covered her face with a hand. "Oh God. Just forget it, okay?" She moaned. "Listen, I promise . . . I'm not trying to be your girlfriend or anything."

Since he'd been working pretty darn hard to get her attention, he was kind of offended. "Why not?"

"Because you're going off to college."

"You are, too, right?"

"I haven't decided yet. I think I'm going to take some classes at Pikes Peak Community College, but I don't know." Her eyes lit up. "You'll have a great time, no doubt. You'll meet everyone and find some sorority girl to date."

"How come you're only going to community college? I thought you did okay in school." Plus, she was rich, so she probably didn't have to depend on a bunch of scholarships to go. She lived in a huge house.

Jen bit her lip, seemed to weigh her words, then said, "Everything is up in the air. I can't decide what I want to do. My mom kind of needs me around."

"She's doing that bad?"

Averting her eyes, Jen shrugged. "She . . . well, she doesn't cope well on her own."

"Really? That's too bad."

Meeting his eyes again, she said, "My family's kind of messed up. That's why I said you're out of my league. There's no reason why you should ever be interested in a girl like me."

"Maybe everything you just said are all reasons I am."

When she bit her lip and gave him a look that said he'd just shocked her, Ryan grinned.

"I mean it, Jen. I don't want to date the female version of me or another girl like Allie or Campbell. I want someone different."

"Like me?" she asked in a wry tone.

"Yeah. You."

Her cheeks flushed but she didn't argue.

That was good. No, it was awesome. Maybe he'd just figured out how to get Jennifer Ferguson to take him seriously. All he had to do was be completely honest and blunt.

He could work with that.

Chapter 12

Jen's scowl would've been funny if she hadn't looked like she was coming over to quit. Kristen pretended to brace herself against the counter.

"Uh-oh. What happened?"

"Campbell happened," she practically growled. "I can't even believe that she's *here*."

Half-entertained and half-dismayed, Kristen raised her eyebrows at her usually easygoing employee. "Am I supposed to know what that means?"

"No."

"Excuse me?"

Suddenly looking embarrassed, Jen sighed. "Sorry. I'm not making much sense, am I?"

"You're not. And I would appreciate it if you would dial your attitude down a notch. I prefer to keep my customers content, not scare them away."

"I'm sorry." After looking around to make sure no one could overhear, Jen said, "A girl I know from school was just here and she was being awful."

"Why? Is something the matter?" Kristen tried to imagine what could have happened.

"Yeah. She's Ryan Halstead's ex-girlfriend."

"Ah." Knowing Jen's mood was because of her love life and not something to do with the store, Kristen relaxed. "So you've got a woman scorned after you?"

"I guess, but it doesn't even make sense. Ryan and I aren't together, we've only gone out once. Plus, Campbell and Ryan were only together for a few weeks and broke up months ago. Why does she even care?"

"Sometimes that happens. If Campbell can't have Ryan, she doesn't want anyone else to have him. Or she didn't think she wanted him, but now that you do, she suddenly wants him back."

Jen wrinkled her nose. "That's crazy, right?"

Kristen shrugged. "I don't know if it is or isn't. It's been my experience that relationships don't always make a lot of sense. Even the good ones can be confusing." Thinking about herself and Greg, she added, "I hate to tell you this, but it isn't necessarily a lot clearer when you get older, either."

"Great." Sharing a smile, Jen added, "I kind of feel like I was thrown into the deep end of the pool and told to swim. I have no idea what I'm doing." Lowering her voice, she added, "I've never really had a boyfriend, Kristen."

"Maybe it's time, then."

"Maybe . . . oh! Not that Ryan has even said he wants to be my boyfriend." She slapped a hand over her face. "And now I officially sound stupid."

Kristen's heart went out to the girl. Jen looked so hopeful but so unsure, too. And who could blame her? "Is Campbell still here?"

"No. She only stayed long enough to make me feel bad. And to embarrass me, too. She had a lot to say about finding me replanting and watering a bunch of perennials."

"I see." It didn't feel great that Jen was embarrassed to

be seen working there—the place that meant everything to Kristen—but she supposed that was only natural. It didn't take much for some teens to locate other people's vulnerabilities.

Kristen was just about to tell her to forget about this Campbell and get back to work when she realized something else was going on. Jen's eyes were glistening; she looked like she was about to start crying. "Jen, why don't you take a break?"

"I don't need a break. I just needed to vent, but I'm fine."

"We're not busy. Go ahead." When Kristen continued to gaze at her steadily, practically daring her to refuse, Jen nodded.

"Thanks. I'll be back in ten minutes. I promise," she said over her shoulder as she hurried out the door.

"Take your time, honey."

After helping a couple who were buying some food for their rosebushes, Kristen leaned against the wall and looked out the front window. Poor Jen. She was such a mess of contradictions. At first glance, it seemed like she had it all. Nice clothes, good looks, and a bright future. However, the more Kristen got to know the girl, the more she worried about her.

Jen never talked about her mother—even seemed to go out of her way to *avoid* talking about her, and learning that she was saving to pay for classes at the community college was confusing, given where the girl lived.

True to her word, Jen walked in the door a few minutes later and went directly to her busywork task of wiping down shelves. Kristen always gave her employees small tasks to do for whenever things were slow.

She was just about to start her own busywork of straightening some stock when a couple with a list came in, followed by Samantha Carter from the fire department. The moment she spied Kristen, she grinned. "Hey!"

After greeting the couple, who said they wanted a few

minutes to look around, she replied, "Hi, Sam. How are you?"

"I'm good, especially since I ran into you. I was hoping to find you here today."

"I'm only open for four hours on Sundays, so you came at the right time. What do you need?"

"Plants, I guess?"

"I think we've got a few of those," Kristen joked. "Want to give me a hint about what you're looking for?"

"I have no idea. Maybe some daisies or something?"

"We can definitely help you with that."

"Thanks. I want to look around, too. After we talked the other night I wanted to stop by and see this place for myself. It's really cute."

"I'm glad you did." She was just about to suggest a tour when she noticed the couple looking visibly confused about something on their list. They were going to need help, too.

Seeing Jen was nearby, Kristen waved her over. "Hey, Jen, this is Samantha. She's a firefighter here in Woodland Park."

Jen's expression perked up. "For real?"

"Yep." Samantha smiled. "For several years, now."

"That's a cool job."

"I think so. I've never wanted to do anything else."

"Hey, Sam, I need to go help another customer, but Jen will take care of you." Turning to Jen, she added, "Take Sam on a quick tour of the nursery, would you, please? She's looking for daisies . . . *maybe*."

"Sure thing." She smiled at Sam. "Let's start at the annuals."

Kristen breathed a sigh of relief. It seems Sam was just what the doctor ordered. Already Jen seemed more animated and happier. Glad everything was right with her again, she helped the couple, who were looking for wind chimes.

After ten minutes, wondering where they'd gotten to,

Kristen took a walk and spied Jen talking to Samantha by a display of herb garden kits. She'd thought Sam would find the tour helpful and that it would take Jen's mind off her troubles. But it seemed that Jen was talking the poor fire-fighter's ear off.

She joined them. "I bet she's good now, Jen. Maybe you could make sure the back nursery is in order?"

"Oh, you don't need to do that," Samantha protested with a chuckle. "We've been having a good conversation."

"Sam said I could come visit her next time she's on shift," Jen said.

"I'm sure you'll enjoy that."

"I would love to show you around. And now I'm going to love to pick up a couple of things." Sam smiled at Kristen. "But I think I'm more of a bird feeder person instead of a plant one."

Thirty minutes later, Jen was helping Sam carry her bags out to the car. Since it was time to close, Kristen counted out the cash register while she watched the two of them talk some more by Sam's SUV.

"You two must have really hit it off," she teased when Jen returned.

"We did. She was so nice! I must have asked her two dozen questions about being a female firefighter."

"Not that there's anything wrong with it, but why all the interest? I thought you were college-bound?"

"I am, but . . . I haven't been too excited about it."

"I'm sure when you start you will be."

"Maybe, but I don't know. I think I really am going to visit her at the station. Being a firefighter sounds a lot more interesting to me than college."

"You're serious, Jen, aren't you?"

She nodded. "I was a decent student, but it was mainly because I didn't have a choice. Plus, college is so expensive. Exploring another route sounds really good."

"I'll look forward to hearing what happens."

Jen shrugged. "Maybe nothing will, but I want to look into it, you know? When it comes to work, I'd like it to be something that I choose instead of what everybody else thinks I should do. Plus, if I don't push myself to go forward, I might really regret staying put."

"I couldn't agree more."

After she closed up the shop and went upstairs to her apartment, Kristen thought more about what Jen had said. She'd made a lot of good points. If you weren't moving forward you risked being stuck and not going anywhere at all.

That was what she'd been doing with her life—with relationships—Kristen realized. It was time to stop being so worried about the bad thing that might happen and start concentrating on all the good things that could.

And that was what helped her make up her mind and give Greg a call. When he didn't answer, she left a message.

"Hey, it's me. I know you're probably on shift. But when you're free, consider yourself invited to dinner here at my place."

Chapter 13

The day after Sam had extended the invitation to tour the fire station, Jen reached out to her brother. Bill was in the middle of work, but he was happy to take her to the firehouse. He had to go to a meeting afterward, so he told her to use his Lyft account to get a ride if she couldn't find one from somebody else.

"Have fun, Jenny, okay?" he asked with a wave as he took off.

She nervously rang the bell at the door of Woodland Park Fire Station Number 1.

It was opened almost immediately by a tall, well-built man with a scarred face. Inwardly Jen gulped. It looked like he'd been seriously hurt in a fire. Could she really do this?

He studied her with a concerned look and said, "Are you okay?"

"Ye-es." Oh, bummer, he could tell how nervous she was! Jen pulled herself together. "My name is Jennifer Ferguson," she tried again. "Samantha Carter told me I could stop by."

"Oh sure. Come on in." He stepped aside so she could enter but didn't move from the small entryway. "Are you her cousin or niece or something?"

"No. I only just met her yesterday." Mentally giving herself a firm kick in the rear, Jen forced herself to sound more confident. "I'm, uh, interested in becoming a firefighter. Sam said the first thing I should do is visit the station." She stood there uneasily while he looked her over. She wasn't exactly short, but she knew she was thin and slight. Both were good when trying on clothes but neither screamed *successful firefighter candidate*.

"So you met her yesterday and then decided to come here?"

"Yeah." When he didn't say anything for a moment, she glanced down at the spiral notebook in her hands. All of a sudden, she felt even younger and more naive than usual. "Sam said I could come over today, but maybe I should have called and made an appointment?"

"You don't need one." He smiled as he motioned her inside. "Sorry if I seemed hesitant. Every once in a while we get a teenager who's in trouble and looking for a safe house. I wanted to be sure you were okay."

"Oh, I see."

"Sam and I are good friends. She's been saying for years that she wants to bring in some female candidates. I guess I'm looking at you so closely because she finally went out and recruited one. That's great."

"Doc, you aren't scaring Jen off, are you?" Sam called out as she strode forward.

He winked at Jen as he closed the door. "Trying not to."

"I was just telling him that you invited me."

"I absolutely did," Sam said as she patted Jen on the shoulder. "And I'm so glad you took me up on the invitation."

"Me, too."

"Now, did this guy even bother to introduce himself?"

What could she say? "Ah, no?"

"Sorry, Sam. I should've done that first off." He held out a hand. "I'm Anderson Kelly, Jen. I'm a firefighter paramedic. That's why a lot of people around here call me Doc."

She shook his hand. "It's nice to meet you."

"I'm going to give her a tour and then maybe see if the cap can spare us a few minutes," Sam said. "Where is he at?"

"He's been in his office for the last hour. I heard he's working on paperwork."

Samantha grimaced. "Well, good to know. Come on, Jen. Let's start that tour. Hopefully by the time we finish, Captain DeWitt will be in a good mood." She lowered her voice. "He hates paperwork."

"Oh." Jen smiled.

"Have a good time, Jen," Anderson said. "We're glad you're here."

Sam, who was in a red polo shirt, dark-blue chinos, and suede tennis shoes, led the way down the hall. "I know you might be tempted to take a lot of notes," she said, "but can I ask you just to relax and look around on this first visit? I want you to get a good feel for the place."

"All right." Jen slipped the pen she was holding back into her purse.

"Okay, here is the captain's office. Next to it is a conference area and next to that are the bathrooms and a private room in case someone comes in who needs assistance or a safe place."

Through the open door Jen could see a twin-sized bed, a chair and table, and a sink and mirror.

"We're a designated safe place," Sam continued, "so, say, a runaway is scared, or a woman is trying to escape an abusive situation, they can come here and we'll help them."

"Have you ever actually had anyone come in?"

"Oh yeah. Not all the time, but three times when I've been on duty."

"Were you worried about what to say to them?"

"No. We're trained for stuff like that." She beckoned Jen to follow her upstairs. "Plus, all of us went into this profession because we want to help people, you know? It's good to be able to help someone without having to save them from a fire."

"I guess it is."

"Here we are in our living quarters." She showed Jen the kitchen, rec room, more showers, and the cubicles where everyone who was on shift could sleep. "Now let's go down to where the good stuff is."

"What's that?"

"The fire engines, of course. That's where all the guys are."

Jen trotted down the stairs after Sam, then followed her down a short hallway and finally out to a huge garage bay.

Three men were working on one of the red fire trucks. One man was polishing chrome, another was doing something with hoses, and Anderson was on one of the steps writing something down.

"Way to get out of polishing chrome, Sam," a man with glasses said.

"Sorry, but I had important work to do. I'm giving a tour. Everyone, this is Jen. Jen, please meet Mark and Dave. You've already met Anderson."

"Are you working on a summer project for school or something?" Dave asked.

"No." She glanced at Sam, then added, "I'm interested in becoming a firefighter."

"You? What are you, in eighth grade or something?"

"No. I just graduated high school."

"Really."

Jen mentally took a step back. Dave wasn't being rude exactly, but it was pretty close. She didn't respond. What could she say?

"Dave, what's up with you?" Sam asked.

"Nothing. I was just asking a question. You gotta admit she looks like a kid."

"That kid is also standing right here," Mark said. Looking apologetic, he added, "Don't let Dave's bad mood get you down."

Feeling everyone's attention on her, Jen shrugged. "I won't. I know I look younger than I am, but I can't help that. Besides, if I ever do get the chance to be a firefighter, I'm going to be covered up anyway, right?"

Mark grinned. "Right."

A new awareness appeared in Sam's expression. "Good for you. Just keep looking at the positive, Jen. That's the best course of action."

Feeling relieved that she hadn't overstepped, Jen exhaled. "Okay."

"Great. Now, let me show you these trucks." Sam's voice grew more animated as she described the operation of the engine, tanker truck, and ladder truck. She even let Jen climb up into the passenger seats, just to get a feel for what that was like.

Finally, after letting Jen heft some of the tools to get an idea of their weight and function, Sam led Jen over to a long line of cubbies on the back wall. Each had a person's last name at the top. Inside were helmets, boots, and other parts of the uniform.

The pants and coat were tan and made of heavy canvas and, before Jen could stop herself, she reached out and touched one.

"What do you think?" Sam asked.

They looked intimidating but she couldn't say that. "They look as heavy as I imagined they'd be."

"Would you like to try my gear on?"

"Is that allowed?"

"Sure it is." Step by step, she showed Jen how to put on the pants and boots, pull up the suspenders, and then fasten on the coat and gloves. Finally, Sam placed the helmet on her head. The whole uniform felt like it weighed fifteen or twenty pounds, and she wasn't even wearing the breathing apparatus.

"What do you think?" Sam asked. The men in the area were watching her, too. No one looked derisive, though. Just curious.

Jen lifted her arms, displaying how the sleeves hung down over her hands. Sam wasn't that much bigger than she was, but those extra three inches—and probably ten pounds of muscle—seemed to make a big difference. "I kind of feel like I'm a little girl trying on her mother's clothes," she joked. "It's also bulky and heavy."

"During training, you do practically everything in turn-out gear," Sam said, "which is really tough, but it's good, because your body needs to be so used to the weight that carrying it feels second nature."

"It sounds awesome."

Anderson smiled at her. "You're really serious about this, aren't you?"

"I am."

"Why?" Dave asked. "I mean, you look like a smart kid. Why aren't you headed to some big campus?"

His direct question caught her off guard, but she realized she was glad to have the opportunity to explain herself. "It's true I did okay in school, but I didn't enjoy it that much. I also don't want to rack up a lot of student debt. I want to help people and I want a job that pushes me both mentally and physically."

"Those are all good reasons, but passing both the written and the physical tests is really hard," he warned.

"A lot of things are hard," she said before wondering if that sounded rude. "That doesn't mean it's not worth it, though."

"All right, then." Dave looked impressed in spite of himself.

"Thanks for letting me try this on, Sam," she said as she

unbuckled the coat. Just as she handed it over, a series of sharp bells rang out.

"MVA ignited a field near Rampart Range Road," a voice called out. "Two alarm."

Immediately, the entire atmosphere in the bays changed. Motor vehicle accidents brought a whole set of problems, but a two-alarm fire ramped everything up to another level. Sam reached for the pants. Jen had barely got out of them before Sam was pulling them on.

Around them, all the men were doing the same. Two of them had radios attached to their topcoats and were speaking into them.

Dave climbed into the first engine and turned on the ignition.

"I'll be in touch," Sam said just before she donned her breathing apparatus.

"Wait until we all get out, then you can leave," Mark yelled Jen's way.

Staying next to the uniform cubbies, she gave him a thumbs-up as two trucks pulled out, lights and sirens going.

When they were out of sight, she gave herself a moment to soak in everything that had just happened: The tour, Dave's doubt, Anderson's kindness. The trucks and the weight of the uniform. And, most of all, the way being there made her feel.

And she realized that she wanted more of that. She wanted to feel like she was a part of something. Part of something greater than her life at home or at work at Werner's . . . or even everything that was going on with Ryan.

"Hey, uh, Jen, right?"

"Yes?"

The speaker came toward her. "I'm John DeWitt, otherwise known as the captain of this firehouse."

She felt her cheeks turning red. "Hi. I'm sorry if I'm in the way, I was just taking a tour and—"

"And I just called everyone out." He finished with a

short laugh. "No worries. I'm on my way to meet them, so I'll walk you out."

"Thank you."

As he closed the garage bays and tapped something in his phone, he asked, "What did you think of our house?"

"I loved it."

"Yeah?"

She nodded. "I want to be a firefighter, Captain DeWitt."

"All right, then. Sounds like we need to talk." He pulled a card out of his pocket. "Leave a message and someone will put you in the schedule. I'll start gathering some materials together for you as well."

"Do you have any suggestions about things I can do to prepare?"

"I'd start getting stronger. Do push-ups, sit-ups, maybe weight training. Run, too—work on your endurance. No need to do anything too crazy—if you end up going into the program, your mentor will guide you about how to push yourself safely. But I won't lie. It's going to be a lot." He eyed her more closely. "Do you feel ready for that?"

"*Yes.*"

"Good." He started toward his truck. "See you soon."

"Thank you, Captain."

She pulled out her phone as she started down the sidewalk. She had one message from Emme, one from Kristen at work, and one from Ryan. She opened his message first.

How's it going?

Smiling, she texted back. **Good. I can't wait to tell you all about it.**

What are you doing now?

A new giddy feeling slid into her. Something really was happening between her and Ryan. The feelings she had for him weren't one-sided. Not at all. She cautioned herself not to sound like a dork and replied. **I'm still at the firehouse.** She was pretty proud of herself for not adding a bunch of emojis.

Do you need a ride?

I'm not sure. Let me check in with my sister.

I'll come get you if you need a ride.

Are you sure you don't mind?

I'm sure. Check with your sister then let me know.

She paused, then texted, **Okay.** Sure, she might have been too nervous to ask him to pick her up, but Ryan had offered!

After she clicked send, she called her sister. She really hoped Emme was too busy to come get her.

Chapter 14

$\mathcal{R}$yan was glad when Jackson and Adam had shown up at his house a couple of hours earlier. He'd just showered after going for a run in the heat. Even after drinking a couple of Gatorades, all he'd wanted to do was hang out in the cool basement. That was fine with the guys.

After playing Xbox for a while, they'd started watching TV from the giant sectional he and his dad had somehow gotten downstairs last winter. Adam had the remote and was flipping channels, Jackson was commenting on the shows, and Ryan was thinking about taking a nap.

But then Jen texted him back.

He was slowly learning that texting Jen was different from texting other girls. The other girls he'd dated had treated their cell phones like an appendage. They looked at their phones constantly, skimming through Instagram, posting Snapchat stories, or texting multiple people at the same time. Being with him didn't change that—it just meant taking selfies and posting them, like hanging out together was news.

Jen, on the other hand, was way too busy for that stuff. She was either working at the nursery, helping out at home, or running and working out. When he was with her she hardly ever looked at her screen. The flip side was that she rarely texted him back right away. He sometimes felt like one of those girls in the rom-coms Campbell loved to watch. More than once he caught himself staring at his phone wondering if she was *ever* going to text him back.

"You must really like this girl," Jackson said when he put his phone down after checking it for the fourth or fifth time that afternoon.

"Why are you calling her 'this girl'? It's Jen Ferguson. You know her." Noticing Jackson's frown, he added, "And, yeah. I do really like her."

"I'm kind of surprised you're so into her."

That pissed him off, but he didn't say anything.

Obviously annoyed by his silence, Jackson said, "Come on. You know what I mean. You can do better."

"I just told you I like her. What's your problem?"

Jackson leaned back and crossed his ankles on the coffee table. "She's not really in our crowd. Plus, she's stuck-up." He elbowed Adam. "Right?"

Adam didn't bother looking away from the screen. "I'm not saying anything."

"Come on. You know I'm right . . . and that I'm not the only one who thinks it, either."

Looking uncomfortable, Adam tossed the remote on the couch. "Jack, let it go."

Ryan glared at them both. "I don't understand what you two think is wrong with her. She's great. Really."

"I never said she wasn't," Adam said.

Glancing impatiently at Adam, Jackson put his feet back on the floor. "Come on, Halstead. She lives in that big house but she never has anyone over."

"How do you know that?"

"Junior year I had to do a group project with her, Eddie, and Molly in American history. We needed a place to meet and it wasn't like I could have anyone over, right?"

Jackson's mom had remarried a couple years ago and popped out two more kids. Going to his house was like stepping into a really loud day care center. "Right."

"Anyway, so I go, 'Jen, how 'bout we use your place?' and she just flat out refused, but would never tell us why. It's like she thought we weren't good enough to walk through her front door."

"Her dad died a couple years back," Adam said. "Maybe her mom didn't want anyone over."

"Oh. Well, whatever. My point is that Jennifer Ferguson isn't very nice. Plus, she's soooo quiet. And she's built like a jock."

"She might not have curves, but she's built just fine," Adam said as he flipped to some reality show.

Ryan whacked him on the shoulder. "Don't talk about how she's built, A. Or you, either, Jackson."

"Sorry. But even if you and her are getting along just fine, why are you dating anyone right now?"

"What's wrong with now?"

"Uh, because you're getting ready to go to college. You don't have to settle for our high school girls. You're going to have your pick from a whole crop of new ones in a month or so."

"Stop."

"Jackson does have a point there, Ryan," Adam said. "The last thing you want to do is go to college with a girl-friend back home."

"I'm only going to be in Pueblo, so it's not like the two of us are going to be across the country from each other." When neither of his buddies spoke, he added, "You guys need to stop talking trash about Jen and make sure no one we know does, either."

"Seriously?" Jackson asked.

"Yeah." Jackson was looking so irritated, Ryan finally blurted, "What's really going on with you? Why do you even care who I'm seeing?"

"I only care because we hardly ever see you anymore. You're always gone or trying to make plans with her."

"He's ticked because all this is new, Halstead," Adam interpreted. "You never used to make plans without us."

"Oh."

"Oh? That's all you've got to say?"

"That's all I've got. Sorry." When his phone dinged, he tapped the screen.

Sorry but Emme can't pick me up. Were you serious about your offer? If you're busy now I can walk home or call a Lyft.

Don't go anywhere. I'll be there in ten.

Are you sure?

Positive. On my way.

He stood up. "Sorry, but I've gotta go."

Adam groaned but stood up, too. "What's going on?"

"Jen needs a ride. I'm going to pick her up."

Jackson was still half reclining on the couch. "So you're just taking off?"

Ryan rolled his eyes. "Yeah, I'm just taking off. Deal with it."

Two minutes later both guys were gone and he was putting on a clean shirt.

"Mom, I'm going to hang out with Jen for a while."

She poked her head out of the laundry room. "Jen from the garden center?"

"Yeah. She's really cool. She's thinking about being a firefighter. She's over at the fire station and needs a ride home." Thinking about how much her mom didn't do for her, he added, "I might take her out to get something to eat, too. Is that okay?"

"Do you have money?"

"Enough."

She pursed her lips. "Come here. At least let me give you a twenty."

"Mom, you don't have to do that."

"All the more reason for you to have this. Either use it for your meal or to help fill up your gas tank."

"I promised you and Dad I wasn't going to mooch off of you two all summer."

"You haven't been. Take it, son. In a couple of months you'll be on campus having to eat dorm food."

"All right. Thanks."

"You tell her hello for me."

"I will."

"Hey, Ryan?"

He turned to face her again. "Yes?"

"I . . . well, I just wanted to say that I like Jen. She's a nice girl. And . . . I think she might need you."

"You think she needs me?"

"Yes, but not in a scary way. It's just that you've got a calm and steady way about you, son. That's a good thing." Suddenly looking embarrassed, she shook her head. "You know what? Forget I said anything. I'm probably the last person you want to get a seal of approval from."

She would be wrong. He leaned down and kissed her cheek. "You're a really good mom, Mom."

"I'll tell your brother and sister that."

$\mathcal{H}$e found Jen standing outside the firehouse, looking perfectly happy to be just leaning against the building.

Pulling up, he rolled down the window. "You ready?"

"Yep. Thanks so much for coming to get me. I wasn't looking forward to walking home."

"I would've been bummed if I learned you walked home instead of texting me. It's really hot out."

Her eyes warmed as she climbed into the passenger seat. "You weren't doing anything, were you?"

"Not really. The guys were over, but I was ready for them to leave."

"You sure?" She nibbled her bottom lip.

"Jen. Stop worrying so much. Now, how was it? Give me the rundown."

"Are you sure you want to hear about everything?"

"Positive . . . as soon as you tell me where you want to go eat."

"We don't have to do that."

"Come on, let's grab something to eat. What do you feel like?"

She shrugged. "Tacos or burgers?"

"How about Mexican?"

"That's good . . . if you're sure?"

"Yes. Stop worrying. I've got some money."

"I do, too. We can each pay for our own."

He grinned at her. "Now, tell me all about it. You met a female firefighter at the garden center, right?"

"Right. Her name is Samantha. She's amazing."

The whole way to the restaurant, Jen told him about the tour and meeting the guys, including the jerk who was trying to give her a hard time.

When she finished with how she had to hurry out of the turnout gear because Sam had to suit up and go to a fire, a chill raced through him.

Imagining Jen one day doing the same thing kind of caught him off guard. He'd been so focused on her goals, he'd forgotten just how dangerous the job really was.

When they got to the restaurant and sat down, he said, "I can totally see you being a firefighter, but I think it's going to freak me out."

"Why?"

"You could get hurt."

Everything in her expression softened. "Ryan, you know that I won't be actually fighting fires for a while, right?"

"Yeah, but that doesn't mean I won't worry about you."

Her cheeks flushed. "If we're still going out then, I'll make sure to be safe."

"Good. Because if we're still going out then, I'll definitely worry about you."

When she smiled at him, Ryan felt like he'd just hit a milestone, though he wasn't sure if it was with himself or with her.

Maybe it was both.

Chapter 15

$\mathcal{A}$ couple of times a year, firefighters from Woodland Park were asked to get together with other departments in the area to help train new recruits. Captain DeWitt always made it clear that no one from WPFD had to help with these sessions, but their participation would be appreciated.

Some people signed up only once a year. Greg, on the other hand, helped out practically every time. He not only felt an obligation to give back, participating helped him keep his skills up to date.

The drills were tough, but not as tough as either basic training or his Officer Candidate School—though he shared that opinion with only Mark and Anderson. It was plenty grueling for the recruits.

Staircase drills in the summer were brutal, for sure. Carrying packs in full gear up and down three flights of stairs was a common drill. It was an easy way for fire departments to see if a probie was in decent physical shape without a series of awkward conversations. Though even the best candidates could have an off day, everyone agreed that if a recruit couldn't easily climb stairs in full gear, they weren't going to be able to handle the job.

The stair climbs also gave the recruits a reality check. If they imagined that fighting a fire meant standing in a parking lot while pointing a hose, the total whipping of climbing stairs carrying seventy pounds of gear would prove otherwise. Doing it at seven thousand feet made it even more of a challenge.

Timothy and Roberta, the two probies from Cripple Creek running stairs with him, had looked like they were in decent shape. They were both in their early twenties and so far had done well in training.

But they were struggling now. Timothy was breathing so hard he might end up needing a shot of oxygen. Roberta just looked freaked out.

Realizing that neither of them was going to give in but both needed a pep talk, he called out to them on the tower's fourth landing. "Time for a break. Stop, you two."

Timothy scowled but didn't argue.

Roberta pressed her palm against the wall but shook her head. "I don't need a break, Greg. I can do this."

"I didn't say you couldn't. But I'd be lying if I told you I didn't notice that both of you were struggling."

"I'm not struggling," she replied. "It's just the heat that's getting to me."

Timothy was almost doubled over. "It is July. I mean, what can you expect?"

That was the wrong question. "I expect both of you to realize that y'all need to step up your workouts. It's obvious y'all aren't in good enough physical shape yet."

"I told you I didn't need to stop," Roberta said. But she was gulping down so much water Greg was afraid she was going to puke.

He was getting annoyed by their attitude. There were moments when he ached to stick someone in an army uniform and put them in front of Mark for a couple of hours. His usually mild-mannered buddy could yell louder than every other guy he knew. Mark Oldum in his drill sergeant glory was something to behold. He'd instilled waves of fear in hundreds of recruits.

"Look. It's hot, yeah, and it's going to be hotter when the whole building is on fire. But you know that, right?"

Timothy shrugged. "I'm fine. Let's go."

"Roberta, it might sound like I'm judging, but I'm not. I'm here to help you. To talk you through this. What are you having the hardest time with? The heat, carrying the weight, the stairs?"

Her lips went into a fine line before she muttered, "The weight, but I'll deal."

"I know you'll deal. But if you can use some ideas, it might be easier if you widen your stance a bit." He demonstrated. "This works different muscles, and it gives others a break."

Roberta gave it a try and trotted up four steps and then back down. "It feels awkward, but I can see it helping."

"Good. If it doesn't help at all, go back to your original stance. Sometimes what helps me is focusing on different things every time I climb a new flight. Try focusing on your legs one flight, then your breathing the next, then carrying the weight the next."

"Got it."

Turning to Timothy, he asked, "Anything I can help you with?"

"Nope."

"All right, then." Speaking into his radio, he said, "We're back on it, Cap."

"Get them to the top, then down here, then do it again."

"Copy." He pointed to the stairwell. "Okay, head up, go back down, then do it again. Go." Roberta and Timothy tore up the stairs. Knowing that Dave was up at the top, Greg elected to remain in position. They were going to need to do the drill on their own, for better or worse. If they couldn't handle being coached, or simply couldn't handle the grueling pace, then all of them needed to know now.

Minutes later, they passed him going down. He looked at his stopwatch, checking their progress. It was too slow, but Roberta, at least, didn't look quite as worn out.

He clapped his hands when they appeared again. "That's right. Good job. You've got this!"

By the time they came back down to his landing, both candidates looked exhausted but neither looked in danger of collapse.

If he had to choose, he reckoned he would rather have Roberta by his side. She might not be as strong as Timothy, but she was honest about her limitations and was willing to be coached. Timothy had simply made excuses.

After all the candidates had finished the drill, Greg descended the stairs. He found Timothy and Roberta with their breathing apparatus off and guzzling water. Neither recruit acknowledged him or spoke to any of the other recruits.

Greg clenched his jaw. Their poor attitude was another strike against them. It was the nature of the job to help one another. Thinking only of oneself would never work.

"What next, Cap?" Greg asked.

The captain's face was impassive as he handed Greg and Dave water bottles. "Let's head back to the station," he said. "I've got a mess of paperwork to get through."

"Roger that."

Without a word, Greg pulled off his breathing apparatus and unfastened his turnout coat. Sweat was dripping from his face and his gray T-shirt was wet enough to wring out. He ignored it as he and Dave rode back to the WP fire station in relative silence with three of the recruits.

After Dave parked the engine, Greg supervised the recruits in putting away their equipment. The second he put away his gear, Timothy pulled out his keys and headed over to his truck.

Roberta, on the other hand, looked like she was building up to something. "Thanks for your help up there," she said. "I did what you suggested and it helped a lot."

"I'm glad to hear it."

"Today was hard." She grimaced. "Obviously. But I'm going to get better. I'm going to practice until I am."

Pleased, he shook her hand. "Good."

She smiled as she reached for her purse. "See you," she called out before walking toward the exit.

"Roberta," Captain called out.

She turned to face him. "Yes, Captain?"

"What do you do now?"

"I'm a substitute teacher."

"Why did you choose that? Are you planning to be a teacher?"

"No, sir. I'm planning to be a firefighter. Substitute teaching was the most flexible job I could find. I'm going to do everything I can to be a successful recruit, sir."

Captain DeWitt nodded. "I know you're hoping to get on at Rifle, but what would you think about coming up here and working with one of our female firefighters? Samantha is one of the best."

"Thank you. I'd like that."

"Are you looking at other companies?"

"I'm looking at wherever will take me. Rifle said they'd be very open to me joining them."

"Rifle's a good house, but there aren't any women firefighters there."

"Yeah, it might be hard, you know?"

"I can see some advantages to working with Sam."

She nodded. "I see that. I'll do whatever it takes to achieve my goal. Uh, sir, does your suggestion mean that I didn't do as poorly as I thought?"

He grinned. "Obviously, you've got a ways to go. But

there's more to firefighting than carrying weight and climbing stairs. Everyone needs someone who has their back. Sam might be a good person to do that for you."

Roberta smiled. "All right. That . . . that sounds great."

"Come in tomorrow about eight. She'll be looking for you."

"Thanks. I'll be here."

The captain smiled. "Good."

After she disappeared, Captain DeWitt sighed.

Worried that the captain felt he should've done something differently with the recruits, Greg asked, "Everything okay, Cap?"

"Yeah. I just felt the need to step in. Oringer told me that Timothy cut corners. And he hip-checked Roberta when they got to the top. He did it hard enough for her to stumble." His lips turned into a flat line. "You know how I feel about that. Our job is not about competition. Yes, we push ourselves and each other to be in top physical and mental shape. We do *not* undercut each other."

"I agree, but I don't think he's going to take being cut easily."

"I'm not cutting him. That's Cliff's job over in Rifle." The captain shrugged. "Cliff might even simply talk to Tim and give him another chance. And, if he changes, he might make it after all."

Greg doubted it but kept that to himself. "Yes, sir."

"Better go shower, yeah?"

Greg nodded and did just that.

He spent the rest of his shift playing cards with Dave and Chip, going on two runs for minor emergencies, and then helping to clean out one of the bays. By the time he got home at seven in the morning, all he wanted to do was sleep.

His goals changed when he checked his phone and saw that Kristen had reached out to him the night before. He called her back.

"Hey, Greg. Is everything okay?"

"Everything's great. I just got off shift and wanted to tell you good morning. I didn't wake you, did I?"

"Not at all. I'm already downstairs watering plants."

"You sound happy."

"I am. I love mornings and I really love summer mornings." She chuckled. "They kind of remind me of home, but, you know, without all the humidity. How are you?"

"I'm good. I try not to take a lot of phone calls when I'm at the station. I learned that we can get cut off at any time."

"There's no reason to apologize. I can imagine the conversations you've cut off over the years."

"That's a fact. So, did you need anything when you called or just wanted to say hi?"

"I did want something. Um . . . I mean, I called to see if you'd like to come over for supper one night soon."

She was asking him out? "I'd love to. Are you cooking?"

"Of course. Do you like fried pork chops?"

"Of course . . . as long as there are mashed potatoes involved."

"I can do that. What night works for you?"

"I'm home the next three nights, then I'm back on for forty-eight hours."

"What about tonight? Or is that too soon? Do you usually just collapse in bed and sleep for twenty-four hours right after a shift?"

"Sometimes I collapse, but I'm feeling good. Tonight's perfect, Kristen. What time do you want me?"

"Six thirty?"

"What can I bring?"

"Only yourself."

"You sure? I can at least pick up a bottle of wine or a six-pack of beer." Remembering how Anderson said he'd won Chelsea over with ice cream, he added, "Or I could pick up a couple of pints of ice cream."

"Thank you for offering, but this is my treat. I'm not inviting you over just to give you an assignment."

"Understood. I'll see you then. Thanks."

"Thanks, Greg." Her voice sounded so soft and sweet.

After they hung up, he forced himself to tamp down his excitement. It was likely that she would keep him strictly in the friend zone and he was going to need to be prepared for that.

But he couldn't help but wonder if he'd finally be able to kiss her good night.

Chapter 16

Kristen knew she was a good cook. She wasn't a gourmet chef, but she could absolutely fry up a batch of pork chops or put together a decent casserole. Her mother had taught her all the basics of southern cooking. Some of it didn't always go over with girlfriends who counted calories, but most men seemed to like her food a lot.

So, she wasn't worried about making a decent meal for Greg.

It was everything else that was sending her into a tailspin. There was something special about him that she couldn't stop thinking about. Sure, he was handsome, but she was captivated by more than just his good looks. Maybe it was the way he had reached out to her but always worried he pushed too hard.

Or the way he'd taken the time to see her at the hospital.

She wished she could pinpoint just what drew her toward him but figured that it maybe didn't matter all that much anyway. What mattered was that she knew he was special and she wanted to get to know him better.

And, maybe, learn to relax around him.

At the moment, she couldn't figure out if she'd gotten too dressed up, fussed with her hair too much, or even went too far in setting the table.

She'd decided to wear a sleeveless black-and-white sheath dress with some strappy black patent leather sandals. Then she'd decided that her hair would look best curled around her shoulders and that her favorite set of gold bangles would go perfectly. Next thing she knew, she looked awfully dressed up for pork chops at her kitchen table.

Or, maybe it was more like she and her table were in sync, but it was too fancy for the casual supper she'd invited Greg to.

Reviewing the floral place mats, mismatched pottery, white cloth napkins, and assortment of flowers arranged in the center of the table, she was sure she'd gone too far. Greg might be from West Virginia, but he'd spent years in the army and as a firefighter up in the mountains of Colorado. His memories of southern tables had likely faded.

She'd insisted she wanted to be friends and she was dressing up the table like they were celebrating an anniversary or something. Talk about sending mixed messages!

"Girl, you've got to calm down and get a hold of yourself," she muttered under her breath. "He's a guy. He probably isn't going to notice anything besides the food."

Unless he noticed everything. In which case she was going to freak him out when he came to the door. Just when she decided to head back to her closet, she heard his knock. Throwing up her hands, she hurried to answer it, eager to stop second-guessing herself.

He was standing on her little landing in a pair of jeans, tennis shoes, and a fitted shirt that was untucked. He smelled like some kind of woodsy cologne and soap.

And he was looking at her like she'd taken him by surprise.

"Kristen, look at you. You're all dressed up."

She swallowed and tried not to let on how awkward she was feeling. "I think I was so excited not to have a date with a flat of begonias tonight that I went a little overboard. You wouldn't believe how much time I spend covered with mud and dirt." When he continued to stare at her, she felt her cheeks heat. "If you'd like, I could change . . ."

"No. I don't want you to change a thing. I think you look real pretty." He smiled. "Will you slap me if I tell you that I like this look on you?"

She chuckled. "As opposed to my shorts and T-shirts at work or in a hospital gown? No, I won't slap you for thinking that."

"You didn't wear a dress when we went to Chip's engagement party."

"I didn't want to look out of place, since most girls wear jeans all the time. I like dresses, though."

"I'm glad you pulled one out for me."

"Well, come on in."

Stepping across the threshold, he handed her a bottle of wine. "I have it on good authority that pinot noir goes with fried pork chops."

"I've heard that same thing," she joked. "Thank you." Putting the wine bottle on the counter, she waved a hand. "So, what do you think about the state of my apartment? Does it smell smoky?"

"Not at all. I might be the wrong person to judge, though. I'm around smoke all the time."

She laughed. "I'm going to pretend it smells fresh and clean. Feel free to pretend, too."

"No reason for that." He did a slow turn around the room. "Kristen, I gotta say that I'm impressed. I didn't know what to expect when you said you had an apartment above your shop. It wasn't this, though. It's so nice in here. You really know how to make things pretty." He ran a finger along her dressed-up table.

"My parents said the same thing when they came out. I

think my dad pictured me with bags of fertilizer stacked up next to my bed," she said with a chuckle. "I really wanted a space that feels like home instead of an extension of the shop."

"You succeeded."

Noticing that he really was looking around with an appreciative look, she said, "Would you like the nickel tour?"

"Of course." He looked down at his shoes. "Want my shoes off?"

"No. I might be feeling fancy, but that's not necessary."

"So, this is the bathroom." She opened the door and turned on the light. "It came with this giant cast-iron bathtub. Sometimes I think that tub is the reason I purchased the building."

"I like the tub and the floor. Was this here, too?" He indicated the black-and-white parquet tiles.

"No. There was some gross linoleum. I put the tile in." Recalling how much she'd stressed about the choice, she added, "I wanted something kind of elegant-looking, so when I took a bath at the end of the day I'd feel like I was someplace different than above the store."

He peered in the open doorway to the right. "And this is your bedroom?"

She led him in. The queen-sized bed, Amish-made quilt, pink sheets, and antique dresser looked as girly as the cast-iron tub had. "Here's the last part." Walking to the last room, which was really a glorified closet, she opened the door so he could peek in.

Greg politely looked inside, then his expression went slack. "Whoa. You've got yourself a little man cave."

"I believe it would be a woman cave." She laughed. "But you're right, it's definitely made for relaxing and watching TV. My dad never wants to do anything but sit in here when he and my mom visit."

Walking into the darkened room, he immediately sat down on the navy-blue velvet couch. "Oh man, this is comfortable. If I sat on this thing to watch movies, I'd fall asleep on it every night. Do you ever do that?"

"Sometimes." Across from the couch was a fifty-five-inch flat-screen TV mounted on a dark-navy wall. Attached to the television was surround sound. Next to the couch in a wicker basket were three neatly folded blankets. An ottoman and two side tables completed the tiny space. "I really like watching movies. And Netflix. And Hallmark. Basically, if it's on a screen, I'm happy."

"Not so much a reader, I guess?"

"I'm an equal-opportunity escape fan, but my all-time-favorite way to relax is to watch movies in the dark. It's probably because I'm outside in the sun talking to folks about plants throughout the day."

"I get that."

Feeling a little embarrassed that the tour had taken so long, she led him back to the kitchen. "What can I get you to drink? We can open your wine, or I have white wine, beer, soda, lemonade . . . water."

"Water's good for me, if you don't mind."

"Not at all." As she retrieved a glass and poured the water, she said, "I have a squash casserole in the oven. It will be done in about fifteen minutes. Would you like to sit down?"

"Sure."

She noticed he was smiling at her. "What?"

"You've taken me by surprise, that's all." When she bit her lip, he added, "Kristen, it's all good. You . . . well, you are just something to see. Here I thought I knew a lot about you, but you've surprised me with everything from your dress to the table to your movie room."

"Surprises are good, right?"

"Yes, ma'am." His expression warmed. "In this case, they're really good."

"What about you? What would I find in your apartment? Are you full of surprises, too?"

Some of the humor faded. "Afraid not. I haven't done much with my place. After the army I trained for firefighting, then moved out here with my buddies. I feel like all I use my place for is to sleep and store my clothes."

"I never asked you much about your life in the army. You were enlisted for a long time, weren't you?"

"I was. Almost twelve years."

"What did you do? Did you like it?"

"I was with an infantry unit. I did like it." A shadow fell over his expression. "I planned to do thirty years. For a while, it was . . . it was everything."

He sounded cryptic. Kristen wanted to respect his privacy but also wanted to get to know him better. "It sounds like you took to military life very well."

His expression turned more positive. "I did. Even though my parents wanted me to get a degree and live nearby, I knew that wasn't for me."

"I imagine it was a lot different than your small town in West Virginia."

"From the very beginning, I felt like I'd found my place. I loved the challenge of learning new things. I loved the structure of it all." He half grinned. "And even the rules."

"Really?"

"I'm one of seven kids. I promise, I was surrounded by rules, being told to pull my weight and wait my turn. A lot of the things some guys had a tough time getting the hang of felt like home to me." He shrugged. "I met some of the best men and women I've ever known there, too."

"Were you stationed all over?"

"Fort Carson, with some stints in Texas and training in North Carolina." His expression faded a little bit more. "And then, of course, our deployments."

"Where did you go?"

"To the sandbox." A muscle in his jaw jumped. "Iraq and Afghanistan."

She knew right then and there that he'd done and seen

things he didn't want to talk about. "You know what? I think dinner is done. Would you mind if we went ahead and ate?"

He stood up. "Not at all." He winked. "If you don't mind, let's not taint all your efforts with army talk at the table."

"Whatever you want, Greg," she said lightly. "Though if you hate my food, do me a favor and don't say so right away."

"I'm not going to hate a thing, sweetheart. I can promise you that."

It wasn't the first time he'd used an endearment, but it was the first time that it affected her so deeply. Here, in the comfort of her little place, all the problems she'd been focused on seemed to evaporate into nothing. It allowed them to simply be two people who felt a connection to each other.

Two people not stressing about fires and hearts and futures. Just a man and a woman hoping to get to know each other better.

Two people knee-deep in a pool of attraction, and neither one anxious to swim into deeper waters or return to the shallow end.

Chapter 17

$\mathcal{G}$reg was beginning to believe that he and Kristen were meant to meet. She was really special. He loved how easygoing she was. How she "got" so many of the things his mother had instilled in him back in West Virginia.

He appreciated how she was easy to talk to but didn't push too hard. She made him want to do everything he could in order to see her again. Very soon.

An hour after Kristen had served him one of the best meals he'd eaten in years, they were sitting on her cushy couch. At her encouragement, he'd kicked off his shoes and propped his feet on the leather ottoman.

After flipping through channels, they'd started watching old episodes of *One Tree Hill*, of all things. Kristen had taken her shoes off as well and had her feet tucked under her. "I used to be so into this," she giggled about the show. "Now all the drama makes me cringe."

"I was just thinking that," Greg said, though that was kind of a lie. As much as he was smiling at the teen angst, his mind wasn't really on the show. They could've been watching *The Love Boat* and he would've been pleased. All he wanted to do was think about Kristen, about how well they were getting along, and debate different approaches to convince her to let him see her again. Like tomorrow. And then the day after that.

Am I kind of obsessed? he thought with a shock. He'd liked Kristen ever since they met, but his feelings were heading into new, uncharted territory.

He wasn't exactly a player, but he'd sure never had a problem finding a girl to go out with.

When he was younger, he'd been full of himself, loving his life and eager to say yes to any challenge or opportunity that came his way. He'd put strict parameters on his dating life, making sure that the women he took out understood that he wasn't ready for anything serious.

He'd even once gone so far as to tell a woman in all seriousness that he was essentially married to the army.

But after Afghanistan, everything changed. He wasn't the same man. He wasn't as confident, he was haunted by memories, and his PTSD episodes hit him at so many unexpected times that he was perpetually on guard.

Then, of course, there was the fear he carried on his shoulders. He was so worried about being thought of as less than everyone else that he'd put up barriers.

Was he willing to pull them down to have a relationship with Kristen? Although the idea scared him, he thought he was ready to do that with her. Not right away, maybe not even soon. But eventually? Yes.

He'd seen how content his parents, his older sisters, and now Anderson were in their marriages. He wanted to give it a try. Maybe all he'd needed in order to change was to meet the right person.

Maybe Kristen was that woman.

"Greg, we can watch something else if you'd like."

He glanced her way. Kristen's earlier look of contentment

had faded into something that looked a lot like apprehension. Hating that he'd caused that, he sat up a little straighter. "Why do you think I want to do that?"

"Because you've been frowning at the wall?"

"Sorry. I like this show fine. My mind just drifted."

"Ah. Okay." She looked back at the television, but her hands were now folded tightly on her lap.

She was closing up. Maybe shielding herself from him. Boy, he was messing this up.

"Hey," he said as he carefully pulled one of her hands into his own. "What I meant to say was that I was sitting here thinking that I haven't had a nicer supper in years. It was wonderful. This is, too. You make me feel so comfortable."

Her hand relaxed. "I'm glad you liked it."

"I've liked everything. The table, the food, sitting here with you." He motioned with his free hand. "Your pretty dress. Even if you did this whole evening just to please yourself, it was special to me. You made me feel like I was worth the effort, and no one's made me feel that way in a long time."

"I did get a little carried away because it's been so long since I had someone over for dinner, but you *are* worth the effort, Greg." Her eyes turned soft. "You're easy to talk to and fun to be around. You're a great guy."

"Does this mean we can get together again soon?"

"I'd like that, but just as friends, okay?"

"Are you sure that you don't want anything more? I mean, you can feel what's happening between us, right?" Even though he'd already cautioned himself not to push too hard, he couldn't help himself. There was something good between them. She had to feel it, too.

No, he didn't want to be sidelined in the friend zone when all he really wanted to do was pull her into his arms and hold her close. And then kiss her until she clung to him.

With obvious reluctance, Kristen pulled her hand away.

"I do feel it, but . . . I still think it would be best if we just kept things friendly between us."

"Is this all because of your loser ex-boyfriend? Or is it something else?" Before she could speak, he blurted, "Is it me? Are you not into me?"

Regret filled her eyes as she softened her voice. "It's not you. You're a great guy. I'm flattered that you want to date me."

"You shouldn't feel flattered. Any guy I know would feel lucky to date you. You're special, Kristen." When it looked like she was pulling away again, he shifted so he could face her. "Look, all I want is to see more of you. We can take things slow, Kristen. Slow as molasses."

"Greg . . ."

"I'm serious. I don't expect you to do anything you don't want to do."

"I'm not trying to be difficult, but I just don't think I'm ready for another relationship. Not yet."

She was so firm. Adamant.

But a sixth sense was telling him that if he stepped away he might never get another chance with her again.

"Tell me why you've got me so firmly in the friend zone."

She blushed. "Does there have to be a reason?"

"Yeah. I think so, because my mind is going to all kinds of stuff I don't want to think about happening to you."

"Greg—"

He interrupted. "Were you hurt? Did someone hurt you physically?"

"Oh my gosh! No."

Well, that was a relief. But he still needed answers. He wasn't trying to be a jerk, but her silence was driving him crazy. "Come on, Kristen," he said, this time more gently. "I can't hide that I'm really starting to fall for you."

Her eyes welled up with tears. Now he really did feel like a jerk. "I'm sorry I pushed you. Just forget I said anything." Standing up, he added, "Thank you for supper. It was great. Nicest meal I've had in a long time."

"I wasn't just in a serious relationship, Greg. I was engaged to be married."

"What happened?"

As Kristen stood up to face him, she said, "He broke things off the day before the wedding." Voice shaking, she elaborated, "Clark broke up with me two hours before our wedding rehearsal at the church."

Greg felt his face go slack. "*What?*"

When she met his eyes, her gaze was filled with pain and embarrassment. "After he broke things off, he . . . he left. I had to tell everyone that he didn't want to marry me—his parents, my parents, the groomsmen, our minister . . ." She swallowed.

"Oh, honey." Aching for her, he tried to pull her into his arms, but she resisted.

"No, I need to do this right. On my own." Taking a deep breath, she continued, "I can honestly say that those next forty-eight hours were the worst of my life. Everyone was upset."

"I'm sure they wanted to wring his neck." He felt like punching the guy and he'd never even seen a picture of him.

"Yes, they were mad at how Clark ended things, but, um, a lot of people resented me. As though I knew Clark didn't want to marry me and tried to push him to go through with it anyway."

"That's stupid."

She chuckled softly. "Maybe, but you know how people are. Once the shock wore off, I heard about hotel bills and the cost of plane tickets. About wedding gifts and wasted weekends."

"Surely not from your family."

"No, they understood."

She didn't look convinced, though. "But?"

"But they had a lot of questions, too." Holding herself

even straighter, she added, "I could be imagining this, but I think there was a part of them that wondered what I'd done wrong. Like, how could Clark have been so committed one day and then walk away the next." She shook her head. "And then there was all the money they lost. Hardly any of the vendors would give them a break."

"It's understandable to be upset, but they shouldn't have put that on *your* shoulders. It was his fault."

"You know what was really funny? My mother and I spent a year planning my dream wedding and within a couple of seconds, it went from everything I thought I could ever want to a bunch of stupid stuff I never wanted to see again."

"Kristen, I've never really been in a serious relationship. Not so serious that I was thinking about marriage, anyway. But I will tell you, with one hundred percent certainty, that I would never ask a woman to marry me if I wasn't all in. There is also no way I would drop a bombshell like that and then walk away like a coward. No way."

Her eyes lit up. "I know, I can't imagine you doing that."

"That's because I wouldn't. Not. Ever." Tired of watching her try to be so stoic, he pulled her into his arms and kissed her brow. "As hard as it was to tell me, I'm glad you did."

She relaxed against him. "I am, too. Greg, I promise I wasn't trying to play games. I just really hate reliving it. I hate remembering how horrible I felt about myself."

He ran his hand along her spine. "I never thought you were playing games, honey."

"At least there's that." Pulling slightly away, she looked into his eyes. "I wanted you to know the truth about it all, but we're just starting out. I didn't want you to look at me differently."

"I don't."

"You're sure?"

"Kristen, even though I haven't been in a serious relationship before, that doesn't mean I don't know what they're like. My parents were married for twenty-five years. Two of my sisters are married. What I'm trying to say is that I have a pretty good idea about how to treat someone I want to marry. It's obvious that this Clark guy didn't have a clue."

She pressed her hand over her eyes. "Well, this is, without a doubt, one of the most awkward dinners I've ever hosted."

He had to grin. "It's been a good night, though."

"How can you say that?"

"Because everything's out in the open." He also knew that the evening's drama wasn't all on her. He could've handled things better. He wished he hadn't been so selfish. "Still, I'm sorry I pushed you to explain yourself."

"I'm kind of glad you did. Now it's out there. I don't have to stress anymore about how to tell you the truth." For a split second she looked panicked before gathering her composure again. "And now, if you don't mind, I think it's time we said good night."

As much as he would've liked to linger, Greg agreed that she probably needed a break. "May I call you later? Call you, still?"

"Yes, if you still want to."

"Of course I do. Look, I wish I was the kind of man who has all the answers ready-made in his head. I want to be the kind of man who says all the right things at the right time. But none of that is me." Struggling, he ran a hand over his head. "It's crazy, but I seem to know exactly what to do if a house is on fire. I knew exactly what to tell guys in my unit to do. But when it comes to relationships, I'm as green as any new recruit."

"That's okay with me."

She was gazing at him intently, obviously soaking up every word. When he continued, he made every effort to convey his sincerity. "I really like you, Kristen Werner. I liked you from the first moment I saw you trying to argue with your doctor while lying on a stretcher. No matter what happens in our future, I want to know you."

"I want to know you, too."

"Now that that's settled, I'll call you soon." He leaned down and brushed his lips against her cheek. "Good night."

"Good night."

She didn't move when he walked to the door and let himself out. As he walked down the steep flight of stairs, he wondered if she was still standing where he'd left her. Looking so alone. Maybe feeling so alone.

When he got home, he took a hot shower, threw on sweats, and got into bed. It was early. Usually he'd turn on a movie or a game and zone out for a couple of hours.

But his head was too full of questions—not for her, but for himself. He had loved growing up in a big family. He'd observed his parents' happy marriage, their mutual dependence. He'd seen his sisters fall in love, their bonds with their husbands. Why had he waited so long to commit his heart?

Was it just a matter of not meeting the right woman until Kristen . . . or was it something else?

Thinking about the anxiety he sometimes felt, his trouble sleeping, the reoccurring nightmares and feelings of guilt he seemed to constantly wrestle with, Greg felt another rush of dismay about the way he'd pushed Kristen.

She had no idea what he wrestled with.

And before this evening's conversation, he'd hoped she would never find out. But now it was obvious that he was going to have to open up to her like she had to him.

Someday.

Chapter 18

*W*hen Emme texted to say that she and Bill were coming over with dinner, Jen warned herself not to expect that Mom would be excited about having all three of them home together. But it was going even worse than she'd expected.

Mom was having a really bad night.

Even though Emme had supposedly told Mom she and Bill were bringing dinner, their mother had forgotten. Now she was glaring at Bill and Emme like they were nosy neighbors instead of her two oldest children.

"Isn't this a nice surprise," Mom said as she got to her feet. "All three of my children are home at the same time."

If they were on an old sitcom, Jen figured their mother's words would cue happy music and sappy looks from all the kids.

Or if Ryan's mother had said it. Mrs. Halstead seemed like the kind of woman who not only would say she was glad all of her kids were home, but she'd mean it, too.

Unfortunately, they weren't on TV, and the living room—and family—were hers.

Which meant Mom wasn't being sweet or sentimental. She was being sarcastic and mean.

Jen sighed. Why did everything always have to be so hard?

Bill noticed. "Jen, you want to go hang out in your room for a little bit while we talk to Mom? The Chinese food I ordered will be here in about half an hour."

"I'll stay here." She wasn't a little kid anymore. She wanted to know what was going on.

"Why do you want to stay here, Jen?" Mom asked in a brittle tone. "Are you just as curious about why Emme and Bill came over together?" Her expression darkened. "Or did you have something to do with this impromptu get-together?"

"I didn't."

"Are you sure?"

Emme, who'd been clearing off the coffee table, scowled. "Mother, there's no need to talk to Jen like that. And for the record, Bill and I decided to come over because we wanted to see what we could do for you."

"You mean for Jen," Mom said as she brushed a crumb from her sweater. "None of you seem to care what I need."

Jennifer gazed at her mother. Really looked at her. Her jeans were looser and the pale-yellow sweater hung on her frame and emphasized how sallow her skin had gotten. It was obvious that she'd lost more weight. The skin around her eyes was stretched tight.

She wondered if Emme and Bill were seeing the same things. Were they as worried about Mom as she was?

"What do you need, Mom?" Bill asked. "Are you sick? Do you want us to take you to the doctor?"

"Of *course* not. I'm *fine*." She lifted her chin. "I'm always fine"—but the chin started to wobble, and she went from anger to sorrow—"all I need is your father, but you can't bring him back!"

Bill flinched.

Her voice rose as she began a familiar rant. "I'm a widow. A widow at fifty." She waved a hand through the air. "This isn't the life I deserve! Your father and I had plans. Big plans. We were going to be so happy together once Jen was out of the house."

Jen turned away. The familiar words still hurt. She knew her parents planned to go on a big trip to Europe as soon as she went off to school. She used to laugh and tell them to be sure to send her a postcard.

But now the reminder of that missed trip made her feel sick to her stomach. Almost like it was her fault for being so much younger than Bill and Emme.

Emme put down the glasses in her hands and walked to Jen's side. She didn't speak, but rested her hand on the middle of her back.

"I'm sorry I upset you, Mom," Bill said. "Let's go sit down at the table."

"Why can't we just sit here?"

"Because we want to talk to you and the food is on the way."

"What did you order, anyway?"

"Chinese food, Mom," Jen said. "They already told us that."

"I'm not hungry."

"Oh, Mom," Emme murmured.

Boy, it was going to be a really bad evening. Their mother was acting out, Emme seemed more upset than usual, and Bill was obviously exhausted.

He walked to the kitchen counter and picked up a pair of coffee cups with hardened stains. "Mom, look around," he said gently. "If Dad was here, he'd be so shocked. You always kept everything nice. Instead, you've got dirty cups and dishes and old mail and who knows what else all over the place. We need to clean up this house."

"And go to the store," Emme said. "I peeked in the pantry, Mom. There's hardly anything in there."

"I did go to the store. Didn't I, Jen?" Mom swayed slightly as she blinked. "When did I go?"

"I don't know."

"How come? Oh yeah. Because you're always working. And going on dates with Ryan What's-his-name." She waved a hand as her voice cracked. "You're so busy, you never think about me. None of you do. Why don't any of you ever think about me?"

Before they could reply—not that there really was anything to say—their mother went into her bedroom and closed the door.

Jen sat down on the couch.

Bill cursed under his breath as he and Emme joined her. "Are you okay?"

She shrugged. "I guess."

"Honey, I think Mom's gotten worse. What do you think?"

"I think she's having a pretty bad day. Most of the time she's not this erratic."

"I know, I was here a couple of days ago when you were at work. She'd showered and gotten dressed, at least." Emme leaned back against the cushions. "I'm out of ideas about how to help her," she said with a sigh. "She's gone to church counseling, doctors, therapists. We've encouraged her to go to AA . . . Nothing seems to help." Her voice flattened. "I know she misses Dad, but it's like she's determined to be miserable. I'm starting to worry about you being stuck here with her, Jen. This isn't good for you."

It wasn't fun, Jen had to admit, but it wasn't like her brother or sister had tons of extra time. They both had more demanding jobs than she did. "I'm almost eighteen. At the end of August I'll legally be an adult. Then I won't have to be here. I can move out." Of course, she had no idea where to go.

Emme wrapped an arm around her shoulders. "Honey, that's true, but you don't even have a driver's license."

"I'll get one. I passed the written test a couple of weeks ago."

"How did you score?"

"I got a perfect score."

Bill, always so patient, smiled. "That's great, squirt. How come you didn't tell me?"

"I don't know."

He gave her a pointed look. "Is it because you didn't want to ask me for driving practice?"

"Maybe." She looked down at her lap. "You and Emme do enough for me."

"I told you that I like helping you out. We'll start driving this week, okay?"

"Okay."

"Good, we'll work on getting your hours, and while we do that, we can talk about what's next."

"I already know, Bill. I want to give firefighting a try."

"Just from taking a tour, you really liked it that much?" Emme asked.

"I did. I even met the captain and he gave me some suggestions for working out. But . . ." She looked away.

Emme leaned forward. "What's wrong, Jen?"

"If I'm training and volunteering at the firehouse all the time, I'm never going to be home. But I don't know how Mom will do if she's alone so much. I mean, she can't live here by herself."

Bill rested his elbows on his knees. "I think we should talk to Mom about living someplace smaller. And . . . maybe call Aunt Julia again."

"Don't do that."

"If Julia came over more often, she could not only help Mom but help you, too."

"No, Bill. I don't like her." Aunt Julia was too rigid. She always acted like Jen couldn't do anything right. Even worse, her aunt seemed to go to great lengths to tell their mother how disappointed she was in her. And, to a lesser extent, in Jen, Bill, and Emme.

Jen *hated* that. Her aunt always acted as if she and her perfect children would be doing really well if Uncle Brett suddenly died. It was like she thought *they* were all weak or something.

"Well, let's think about it." He looked at their mother's closed door for a moment, then said, "So, I have some news. I was going to tell Mom, but maybe it's better to wait." He took a deep breath. "I asked Brittany to marry me and she said yes."

"Bill! Oh my gosh!" Emme jumped to her feet and hugged him tight. "I'm so happy for you. I would say that I hope she knows what she's getting into, but you two are so good together."

"Thanks. I love her." He laughed. "I mean, I'm crazy about her." He looked over at Jen, who'd gotten to her feet as well. "What do you think?"

"I was just waiting for Emme to move." She hugged him, too. "I like Brittany a lot and I know she loves you. Congratulations."

"Thanks, squirt."

Bill looked so proud. "Does Brittany have a ring yet?"

"Of course I got her a ring. I even had lunch with her father. And, I got down on one knee and pretty much begged her to say yes."

"I can just imagine that!" Emme said. "Are you sure she didn't feel sorry for you?"

"Heck, no. She said it was the sweetest proposal ever. I did it up right."

"When are you going to get married?" Jen asked. "Have you picked a date?"

"We haven't gotten that far, but probably pretty soon. We don't want to wait much longer. We've been together forever, you know."

Jen nodded. "Since high school."

"We've been through a lot, that's for sure." He smiled. "Jen, Brittany brought this up—what do you think about moving in with *us*?" When she gaped at him, he added, "I know we were just talking about you living on your own, but if you're training to be a firefighter you probably aren't going to want to worry about paying rent and utilities and stuff."

"Why would you want me there?"

"Any number of reasons. Because you've got a lot going on. Because I'm making plenty of money and Brittany has a good job, too. Because if you were with us, then you could maybe be a kid again." He gave her a pointed look. "Or . . . maybe take care of yourself and attend an Al-Anon meeting."

"Bill, I'm not sure . . ."

"Okay, how about this? If we change some of our living arrangements, then maybe you won't always feel like you need to take care of Mom."

"You've really been thinking about this."

"I have. I know things have been hard for you. Sometimes I feel like you've been isolating yourself on purpose. Maybe if you were at my place you could have people over instead of trying to keep them away."

She hadn't realized that Bill knew she did that. All of what he was saying sounded great. Except for one thing. "What about Mom?"

"I think you moving out might help her."

"I agree with Bill," Emme said before Jen could disagree. "Jenny, the truth is that we need a new plan because it's obvious that what the three of us are doing isn't working. Instead of getting better, Mom's just getting worse."

"I've been trying to help her."

"Honey, I'm not being critical. Mom's leaning on you to do everything. If you were out of the house, she'd be forced to take care of herself—or get help."

Her brother and sister were making everything sound so easy, like Jen's moving out would flip a switch and suddenly their mother would stop drinking and crying all day and be able to function normally again. As far as Jen was concerned, those chances were pretty slim. "I don't know."

"Just think about it, okay?"

Bill took her hands in his. "I know you love Mom. We love her, too. But this burden on you isn't fair."

Even thinking about not having to worry about what her mother was going to say to her every time she opened the door felt like a huge relief. "I'll think about it."

"Good," Emme said. She smiled at Bill.

"Wait, this is starting to feel like you two had this all planned out." She turned to her sister. "Emme, did you already know about Bill proposing to Brittany?"

"Not at all. But Bill and I have been talking. We've been thinking that you need a change. I was thinking about having you move in with me, but I live farther away and I'm not making all that much. Not like our big brother here."

"Bill, are you sure that Brittany would be okay with me living at your house?"

"I'm very sure. I promise. She likes you a lot. Plus, she knows that I worry about you being here. If you're just down the hall, I might be able to sleep at night."

"I really will think about it." She noticed her siblings exchange glances again.

"I hope so." Bill squeezed her shoulder just as the doorbell rang.

Emme got their order and placed everything on the table. After their mom refused to come out to eat, Bill and Jen pulled out three plates, a bottle of soy sauce, and a bunch of napkins.

After they filled their plates, Bill said, "Come on, tell us about your tour of the station."

In between bites of moo shu chicken and fried rice, Jen filled them in, growing ever more animated until she finished with, "This female firefighter I met is amazing. Her name is Samantha and she's really cool. She's kind of hinted that she might be willing to be my mentor."

"That would be awesome," Emme said.

"I guess she's warned you how hard firefighting is in Colorado?" Bill asked. "Forest fires are no joke."

"I didn't think they were. I know it's going to be a hard job and that the training is, too. But I think I can do it. I've always been athletic."

Bill studied her for a moment. "Okay, then. How can I help?"

She blinked. "That's it? You aren't going to try to talk me out of it?" She looked at Emme. "Neither of you?"

"Jenny, I've always known you weren't looking forward to college. If you want to give firefighting a try, you should. But keep an open mind, okay? It might not be what you think it is."

"If I call the station house and ask if I can stop by again, would one of you be able to take me?"

"Of course. You can drive my car," Bill said. "You need to get your license. The sooner the better."

"I agree," Emme said.

"I agree, too. Thanks, guys."

Emme put her chopsticks on her plate. "Jen, remember something, okay? Whether you live with Bill and Brittany or you stay here with Mom, we're going to have your back. You don't have to hesitate to ask for rides or for help around the house. You are not alone."

Realizing that she felt like she was about to cry, she smiled again.

"Are you two ready to clean?" Emme asked.

Bill rolled up his sleeves, saying, "Yep. I call the kitchen. You guys can do the bathrooms."

"Fine, but you aren't getting out of grocery shopping with us."

"Fine, but we better not be there over an hour."

Jen giggled. Their brother hated grocery shopping. Even back when he was in high school he'd always try to get out of it.

Emme winked at Jen. "Some things never change. We'll have to make sure Brittany knows not to expect him to come home with groceries."

Jen felt so much better. Everything was still far from perfect, but her big brother and sister still had her back. Just like they always had.

Chapter 19

Ryan was sick of hearing the guys talk about their big trip to California. He waited impatiently for them to get on the road so he didn't have to hear another word about the VRBO they'd reserved, the parties they were sure were going to be happening nonstop, and girls in bikinis on the beach.

"Are you sure you won't change your mind and come with us?" Grant asked.

"Positive."

Jackson frowned. "Isn't Coach Mann paying you to help out with practice at the middle school?"

"He is, but I've got to save that money for school."

"That sucks," Grant murmured.

"It's fine." Ryan shrugged like he didn't want to party on the beach with his friends anyway. Who knows? Maybe it was even true. Not only were he and Jen seeing each other a lot, he had a big week coming up. The coach at Colorado State–Pueblo had called and asked him to try out for the team. Their second-string receiver was nursing an injury and they wanted to have someone on hand just in case their star senior receiver got hurt.

Not only did he enjoy playing, but being on the team would mean a break on tuition, so Ryan had a lot riding on his meeting with the coach in a couple of hours.

He was trying not to get his hopes up. After all, this was just a "conversation," followed by a tour of the sports facility and some brief drills. They might hate him, or they could be bringing in a bunch of other guys today as well.

But the coach had said that he liked what he saw on Ryan's game tapes.

Ryan hadn't even told his parents about it. He was nervous enough without feeling extra pressure. He didn't want to be swayed either by his parents or the guys whether to join the team or not. There were a lot of benefits to playing . . . but he didn't want to play for a coach or a team he didn't like. Football was not easy. Early-morning practices, getting tackled during drills, the frustration of warming the bench most games . . .

If only his friends would be on their way so he could take a shower and get ready to drive the hour south.

"Last chance," Aaron said with a grin. "I bet you could get your stuff together in ten minutes. You won't need much. Come on, it's our last summer together, you know."

"Yeah . . . until next summer."

"Who knows what that'll be like?" Jackson asked. "I'll be in Fort Collins, Adam's going to Mizzou. Grant's going all the way to Ohio."

And he would be in Pueblo. "You're right. It's gonna be different."

"Okay, see you when we get back," Jackson said as he and Aaron went into Grant's garage to grab the cooler they'd packed.

After looking around to make sure no one could overhear, Grant added, "My parents said that they could help you out if you're worried about the cost. It could be a graduation present."

"Thanks, but I really can't go."

Grant looked even more confused. "If it's not the money, what's the problem? Don't tell me you're so hooked on Jen Ferguson that you can't leave her for seven days."

"It is about the money, but it's also about other stuff, too. And you better watch what you say about Jen."

"Man, you really like her that much?"

"Yeah."

"You guys went out to the movies once and it's a big romance?"

"I've seen her a lot more than that."

"Whoa."

"What does that mean?"

"I feel like you're not telling me everything."

"Maybe I'm not."

Grant folded his arms across his chest. "What, so you've got a secret?"

The guy was pissing Ryan off. "Yeah. I've got a secret. Happy?"

Hurt burned Grant's expression. "Not really. I thought we were friends."

Ryan mentally rolled his eyes. "We are, but that doesn't mean I want to share every single thing I'm thinking or doing."

"Fine. See you around." Grant stormed off to his garage.

Ryan got in his truck and headed home. As he drove slowly through the neighborhood, he wondered if he should've just told the guys about the phone call from the coach.

But as soon as he considered it, he pushed it aside. The guys would have had no problem giving their opinions—and then sharing the news with everyone they knew, even after promising that they'd keep it a secret.

Glad that no one was home, Ryan headed down the hall to his room. He packed a duffel bag with cleats and a change of clothes. For a moment he wondered if he should wear something better than his favorite workout gear, but figured the team cared about how fast he could run and how well he could catch a football, not how he dressed.

Satisfied, he headed out.

Of course he was too early, so he swung by the nursery.

When he arrived, he spied Jen helping a pair of guys in their early twenties. Though he was tempted to walk right over and pull her into his arms, he knew Jen wouldn't be pleased about that one bit.

Instead, he simply kept watch, as inconspicuously as possible, hoping that he looked unconcerned.

"You look like a concerned boyfriend," said Kristen, Jen's boss. "Is she having a problem?"

"No. I was, um, just watching." *Great, I sound like a stalker.*

Putting down the plant she'd been holding, Kristen watched Jen for a moment as well. "Those guys don't look like they're bothering her any."

"Yeah."

"Still, I'm impressed you haven't gone over there."

"I'm not going to interfere with her doing her job. Plus, she'd kill me if I marched over there like—" He caught himself just in time. It wouldn't be fair to say he was Jen's boyfriend. At least, not before he made sure she was good with that.

She chuckled. "Yeah, I think she probably would get upset if you got in her business. Jen's pretty independent." Folding her arms over her chest, Kristen continued to watch. "She's holding her own anyway."

"I know." He tried to think about that in a positive way—when she glanced up and obviously noticed both him and her boss watching her.

She said something to the two guys and headed their way. A line had formed between her eyebrows. "Hi," she said. "Is everything all right?"

"Totally. I only came over to say hello to Ryan," Kristen said.

Jen turned her gaze to his. "I didn't know you were coming by today."

"I know. I had some time to kill before an appointment, so I thought I'd say hi. But you looked pretty busy, and I didn't want to bother you."

She rolled her eyes. "Those guys were asking about organic weed killer. I showed them what we have but they were pretty clueless."

"Yeah." Or they were just acting clueless as an excuse to keep talking to her.

Kristen made a big deal out of checking her watch. "You know, Jen, it's pretty quiet right now. Why don't you take a fifteen-minute break?"

"You don't mind?"

"Not at all. But take off your apron if you're going to stay here, okay? I don't want anyone to think you're ignoring them."

"Thanks, Kristen." Jen untied her apron and pulled it over her head.

The top strap got caught on her ponytail. Unable to help himself, Ryan reached over and freed it. Right away Jen's cheeks flushed.

God, he loved that. He loved how she didn't know how to hide what she was feeling. He loved not having to guess. "Here," he said, handing her the canvas apron.

"Thanks."

"Hey, want to go sit in my truck? I parked in the shade."

"Sure."

Before he knew what he was doing, Ryan reached for her hand, and she let him keep it nestled in his. Since they just happened to be walking by the guys who'd been flirting with her, he gave one of them a chin lift.

When they got in his truck, she grinned at him. "Okay, Ryan, what's going on?"

"Nothing. It's like I told you. I've got a meeting and had some time."

"What meeting?"

The realization hit him hard. Yeah, he'd had some time to kill, but the real reason he'd come was that she was the only person he wanted to talk to about the tryout. Jen was so sweet and supportive. "The coach at CSU-Pueblo asked me to come talk to them today," he said, and explained about the "conversation." When she still looked confused, he told her about the second-string receiver position.

"What? Oh my gosh. That's great!"

"It's nothing yet." He couldn't help but grin, though. "But it's really cool."

"What did your parents say?"

"I haven't told them. You're the only person I've told."

Her eyes widened. "Really? You didn't even tell the guys?"

"No way. They'd all have something to say about it . . . right before one of them put it on social media. Besides, it's just a tryout, not a done deal."

"Well, I'm going to think good thoughts."

"Thanks." He reached for her hand again. "Sorry if I was glaring at those guys."

"I don't care, but Ryan, I don't know why you would."

"You know why, Jen." He reached for her other hand and pulled her closer. "You know I like you."

"Yeah, but what if you make the team?"

"What about it?"

"Well, wouldn't you rather not have a girlfriend distracting you?" Her eyes widened. "Never mind. I didn't mean that."

"Jen, it's not going to matter if I'm on the team or not. I'll still like you." Leaning close, he added, "A lot."

When she smiled at him, he brushed his lips against hers. It wasn't much of a kiss, but it was enough to send a zing of excitement through his blood.

"I better let you go."

She reached for her door handle. "Will you call me later and let me know how it goes?"

"Yeah." Realizing that she looked a little stressed out, he blurted, "Hey, Jen, are you okay?"

"I'm fine." She pasted a smile on her lips. "I'm so excited for you."

"Jen, come on. What's wrong?"

She tucked her hair behind her ear and said, "There's some stuff going on at home, but I'll figure it out."

"Sorry I didn't ask you earlier."

"Don't worry. It's nothing bad."

"Promise?"

"I promise. Now, go break a leg or whatever they tell you to do before a tryout." She smiled at him, hopped down, and walked back through the parking lot.

He watched her until she disappeared into the nursery, then pulled out of the parking lot. The GPS said he'd arrive twenty minutes early. Early enough to stretch and pull himself together.

And maybe even dream for a little bit about being on the team.

Chapter 20

"*H*ey, hot stuff!" Samantha called out when Greg pulled into the parking lot at eight that morning.

Greg raised his eyebrows as he got out of his SUV and grabbed his tote bag. "Didn't you give me enough grief last night, Cat?"

She shut the door of her Jeep and tossed her bag over her shoulder. "Let's see . . . ah, nope."

"You're going to ride me all year about that stupid calendar, aren't you?"

Her grin got even bigger. "Yep."

"Great." He started walking to the open bays, hoping he looked immune to her teasing. He doubted he was putting up a very good front, however. Inside, he was cringing. Not as much as he had the night before, but pretty darn close.

When Emory, Woodland Park's marketing director, asked him to be part of the inaugural "Heroes of Woodland Park" calendar, he was flattered. He knew lots of charities sold calendars—this one would raise money for both the fire and police departments—but he didn't give much thought to what the process would actually be like. On the day of his photo shoot, he'd brought both his dress uniform and his usual "uniform" of jeans and a WPFD navy polo. It turned out that the photographer had something completely different in mind. Next thing he knew, he was wearing a pair of WPFD shorts, baby oil, and nothing else.

Last night's gala to celebrate the publication of the calendar was extremely awkward, with women of all ages hooting and hollering as he was unveiled as Mr. March. Of course, it wouldn't have been so bad if the whole gang from the station house hadn't been there to witness it.

There was no way he was going to let anyone know that he regretted taking the bait, though. If he even hinted that he wasn't in on the joke, the whole firehouse would yuk it up even more. Instead of making them feel more sympathetic, the opposite would happen. He'd get grief not only for posing in the almost buff but for being embarrassed about it. And who could blame them? He would do the same thing to any one of them—even Sam.

"Why you wearing so many clothes today, Tebo?" one of the guys in the bay called out.

Greg put on his best cocky attitude. "I thought I'd spare you today, since come March you're going to see me up on the wall in the kitchen all the time."

"I ordered two calendars. You're going to be hanging on *my* kitchen wall"—Sam winked—"*and* my parents'."

"Glad to hear it."

When they reached the open bays, Anderson and Mark were waiting. Anderson whistled low. "You look good in baby oil, buddy."

"Shut up. How did *you* see the calendar?" They weren't at the gala because they'd been on duty.

"The shindig was livestreamed," said Mark.

What in the world? It took everything he had not to blush. "I didn't know that."

"You looked good in that suit, bro."

He rolled his eyes. "I'm just glad it's over."

"Seriously, you did a good job last night," Anderson said. "Cap told me that the station got a big chunk of money in donations. Maybe even enough to finally purchase another tanker truck. We heard Jefferson County has two that are about to go on the market."

"That's great. I sure wish I hadn't been the only one from this station, though. It would've been better if all of us were in the calendar." He still didn't understand why he'd been the one selected.

Anderson put up his hands. "Believe it or not, they asked me, but there was no way I was going to show off my scars like that. I'm all for charity, but that's going above and beyond."

"What do you mean?" He would've loved to have had one of his old army buddies up there beside him.

"My fiancée likes that she's the only one to see me in all my glory," Chip threw in.

"I told them modeling wasn't my thing," Mark said.

Greg's head was spinning. "Wait, so I was only chosen because y'all said no?"

"But you did good," Mark said.

"You looked good, too," Sam added. Her eyes were sparkling.

Well, now he felt even more stupid. Why hadn't he just said no like the rest of them? "I'm going to go put my stuff up."

"Check in with Cap, too," Mark called out.

"Will do." He hustled inside, climbed the stairs to the lockers, and stowed his gear before heading back down to the captain's office.

Captain DeWitt was sitting behind his desk staring at the computer when Greg tapped on his door. Looking relieved, he waved Greg in.

"Hey, Tebo." He motioned for Greg to take a chair. "So, are you all recovered from last night?"

"Not necessary, sir. I didn't drink." He knew better than to start a shift hungover.

Captain DeWitt grinned. "I meant recovered from all the frisky women in the audience."

At last Greg relaxed enough to laugh. "It wasn't too bad. The ladies were complimentary."

"I bet they were. Cara told me that she almost went to rescue you a couple of times."

"Mrs. DeWitt is a good woman."

Cap smiled again. "She is, at that."

"I heard you wanted to see me?"

"Yep." He shuffled through a couple of papers on his desk and pulled out an envelope. Placing it on his desk in front of Greg, he said, "This is for you. Emory gave it to me last night. It's a gift certificate for a weekend at The Broadmoor for you and a guest."

Greg stared at the cream-colored envelope with his name written in gold calligraphy. The Broadmoor in southern Colorado Springs was considered one of the best resorts in the whole country. He'd never been, but it was in all the magazines and papers at least once a month with news of the rich and beautiful people who vacationed there, hiking and relaxing at the spa in the winter and golfing in the summer. There was also a lake, a pool, a bunch of restaurants and bars . . . every bit of it with a hefty price tag. "I don't understand."

"It's a thank-you from Woodland Park to the participants in the calendar."

"I did it for charity. I don't want a gift for doing my part."

"Copy that, but take it anyway."

It still felt wrong. "Sir, how about you and Cara go?"

"That's nice of you to offer, but no."

"Sir—"

"I understand your reluctance, Greg, but I think you should accept. The Broadmoor donated the gift certificates, so it's not costing the city anything."

Then he added, "The only catch is you have to go this

month, which is only ten more days. Is there someone you could take?"

Of course he thought about Kristen, but he wasn't sure if they were ready for that. Not after her big reveal at the end of their date. "Maybe. I'm not sure."

Captain DeWitt brightened. "What about your mom?"

"My mom?" He was just about to shake his head . . . and then realized that Cap was right. "That's perfect. My mother would love it."

"She's on her own, right?"

Greg nodded. "She is. She's worked really hard all her life. Getting pampered at The Broadmoor would be really special for her."

"Then I can't think of a better person to take. Everyone's got a ma they owe big. Take yours down to the Springs and do something nice for her."

"You're right. Thank you."

Captain DeWitt shrugged it off. "We'll do a check in ten minutes."

"Yes, sir," he said again as he walked out of the office. Deciding not to wait another minute, he went out into the hall, pulled out his cell phone, and gave his mom a call.

She answered on the first ring. "Greg?"

"Hey, Momma."

"Hey back. Why are you calling?" Her voice thickened with worry. "Is everything okay? I thought you were back on duty this morning."

"I'm good. Don't worry so much. I called about something fun."

"Really? What?"

After filling her in about the calendar and the party, he told her about the gift certificate for The Broadmoor. He wasn't surprised that she'd heard of the hotel. "I want you to come with me, Mom," he said at last.

"Me? Are you sure you don't have anyone special you'd rather take?"

"You're special!"

"Honey, you know what I mean."

"I promise, you were the first person I thought of." Okay, he would've gotten there sooner or later.

"Are you sure?" She sounded pleased but hesitant. "Maybe you want to take one of your sisters?"

"No way am I taking one of the girls and not another. Momma, just say yes."

"Fine. Yes." She giggled. "Thank you, Gregory."

"You're welcome. I'll fill you in on all the details when I get back home in a couple of days."

"Sounds good. I'm pleased as punch about this."

"Me, too. You're the perfect date. We'll have a grand time."

"That's laying it on a little thick, dear."

"Not really. You're fun, easy to talk to, and we can have a good time together without worrying about the future."

She chuckled. "One day you're gonna fall head over heels for someone. I promise, you won't be worrying about the future then, you'll be looking forward to it."

"Yes, ma'am." He smiled when he hung up, thinking about Kristen. He wondered if she really was the one.

Knowing it would do no good to dwell on it at the moment, he joined the others for the captain's quick overview of what had been happening, and then hustled back to the bays, ready to work.

"Where do you guys want me?"

Dave waved him over. "Could you give me a hand with this order? It's taking forever since I've been double-checking each item in the supply closet and in the ambulance."

"Will do." Counting supplies sounded like a perfect activity to take his mind off everything else.

Of course, as soon as he walked into the supply closet, he was greeted by a two-foot-by-three-foot poster of himself. Someone had taken a red marker and put a heart on his bare chest, then wrote *Mr. March* across his groin. The whole thing was tacky and humiliating and funny as all get-out.

"Ah, man."

Dave poked his head in. "Anderson and Mark put that up before they got off shift. What do you think, Tebo?"

"I think life-sized would have been even better," he joked.

Laughter broke out—just as bells rang.

Everyone froze as the dispatcher called out codes. Realizing that it was an MVA, Greg headed for the door. "All of us, Cap?"

"Sam, it's your turn to stay back. Probie Mick is here, too. Have him help with the laundry if you don't need him for something else."

"Roger that, Cap," Sam said. Greg thought she looked a little bummed but agreeable. Greg got that. It was standard procedure to never leave the station empty in case someone stopped by in need of assistance.

"Greg and Dave, let's go."

"On it."

Greg put on his turnout gear in sixty seconds, then climbed into the back of the truck with the captain just as Dave started the engine.

Five minutes later, they were heading down the highway. When they got to the scene, they found a vehicle on fire. A man was standing nearby, shouting that his wife was still inside the sedan. Two more vehicles were off to the side of the road, their drivers leaning against the guardrail.

Immediately the captain called out orders and Greg went to work, pulling hoses and spraying the vehicle with flame-retardant foam. As he did this, he was vaguely aware of Captain DeWitt attempting to calm the man down while he checked for injuries.

The fire was extinguished easily, but Greg wasn't sure if they'd made it in time to save the woman trapped inside.

Another fire truck arrived, bringing along two more

guys from another station. They immediately brought out the Jaws of Life, and Greg worked with their probie to slice through the metal.

Once they got an opening, Greg called out, "Ma'am? Can you hear me, ma'am?"

"Sit rep?" Captain called out.

"Unresponsive." As the probie pulled out another section of metal, Greg cut the woman's seat belt. "Ma'am?" There was no response. Frustrated, he called out to the captain, "Do we have a name yet?"

"Terri."

Greg concentrated on speaking slow and steady. "Terri? Terri, I'm Greg. I'm with the fire department and we're going to get you to the hospital."

He placed his fingers on her neck, searching for a pulse. It was there but faint.

Dave joined him. After they got Terri out of the vehicle and onto a stretcher, Greg put on a stethoscope and listened for a heartbeat.

Hearing nothing, his adrenaline kicked in. "We're losing her!" he said as he began chest compressions.

While the other team pulled out the defibrillator, Dave stayed by Greg's side, counting compressions.

When she was still unresponsive, they attached the defibrillator electrodes to her chest.

"Clear!" Dave shouted. When there was no response, he tried again as soon as the AED, the automated external defibrillator, recalibrated. And again.

Ten minutes later, it was apparent to everyone that Terri hadn't made it.

"Damn it," Dave said under his breath.

Gazing at Terri's lifeless body, a wave of dizziness overtook Greg. He closed his eyes and tried to regain his composure.

Then he heard a new voice over his shoulder. "Is my wife okay?"

The man's question pulled him out of his downward spiral but launched him into a whole new place of pain. "Sir, you need—"

"I got this, Tebo," Captain DeWitt murmured before wrapping his arm around the husband and guiding him away. "Ken, I need you to stand to one side. We need to wait for the ambulance to take her to the hospital."

Unable to look away, Greg watched the man process the news. "Can I see her?"

Again his captain redirected Terri's husband. "It's best if we stay to one side and let them work."

As the ambulance pulled up, Ken clasped two hands over his mouth. "Oh my God. Oh my God! It's bad, isn't it? How could this have happened?"

Greg stood to one side as Ken peppered the captain with questions. Dave and the paramedic took care of transporting Terri to the hospital. Minutes later, a policeman escorted Ken into a squad car and left the scene.

Greg walked back to the truck as the fire chief arrived. He'd stay with the vehicle while a team of investigators took notes and photos of the accident scene.

While the police took over, Greg's team headed back in silence. Greg kept reviewing everything in his head, wondering what he could have done differently.

Unfortunately, nothing came to mind. That was almost worse.

Almost as bad as knowing that he still had something like another forty-three hours of a forty-eight-hour shift to get through when all he really wanted to do was go home and collapse.

"What would you like me to do now?" Mick asked when they got back to the station.

"You can help us do what we always do," Greg replied. "Clean the truck, check supplies, and get ready for the next run."

"Hold on, what happened? Is everyone okay?"

Dave shook his head. "Nope."

"Greg? What does he mean?"

"He means that one of the victims died."

Mick's eyes widened. It was obvious that he wanted to hear the whole story, but Greg wasn't in the right frame of mind at that moment.

"Listen, let's clean the truck now. I'll talk to you about it later."

"But—"

"Later, okay?"

Mick stared at him for a long moment, then finally nodded. "Okay. So, um, should I get out the hose and start washing?"

"Yep." He smiled slightly. "Don't embarrass us, probie. Make sure this truck looks sharp."

"I'm on it."

Greg pulled off his turnout gear, neatly hung it up, and then pitched in to help.

Chapter 21

The phone rang three times before Greg was awake enough to check who it was. As tempting as it was to let his mother go to voice mail, he couldn't do it.

"Hey, Momma. You okay?"

"Hi, Greg. Oh, you sound tired. Are you exhausted?"

"I kind of am." He lay back down and closed his eyes. "Can I call you back? I didn't get any sleep last shift."

"Of course. But I did call for a reason." She took a breath. "I'm very sorry, but I can't go to The Broadmoor after all."

His eyes popped open. "Why not?"

"Meg fell and broke her wrist and needs surgery, so Rachel and Nash need me to help with the other kids. Plus Kristie and Drew and baby Jamie have the flu."

So far she'd listed his two oldest siblings. There were four others who could help out Rachel and Nash. "Can't Rachel ask her mother-in-law to help out with Meg for a spell?"

"Oh, you know how nervous Caroline makes your sister. She needs me."

"What about Stacey or Hope?"

"Hope is heading back to college, son. And Stacey . . . well, you know."

Stacey was flighty. "So it's up to you to be there."

"I'm sorry, but yes. See, Drew and Kristie were going to help out but they're really sick." She lowered her voice. "They just got tested for you-know-what."

His mother treated the word *Covid* like a profanity. "I see."

As much as he felt for little Meg, he hated how Rachel always acted like their mother was the only person capable of giving her a helping hand. "I guess it's too much to think of Quinn or Copeland to step up."

"You know Quinn is working full-time and it's Copeland's National Guard weekend." Sounding more distressed, she said, "Honey, I promise I tried to find someone else to take my place."

He was tempted to call every one of his six brothers and sisters and tell them not to deprive their mother of this much-deserved weekend at The Broadmoor, but he couldn't. One of them would complain to Mom and she would have plenty to say about that.

"Mom, I'm really disappointed. Can't Rachel and Nash figure *something* out? Don't forget I already bought you a plane ticket."

"I know, honey, but changing it wasn't a problem. I already called the airline. A nice lady named Sue couldn't have been more sympathetic. She said that she has grandchildren, too."

So, she'd already made up her mind. "Mom—"

"I'm going to come out around the middle of August. I'm sure we'll still have a good time. We always do when we're together."

"Yes, ma'am. But—"

She cut him off again. "Please don't be mad, honey. I know you're used to army life and now saving lives and whatnot, but everyone else is used to depending on me."

"Yes, ma'am. I was just really looking forward to giving you this." Because, well, between the army and living out west, he'd been awfully out of touch.

"Gregory, as much as I'd like to tell you that I can leave everyone in the lurch, I just can't." When he didn't answer immediately, she added, "I really can't, honey."

He bit back his disappointment. Yeah, he was feeling a little salty with Rachel, but he also realized that Mom *liked* being in the thick of things. It made her feel useful. There was simply no way she could physically bring herself to leave Meg when she was having surgery. "I understand."

His mother proved that she was still as perceptive as ever when she softened her voice even more. "Honey, it's okay if you don't. I know you may feel like I'm putting everyone else in the family ahead of you, but I really am trying my best."

All of a sudden Greg remembered getting his appendix out just after graduating from officer training. The whole family had caravanned to North Carolina to see him get his bars. Two days later, while he was out partying, he was struck by the most horrific pain he'd ever had. By the time he got to the emergency room, he barely had time to call his mom before the doctors rushed him into surgery.

In her sweet, calm voice, she reassured him that she was praying for him and he would be all right.

Greg learned later that she'd called all his siblings and her pastor, then got on a plane that night.

All he knew was that when he woke up the next morning, she was sitting next to his hospital bed, reading a magazine and sipping a Diet Coke like there was nowhere else she'd rather be.

To his shame, he realized that all this time he hadn't thought to wonder how she'd managed to do that.

It was the same after he got back from his deployment and Quinn found out he was suffering from nightmares. Mom made a dozen phone calls, found him a therapist, and lived in his crappy apartment for a week, cooking for him, doing laundry, and decorating the dingy place like she had an unlimited budget.

When he tried to stop her, she simply smiled and told him to stop fussing.

That's how she was.

Armed with the memories—and the knowledge that she wasn't perfect, but she was perfect for him—he said, "I love you, Momma. Don't worry about it."

"Maybe you can reschedule for August? That resort does sound awfully nice."

"I wish I could, but the room is just for this upcoming weekend."

"Honestly, honey, I can see you having a good time on your own. You'd get to relax. But is there someone else you could take?"

"Maybe. I have a friend I might be able to ask. She'd love the place almost as much as you. If she can't go, then I'll pass the tickets on to someone else at the station."

"She?" Mom's voice perked up. "Gregory, do you have a girlfriend?"

"Not exactly."

"Who is it? Is it Kristen?"

Pleased his mother had remembered, he smiled. "It is."

"Where's she from?"

Knowing that she'd like hearing that Kristen was kinda, sorta from their background, he couldn't help but grin. "Texas."

As expected, she sounded like he'd just found the perfect woman. "Oh, Greg. How nice is that? You found a nice southern girl right in the middle of Colorado."

He chuckled. "Mom, she's a nice woman, yeah?"

"Whatever. What matters is that you're seeing someone. Tell me about her. What does she do?"

No way was he going to dive down that rabbit hole. If he answered one question his mother would ask two dozen more. "That's a discussion for another time, I think. I really am exhausted."

"Oh. Of course. I'll call you soon. Get some rest now. And, Greg, thank you for understanding."

"There's nothing to understand. Rachel and Meg need you." And she needed to be needed. "I love you, Mom."

"I love you, too. Now, tell me the truth. Did you get hurt on your shift?"

"No, Momma. Just tired."

When he hung up, he stared at the ceiling and wondered how to ask Kristen to spend the night with him at a fancy hotel.

He had a feeling it might take a little more finesse than he was capable of.

The next morning, sitting across from Kristen at Jo's Kolache Hut, Greg explained all about the calendar, the gift certificate, his mother, and Meg's wrist.

Throughout his spiel, a variety of expressions flitted across Kristen's face—amusement, surprise, admiration, and concern. She stayed quiet, just taking in the whole shebang—whether she did it for his benefit or hers, he didn't know.

"That's quite a story," she murmured when he finally stopped. "I don't know what to say. Is Meg okay?"

He nodded. "I called Rachel early this morning. Meg had some problems with the anesthesia, so they're keeping her overnight. She should be heading home tomorrow, though."

"That's a relief, isn't it?"

He nodded. "I'm sure my sister's glad Mom arrived. My mother is the best 'sick mom' around. I don't know if it's because she had seven of us or if she's just special. She really does have the patience of a saint, though."

"She definitely does sound rather saintlike."

He winced. He really had made it sound like his mother walked on water. "I guess I exaggerated. She's not a saint, of course. She can yell orders like a drill sergeant. All seven of us are pretty different, but not a one of us willingly tells her no."

Kristen reached out and squeezed his hand. "Greg, I'm teasing you. It's a blessing to have a mother like yours. You're lucky—and she's lucky to have children and grand-children who appreciate her, too."

"I promise I didn't ask you to breakfast just so you could hear me sing my mother's praises. I really *do* want you to be my date for this weekend. The Broadmoor is too nice a place to visit alone."

"Thank you, but—"

"Listen, I don't expect anything other than for us to have a good time together."

"Are you sure?"

"I haven't forgotten our conversation at your place, honey."

She ran a finger around the rim of her coffee cup before meeting his gaze. "I don't know how to say this, but, uh, I'm still not ready for us to take things further. I don't want you to be disappointed." Looking even more awkward, she added, "And yes, I realize that I sound like I'm the biggest—"

He rushed to interrupt. "You don't. All I want is a fun weekend at a ritzy resort."

"Are you sure? I don't want you to feel like I'm giving you mixed messages."

"Babe, I'm positive. I already made sure the room will have two queen beds. I'm not going to do anything to sabo-tage where our relationship is going."

Kristen gave him a searching look. Picked up her coffee, took a long sip, and then set it back down. "Okay."

"Yeah?"

"Yeah." She smiled. "But I'm warning you, I'm going to want to explore the whole resort."

"I can handle that."

"Oh, I bet." Lowering her voice, she added, "And, just for the record, I'm going to want one of those calendars with your autograph, Mr. March."

"No way."

Eyes dancing, she folded her hands on the table. "Oh yeah. If you want me to go to The Broadmoor with you, I'm going to want a signed calendar."

"If I say no?"

"You'll be going to the resort without me, and I'm not only going to buy a dozen calendars, I'm going to reach out to the photographer—for all the outtakes. I'm sure he or she took tons of photos."

He was both amused and impressed. "You know what? You look mild-mannered, but there's a lot more to you than meets the eye. You're pretty scrappy, aren't you?"

"Oh, Greg. You have no idea."

Feeling like he could finally breathe again, he laughed. He couldn't wait to take her someplace special. He wanted to spend a lot of time with her so they could get to know each other. He wanted to show her off.

He wanted to hold her in his arms and kiss her until they both regretted their promise to sleep in separate beds.

Yep, without a doubt, she was special. Sweet yet fiery, stubborn but kind. He was starting to hate the idea of ever being out of Kristen Werner's life.

Chapter 22

Sam was standing outside one of the garage bays, sipping a cup of coffee, when Bill pulled up to the fire station. When Sam spied Jen, she waved.

"Do you know her?" Bill asked his sister.

"Yes. Her name is Samantha Carter. She's who I talked to at the garden center."

"So she's the reason you're here."

"Kind of."

Noting that Sam still had her eyes on her, Jen lifted a hand in a half wave. "I better go." She reached for her backpack. "Thanks for the ride."

Bill put his car in park. "Would you like me to walk over with you?"

"What, like it's the first day of second grade? No."

"Fine. Call if you need a lift home, okay? If I can't get you, I bet Brittany can take off work."

"Thanks, but I bet I won't." Sam had said if they weren't on a call then one of the probies could probably run her home, since it wasn't very far at all. Or she could walk. She opened her door.

"Wait a second. I think you should call me when you're done, no matter what."

"Why?"

He shrugged. "I'll want to know how it went."

"Because?"

"Because I'm going to want to know that you're okay and didn't hurt yourself."

If Bill wasn't such a great brother, Jen would probably roll her eyes or something. But he'd come through for her again and again. Whether it was making sure she had food at home, or helping out with her homework, or just giving her hugs and offering an ear to vent to. "Okay, I'll call, but I think I'll be fine."

"I hope you will be." Turning to face her, he added, "I better not hear you decided to walk home because you didn't want to bother anyone. Call."

"Fine. I will." She opened her door.

"Hey, Jen?"

Someone else was now standing with Sam watching her. "Bill, I've got to go."

"All I want to say is good luck, Jenny. I'm proud of you."

"Thanks." Her heart felt full as she smiled at him. "Bye."

As soon as she closed the passenger door, he pulled into a parking space and turned around. She looked back over at Sam. Anderson Kelly had joined her. She remembered him well because he had scars on his arms and face.

She mentally prepared herself. They were probably wondering how she could be a firefighter if she couldn't even drive herself to the station. On that thought's heels was her subconscious reminding her to stop overthinking everything. Armed with that mental boost, she approached the pair.

"Good morning," she said simply.

"Hi, Jen," Sam replied with a smile. "It's good to see you. You've met Anderson."

He held out his hand. "Hello, Jen. Glad you could join us today."

"Who was that dropping you off?" Sam asked.

"That was my brother, Bill."

Anderson gave her a knowing look. "Let me guess, he wanted to check things out?"

"Maybe, but he's a cool guy. He helps me out a lot."

"You're lucky to have him," Sam said.

"I think so, too." Figuring it was better to tell the truth than try and cover it up, she added, "Sam, I know I told you that I might need a ride home, but it's not just because I don't have a car. It's because I haven't gotten my driver's license yet. Bill was dropping me off because of that."

"Ah."

Jen added, "I'm going to get my license soon, though. I mean, as soon as I get all my practice hours in." Now she was wishing she'd taken Bill up on his offer to let her drive to the firehouse.

Sam shrugged. "Jen, it doesn't matter to me how you get here, as long as you get here on time. And you did."

"Okay." She was beginning to feel even younger and smaller than she already was. "Thanks for letting me come here again."

"Of course. I thought we could start with a more comprehensive tour, then you and I have an appointment with the captain about forty minutes from now."

"I already met him last time I was here."

"I know, but this time it will be more formal."

"Okay."

"Don't worry," Anderson said. "He does this with everyone who wants to join the department. Captain DeWitt is a good guy. He's also great with questions, so if there's anything you've been curious about, don't be afraid to ask whatever you want."

"All right." She rearranged the backpack on her shoulder.

"Come on in. There are some hooks near the lockers.

You can hang up your backpack on one of those. It'll be safe there."

"I don't mind holding on to it."

"But you don't need to. Firefighting is all about teamwork. And accepting help when it's offered."

After that tidbit, Jen strode into the garage and put her backpack up. Then Sam took her around again. But this time, instead of just showing Jen everything, she explained in detail what each person on the crew did, and the chores probies and candidates performed around the firehouse.

By the time they stood outside the captain's office, Jen was torn between wanting to sign up for classes right away and feeling completely overwhelmed and stupid for even imagining that she could one day be a firefighter.

"Come on in," Captain DeWitt said.

When they entered, Jen immediately felt better. The captain did look like a really nice man.

"Good to see you, Jen," said Captain DeWitt as he waved her and Sam to the two chairs across from his desk. "Sam told me you were going to be visiting again today. How did it go?"

She glanced warily at Sam, who gave her a chin lift. Jen exhaled. "I want to be a firefighter one day, sir, but I don't know if I'll be able to do it."

He grinned. "That's a good answer."

"Really?"

"Yeah. If you thought becoming part of this team was going to be easy, I'd be worried. I'm sure Sam or some of the others have told you that training is intense. No matter how you slice it, it's going to test you and push your limits." Looking more stern, he added, "But that's necessary, Jen. No matter how hard your training is, there will be many moments on the line that will be far harder."

She gulped. "Yes, sir."

After glancing at Sam, Captain DeWitt said, "Tell us about you."

"Me? Well, I just graduated from Woodland Park and I'm working over at Werner's Garden Center. That's where I met Sam."

He frowned. "We were called out there a couple of weeks ago."

"I know."

"Were you there then?"

"No, sir. I heard about it, though. My boss was rescued and had to go to the hospital."

Sam smiled. "And now she and Greg are dating."

The captain grinned. "It's starting to feel like you were meant to be around all of us. Have you met Greg Tebo?"

"I have. When he comes to the nursery he spends most of his time with Kristen."

"That sounds like Tebo." Looking at her more intently, he said, "Tell me what your long-term plans are. Do you want to eventually go to college?"

"I've debated taking some courses at Pikes Peak Community College, but I don't want to get my degree. I just really want to learn what I need in order to be a part of the fire department one day."

"I see. Some bigger departments have a longer and more formal training process," he warned. "Because we're such a small town, we have a more lenient one, but that doesn't mean it's easy. Being a firefighter carries an enormous responsibility."

She understood why he was treating her somewhat skeptically. She was just out of high school and hadn't even taken one of the junior firefighting classes that were popular at the tech high schools. He was probably imagining that she was feeling a little bit bored and a little bit lost and so she'd grabbed hold of firefighting.

Maybe that was true—at least to some extent.

But it wasn't everything.

"I understand," she said. "I promise, this isn't a sudden whim."

The captain exchanged glances with Samantha. He must have seen something in her eyes that he'd been looking for, because he turned to more practical matters. "All right, then. Here's what it's going to take. To get on here, you'll go through a series of interviews. Not just with me but with the chief. You're also going to have to do a lot of studying and take a bunch of tests. While you do that, we'll let you volunteer here, if that's something you want to do."

"I do," she said quickly.

"It's going to be a lot of grunt work," he warned. "You'll be cleaning trucks and cleaning bathrooms. If you go on calls, it will only be to observe. You'll also be doing PT with us."

"PT?" Jen asked.

"Physical training," Sam supplied. "Obviously, everyone on the line needs to be in top physical shape."

"I understand."

"I doubt you do," Sam said. "I thought I did, but I completely underestimated just how hard it was. Some days you'll wonder why you're doing it, but it's worth it in the end, I promise."

The captain continued. "When you start passing some tests and interviews, you'll get more responsibility and eventually start coming out on calls. And then, when you're accepted into the program as a probie, things will get more intense. You'll be expected to push yourself both in training exercises and in volunteer activities. You're not going to have much of a life."

Jen imagined that was true, but she figured she'd be gaining something she didn't have in her life. A sense of belonging. A sense of purpose.

Honestly, she couldn't wait to have both of those things.

"Okay. When can I start volunteering?"

"Are you sure you don't want to think about this? Maybe talk it over with your parents?" Sam asked. "If you start and then quit, it's not exactly going to make things easier if you decide to come back."

"My dad died and my mom . . . well, she's not all that involved in my life. She won't really care what I do, as long as I'm not at home much."

The captain's expression turned more serious. "Let me look at everyone's schedules to be sure, but you can start volunteering here as soon as you're ready."

"That soon?" *Whoa, dial it down, Jen. You're probably bouncing up and down like a kid.*

He laughed. "We need good people, Jen. We really need people who are eager to work and train. You're young, but that's not a bad thing." He handed her his card. "I know you're excited, but take at least a day or two and really think about this. If you say you're serious, then we're going to assume you are. We'll assign you a mentor, hand you a bunch of textbooks, and expect you to show up regularly, without fail." When she was about to interrupt, he held up his hand. "I'm not saying you won't, but even old guys like me remember what it's like to be your age. You're going to be giving up weekends and maybe nights out with your friends. You're going to be sore and tired and studying and spending days doing stuff you might never have done. There's nothing wrong with wanting to take a couple of weeks before diving in."

"Okay."

"Good. Call me whenever you're ready to begin. We'll go from there."

Sam stood up. "Thanks, Cap."

"Thank you. Thank you both."

When they exited the office, Samantha led her down the hall and said, "So, how are you doing?"

"I'm fine."

She looked skeptical. "Captain DeWitt can get intense. Do you have any questions?"

She did, but there was no way she was going to risk sounding even more naive than she already did. "No."

"Get out your phone and punch in my number." After Jen did what she said, Sam added, "Feel free to text me any questions that pop up. You can even reach out to meet for breakfast or something and talk some more, okay?"

"Okay."

"Listen, what Cap told you about being sure was good advice. We've got a hard job and it's pretty much always intense."

"I understand."

"Just for the record, Cap wasn't being discouraging because you're a seventeen-year-old girl," Sam added. "He gives everyone that spiel."

That made her feel better, though she wouldn't have been surprised if he pulled out that speech only for young recruits. Ironically, though, his warnings had made her more determined instead of wary. "I'm glad he told me everything, but I'm not scared. I want to get started."

"Listen, I had a hunch you'd say that, so I took the liberty of getting you one of the manuals. You'll need to read it and then read it again. Do you want it today?"

"Yes."

Sam still hesitated. "I just want to say this. Jen, I take my job very seriously. As the only woman on my crew, it took me a while to win everyone's respect. If I become your mentor, I'm going to be hard on you. Not just because you'll need to learn discipline, but also because I don't want you to let me down."

"I'm not going to let you down."

"Okay, then." Sam smiled. "I think some of the guys are in the lounge. I'll introduce you, and then you can help me in the kitchen. I'm in charge of supper today." She quirked an eyebrow. "Any chance you know how to cook?"

"I can make basic stuff, like spaghetti and casseroles."

"It's probably more than I can make." She grinned. "Jen, I have a feeling we're going to get along just fine."

"I think so, too. Thanks for giving me a chance."

"You're going to be great, little miss. We need good people and I'm excited to work with another woman. You're going to bring a lot to our team. Remember that, okay?"

"I will. Now, tell me what I can help with."

"Grab an onion and start dicing."

For the first time since she'd arrived, Jen felt herself relax. Even though the task wasn't firefighting, she was doing something useful.

Chapter 23

Four hours after Jen met with Captain DeWitt, Ryan pulled up in his truck. When he'd texted and she told him what she was doing, right away he asked if she had a ride home and offered to pick her up. She'd immediately accepted and let Bill know what was going on.

When Ryan texted to say that he was in the parking lot, she told Samantha that she'd be back in two days, grabbed her backpack and new manual, and hurried outside.

Ryan had stayed in his truck, but he was staring at the front door like he was afraid he was going to miss her when she stepped outside. He smiled when he saw her.

She stood for a couple of seconds just drinking it in—she couldn't help it. Sometimes she just couldn't believe that he liked her so much. She'd had the biggest crush on Ryan for two years, sure that he didn't even know her name.

Of course, she'd since learned that he knew her name. They just ran in completely different circles.

Now, though, everything had changed. He called and texted her and made plans and even picked her up when she needed a ride. Her reality was so far above what she'd ever imagined, she could hardly believe it. She almost wished she could give a pep talk to her younger self and reassure *that* Jen that all her wishing and hoping weren't going to be for nothing after all.

Now, whenever she thought about all the hours she'd spent secretly thinking about him, she blushed. She hoped he never found out just how much she used to watch him.

Frowning, he rolled down his window. "What's wrong? Did you forget something?"

"Sorry. I, uh, thought I did, but I'm good. Thanks for coming to get me," she added as she climbed in the passenger side.

"You're welcome. It was no trouble. Plus it gave me a reason to see you today."

"I'm glad about that, too."

"Good." He leaned close and kissed her brow.

She hadn't expected that. Before she could stop it, she was sure a goofy smile lit her face.

He chuckled as he put the truck into gear. "I was done working out and about to grab a late lunch. What do you think? Are you hungry?"

"Yes." She'd helped Sam in the kitchen, but she hadn't eaten a thing.

"You good with barbecue?"

She nodded. "That sounds perfect."

"So, how did today go?"

"It went great. I learned more about how firefighters train and how hard it's going to be to become one. Then I met with the captain and got a manual to study. Then I did a bunch of chores like cleaning and food prep."

"I can't believe they already have you working."

"I'm glad they do. I have an interview with the chief next week, and then I have to do a basic physical assessment."

"What's that?"

"They want to see how fast I can run, how many sit-ups and push-ups, that kind of thing."

"Are you ready for that?"

"I think so." She wondered if she sounded as worried as she felt. "It's going to be hard, but I'm excited."

He braked at a stop sign. "Yeah?"

She liked how he wasn't assuming he knew how she felt—or how she should feel. He was listening to her. Finally able to be completely honest, she said, "I'm excited, but I'm not sure if I'm going to be able to do everything, Ryan. And everything matters so much. I mean, it's not like I can only learn some things about the job but not others."

"You'll do it."

"I hope so."

He glanced at her as he turned right. "I'm sure you can do whatever you set your mind to. But I also understand your hesitation. I'm pretty sure there's a reason there aren't a ton of women firefighters. You're signing up to run into a burning building and maybe even carry someone out."

"Exactly. I feel like I can learn to fight a fire and eventually get strong enough to carry someone on my shoulder out of a building. But what if I can't do it in the actual moment? What if the flames scare me half to death or I freeze in an emergency?"

"What if you don't? What if everything feels right?"

She liked his positivity, but she couldn't help thinking about messing up. Her mouth went dry as she imagined failing—and someone getting hurt because she wasn't good enough. "It feels like every time I head over there I realize how much more there is to learn." She swallowed. "Plus, Sam told me that she doesn't want me to embarrass her."

"She told you that?"

"Well, not in so many words, but I get what she meant. She doesn't want to stand up for me only to have me change my mind or flunk out."

"One step at a time, right?"

"Yes, but . . ." She stopped herself before she sounded completely pathetic.

He frowned. "They don't expect you to know how to fight fires already, do they?"

"Not at all."

"Then no one can get upset with you if you mess up." He said it with such confidence she had to smile.

He turned into the Smokin' Hot BBQ parking lot. It was a hole-in-the-wall barbecue restaurant that seemed to have been in Woodland Park forever.

"Maybe," she allowed, "unless I mess up something important."

He smiled at her. "You won't, Jen. You're cautious and thoughtful. You don't say and do stupid stuff. We might not have been close when we were in school together, but I knew that much about you."

"Thanks for being so positive."

"Nothing to thank me for; it's all true."

"What about you?" she asked. "Why were you working out all day and skipping lunch?"

His eyes lit up as they walked to the entrance. "I got the official news this morning. The coach at Colorado State put me on the team. I'm going to be a Thunderwolf in Pueblo."

"Ryan! Congratulations!"

"Thanks. I can hardly believe it."

He sounded so happy, Jen couldn't help herself. She tossed her bag on the ground and threw her arms around him. Ryan wrapped his arms around her waist and held her close. "You're going to be amazing, Ryan."

"Now it's my turn to say I'm not so sure what I just signed up for. I know how to play football, but not college ball. Things are going to be really different."

"The coaches must think you can handle it, though."

"I hope so." He grinned as he released her. "When the coach called me this morning, I couldn't believe what he had to say." Suddenly looking embarrassed, he added, "I'm not going to be starting or anything. I'll probably only be keeping the bench warm, but it's still cool."

"What did your mom say?" She could only imagine how excited she must have been. He had the best mom.

"She went nuts and called Dad." He shook his head. "She's making a cake so we can celebrate tonight."

"That's wonderful."

"Yeah. I just hope they don't get their hopes up or anything. I probably won't get to play too much."

"Hey, you made the team! Enjoy it!" she said as they started walking again.

He shrugged as he opened the door to Smokin' Hot. "Thanks. Listen, don't say anything to anyone, okay? I don't want any of the guys to know yet."

She would've thought he had already called them all. "Why is it a secret?"

For the first time, he looked really uncomfortable. "If I tell the guys, they'll either get upset that I didn't tell them I was going out for the team or they're going to expect too much of me."

Jen wasn't sure either was the case, but she held her tongue as they got in line and placed their orders. Then they took their number and sat down at a table to wait for someone to deliver the food.

Now that they were alone again, she returned to the conversation. "What did you mean about the guys expecting too much—for you to start or something?"

He nodded. "Or to get them tickets or go to parties . . . I don't know." After a pause, Ryan added, "Or they're going to bring me down."

Jen couldn't hide her surprise. "I might not be friends with all those guys, but I've seen them with you," she said. "You're all really good friends. Jackson can be kind of a pain, but he's not mean. And Aaron is great. I'm sure they'll be happy for you."

"I guess."

A server came with their food. Ryan thanked her and then sorted out their plates. While he took a big first bite, she said, "Why do you think they'd bring you down?" He didn't respond immediately, and she added, "I'm not trying to make you upset, I . . . I just don't understand."

He darted a look her way. "Some people can't handle it if a friend all of a sudden gets a lot more attention or gets better at something and they're kind of left behind."

After chewing her bite of pulled pork, she asked, "Did that ever happen in high school?"

"Yeah. For a lot of guys, playing varsity football was a really big goal, you know?"

"The pep rallies and the decorated lockers . . ."

"Yeah. And the girls, and the fact that no one messes with you." He rubbed a hand over his face. "I know I sound like an ass, but that's how it was. The guys who were never that good seemed to be okay with not making varsity, but the guys who were kind of good? Or who thought they were better than they were? Well, they made sure everyone knew that they didn't think it was fair, and they didn't want to hang out anymore."

"And now it might happen again with college."

"Yeah. Guys like Grant and Jackson and Aaron were right by my side when we played on JV and then varsity. I knew that they didn't get as much playing time as me, but it didn't matter. We all assumed we'd never play seriously again, but now . . ."

Eventually, they changed topics and discussed movies and favorite foods and some of the clips they'd seen on social media. It was all nothing important, but kind of special, too. Little by little they were getting to know each other a lot better.

After they finished their meal and threw everything in the trash can, Jen picked up the conversation about playing football in college. "What changed, Ryan? Have you gotten a whole lot better?"

"I needed scholarship money and Jackson and Aaron didn't. After football season, Coach suggested I show some tapes to scouts and try to get recruited. He warned my parents and me that it was unlikely to lead to anything but it was worth a chance."

"Then something did happen."

"Yeah." He grinned a disbelieving grin. "It really is crazy."

"You shouldn't be so shocked."

"I can't help it. I wasn't like Austin Brown, Jen. Austin had scouts after him all the time and he got an offer to play D1 ball, which is the real deal." He lowered his voice. "But I hoped. So I worked out and I ran constantly."

"And the coaches at CSU-Pueblo noticed."

"Yeah." He rubbed a hand through his hair as they walked to his truck and got in. "When the guys find out, they're going to be happy for me, I know they will. But some of them might be jealous." He drove out of the parking lot. "Jackson's definitely going to be mad that I didn't tell him I was trying out for the team."

"Maybe not."

"No, he is. He's a good friend, but I know him pretty well."

He looked so bummed, she reached out and squeezed his forearm. "I'm sorry."

"Oh, it's no big deal in the grand scheme of things. I just haven't told them yet . . ."

"I won't say a word, but I have a feeling that the longer you wait, the worse it's going to be."

"I know you're right." He shook his head, as if to clear it. "Enough about me. What's going on at home?"

"My brother is still asking if I want to live with him."

"What's holding you back?"

"My mom." Realizing that she needed to be honest with him—as honest as he was with her—she went on, "We're all kind of realizing that our mom doesn't actually want to change or get better. I'm really afraid what will happen to her if I'm not there." Thinking of how much she'd changed,

Jen added, "She's pretty bad most of the time. When my dad first died, we all wanted to be there for her and support her, because she was in shock, but it's been two years now."

"I don't want to talk out of turn, but I think *she* should've been there for *you*, Jen." He pounded the steering wheel for emphasis as he turned left into her neighborhood. "You were just a kid."

"Yeah. I've thought that same thing." Pushing the pain away like she always did, she added, "Anyway, I've been doing more and more for her without hardly realizing it."

"Which is hard."

Glad Ryan understood, she nodded. "I don't really have much of a life. I work and then try to take care of my mom and the house. Going out with you—and deciding to become a firefighter—is a really big step for me. Emme and Bill think that if I step away it will force her to get her act together."

"They want her to either sink or swim."

Reluctantly, she nodded again. It was a good analogy . . . except for the fact that she was terrified her mother was going to sink instead of pull herself out of her funk and start swimming.

"What are you going to do?"

"I don't know. Bill is great; he's acted like a dad for two years now. But he's engaged. It might be weird living with them."

"What are your other options?"

"I could go live with Emme, but she lives in the Springs."

"Couldn't you try to be a firefighter there?"

"I could, but Colorado Springs is a big place. Things aren't lax in Woodland Park, but it's a lot more small-town, you know? Plus, everyone has been really nice to me there. I know it's not going to be easy, but I don't feel like I'm on my own. I feel like everyone in the department is rooting for me."

Ryan reached for her hand and linked their fingers together. She loved that he seemed to know that she needed that connection with him.

"How did you leave things with your brother?" he asked.

"I told Bill that I was going to need some more time to think about it."

Ryan nodded like her answer made perfect sense. "Then I guess that's what you'll do, huh? Take some time and figure out what you want to do next."

"Yeah."

He pulled up in front of her house. "Hey, do you want some company? I could come over for a little bit."

"I would like that, but I'm not ready for you to see how things are."

He lightly squeezed her hand. "Jen, are you sure? No matter what your mom does, I'm not going to judge you."

Jen stared at the way her hand was cradled in his and wished that she were brave enough to push all her insecurities away for him. But she wasn't. She needed Ryan in her life. Not just because she was at last dating her crush but because he made her feel like she was no longer stuck in some awful spin cycle. She was scared to death of scaring him away.

"Jen?"

"Sorry." Pulling her hand away, she unbuckled her seat belt. "Ryan, I know you won't judge me, but . . . well, I just don't know how she is right now. If she's really bad, it'll be something you can't unsee." Her whole body felt like it was on edge. She'd never been so honest with anyone about the awful shape her mother was in.

"But if she's really bad, at least you wouldn't have to deal with her alone, right?"

Hearing him say that she wasn't alone, she felt a lump form in her throat. "Thank you, but not yet. I appreciate you taking me home, though."

"I want to see you as much as I can before I head down to Pueblo. Just let me know when you're free or if you need a ride, okay?"

"Okay." Their eyes met and she felt a pull toward him that was as intense as any she'd ever seen in the movies. As much as it hurt, Jen forced herself to remember that they were about to be far apart. In just a couple of weeks, they were going to be in two different places, an hour apart. "I'll see ya," she said.

"Hold on."

"What?"

"Come here. Let me kiss you good-bye."

"Careful, hotshot college football player." She leaned forward. "Picking me up, kissing me good-bye . . . it's practically like we're a couple."

"What? You don't want to be my girlfriend?"

"Are you asking me to be?" Immediately, Jen wanted to eat her words. Man, she hated being so inexperienced.

He didn't smirk, though. "Jennifer, will you be my girl?"

She blinked. Waited a couple of seconds, just to make sure he wasn't being sarcastic. "Yes?"

For the first time, he looked wary. "You aren't sure?"

He was being completely serious. "No, I am." She mentally pulled her shoulders back. "I meant to say yes, Ryan. Yes, of course I'll be your girlfriend."

He exhaled a rush of air as though he'd been holding it. "You make me crazy, Jen."

His voice was a little husky. It sent chills down her spine, which felt stupid, but there it was. She liked him so much. "You make me feel the same way."

"Good."

His eyes lit up, which made her giggle. So she leaned close enough to place her hand on his chest . . . and kissed him. Ryan responded but let her take the lead . . . for about five seconds.

Then his hands went to her face, he cradled her cheeks,

and he kissed her again. His lips parted, he nibbled her bottom lip, and then everything deepened. She held on tight as she felt a spiral of desire twist inside her, felt her body practically become limp in his arms. It was amazing and shocking and everything she'd imagined.

Until she pulled away, breathless.

"You're too sweet," he murmured. "I don't know how I got so lucky."

His words were beautiful. The kind of words boys said in old movies—or in daydreams when she was a lot younger. Back when she'd thought that high school was going to be different from junior high.

They kissed again, but this time it was tamer, sweeter. They were both holding back and she was grateful for that. Right at that second, she wasn't sure what she would do if Ryan lost control. She enjoyed being in his arms too much. With him, everything else fell away like it didn't matter.

Finally, she got out of his truck and went inside her house.

The interior was dark again. Her mother hadn't gotten up to turn on any lights. She flicked on the entryway light, illuminating the sadness that seemed to permeate every inch of their house.

"Jen?" her mother called out.

"Yeah." Only duty made her walk into the living room. It was obvious that her mother had been there all day. A couple of glasses, two cans of diet soda, and an empty box of crackers sat on the table. Her mom had been mixing the soda with bourbon. Likely for hours. "Hey."

Her mother blinked twice. "Where have you been?"

"Bill picked me up and took me to the fire station. I was there for a couple of hours, then I went out with Ryan and he brought me home."

Mom looked dazedly at Jen. Was she trying to place the name Ryan, or deciding whether to complain about Jen being gone?

At last, her mom shifted the pillow behind her back. "You should've called, Jennifer. You still live here, you know."

"I know."

"I was worried."

Jen's mean side wanted to point out that Mom hadn't called or texted her. But saying stuff like that would either make her mother cry—or make her really mad. Jen wasn't up for either.

"I'm sorry," she said. "Next time, I'll call."

"Good." Mom turned up the volume on the television and picked up her drink.

Relieved not only that Ryan had taken her to get something to eat but also to be forgotten again, Jen went to the kitchen, poured a big glass of water, and headed to her room.

Only when she got there did she relax. Her room was clean and organized and pretty. It even had its own bathroom. It was everything people probably pictured when they saw the big house from the street.

All Jen cared about was that it was her haven.

She kicked off her shoes, put them in the closet, then washed her hands and face.

A couple of weeks ago, she would've been feeling bummed. Now, though, Bill had offered her a choice, the visit to the firehouse had offered a future, and Ryan had asked her to be his girlfriend.

Lying down on her bed, she rolled to her side and hugged one of her pillows to her chest.

Nothing was going to spoil her mood.

Not even being home again.

Chapter 24

$\mathcal{L}$ooking at all the dresses, shoes, and purses strewn across her neatly made bed, Kristen whistled. "When I asked if y'all could help me out with something to wear, I was hoping maybe one of you had a cocktail dress that was newer than four years old. This is incredible."

Chelsea, Mallory, and Kaylee all laughed. "After you called me, I called for reinforcements," Chelsea explained. "I don't have the greatest dating wardrobe. I wear mostly leggings and Anderson's old army T-shirts."

"Chelsea isn't lying," Mallory said. "There was no way we were going to let you rely on her help. No offense, Chels, but Kristen would look like she was about to go on a run."

"Yep. Next thing we knew, we had a group text going," Kaylee added. "It's been a ton of fun."

Jen smiled at them. "I really appreciate it."

Chelsea folded her arms over her chest. "All you had to say was Greg Tebo and The Broadmoor to spur us into action."

Mallory chuckled. "All you had to say was 'firemen calendar.' You've got yourself a bona fide hunk-of-the-month."

"Don't ever say that around Greg. He's so embarrassed by all the ribbing he's getting."

"Fine. But it is awesome." Kaylee lowered her voice. "And Greg really is gorgeous."

Somehow, Kaylee's praise of Greg made Kristen only more nervous. She was pretty happy with her looks, but she was enough of a realist to know that no one was going to ask her to be on any calendars anytime soon. She didn't need that to happen, of course . . . but his new calendar status did make her feel a little off-kilter. "I hope we have a good time there."

"You will," Mallory said. "I got to go to The Broadmoor last year when my parents came to visit. It's incredible. You're going to have the best time."

"I hope so."

"Of course you will. And Greg will, too." With a grin, Chelsea said, "I promise, Greg is going to be so glad he isn't taking his mother."

Thinking of their awkward conversation, Kristen said, "I think I can be a good date, as long as things don't get uncomfortable. Do you think it's awful that I set ground rules?"

All three women shook their heads.

"I, for one, am sick and tired of women being expected to go to bed with someone just because they spend money on me," Kaylee said. "It's degrading."

"I agree one hundred percent. Good for you, Kristen," Mallory said.

Wondering whether she'd shared too much, Kristen brushed hair out of her face and said, "Well, I wasn't trying to make a point . . . I'm just not ready to go there with Greg."

"I think it was smart to get everything out in the open. Now you won't be worried about Greg's expectations."

"I don't think he would've pressured you," Chelsea said. "He's not that kind of guy."

"Still, it would've been the elephant in the room."

"You and your sayings, Mallory," Chelsea teased. "Now, let's get Kristen ready to look fabulous. Start trying things on, girl."

Feeling a little bit like Cinderella getting ready to go to the ball, Kristen pulled off her T-shirt and shorts and put on one of Kaylee's gorgeous cocktail dresses. This one was a deep pink and made of some kind of stretchy silk charmeuse. Even though she was slightly curvier than Kaylee, the dress was so well made it conformed to her figure easily.

After smoothing it down her hips, Kristen padded over to the full-length mirror in the corner of her bedroom. Turning this way and that, she imagined what Greg would think. Did she come off like a tomboy dressing up in her older sister's dress?

As she eyed it critically, she noticed the three other women in the background.

"What do you think?"

"You look fabulous," Chelsea said.

Mallory nodded. "To be honest, I wasn't sure if it was the right style for you, it's so girly."

"I actually love that it's so girly."

"You've been holding out on us, Kristen," Chelsea said. "I didn't know you liked girly-girl dresses."

"I know I work around dirt, trees, and plants all day, but I actually do enjoy dressing up."

"I think this one is a winner," Kaylee said, "but try on Chelsea's black jersey dress next. That neckline is to die for and you've got enough going on to do it justice."

Never had she thought the fifteen extra pounds she was carrying around were going to be good for anything . . . but maybe she'd been wrong. Pulling off the pink dress, she shook the black one out.

"Did you make this one, too, Kaylee?" Kristen asked.

"Nope. I'm just a fan.'

"I bought it online," Chelsea said as Kristen pulled it on. "Anderson's mother actually told me about the site. They get a small number of a designer dress—just a couple of sizes for each item. I got lucky with this one." Her eyes widened. "Wow, Kristen. It looks like it was made for you."

Turning, Kristen smiled at her reflection—until she took in the top of her scar, which was visible above the deep neckline. "This won't work," she muttered.

"Why not?" Mallory came to her side in front of the mirror. She put her hands on Kristen's shoulders and turned her. "Look how the crisscross straps show off your back."

"It's a beautiful dress, but it—it shows my scar."

Chelsea frowned. "What scar?"

I can't believe you're acting like it's somehow invisible, thought Kristen. "Uh, the giant one in the center of my chest."

Chelsea frowned. "I see a faint red line, but it's not giant. It's not obvious at all."

"It's plenty obvious, and I don't want everyone to stare at it." *Okay, I don't want Greg to stare at it.*

Looking confused, Chelsea turned to the others. "What do you think?"

"I don't think it's that noticeable, either," Mallory said.

"Me, neither. I didn't notice it until you pointed it out," said Kaylee, "but if you don't feel comfortable, that's all that matters."

"I don't feel comfortable." Kristen picked up a pale-green dress. "I'll try on this one next. Whose is this?"

"It's mine," Mallory said. "I wore it in a wedding last year. I know I'm bigger than you, but I thought if you liked it Kaylee could probably take it in for you. I won't wear it again." She stood behind Kristen and zipped it up. "Oh."

"Oh?" Moving in front of the mirror, Kristen winced. It was every woman's nightmare bridesmaid dress. Cheap fabric, puffy seams, and an unforgiving design. "I look like I just gained ten pounds."

"I was hoping it would look better on you than me, but . . ."

"Sorry, Mal, I think you need to donate that dress," Kaylee said. "Remove it from your life."

She chuckled. "You're right."

"One more choice for you," Kaylee said. "Try this one on."

She held up a dress that could only be called a statement. It was longer than the others, in a bold geometric design of teal, peacock blue, black, and yellow.

Kristen looked concerned. "Um, I don't think it's really me."

"Everyone says that until they put it on."

She dutifully slipped it over her head and then gazed at herself in the mirror. "Wow."

Kaylee grinned. "You look fabulous."

"I agree," Mallory said. "It makes you look like the kick-ass woman you are. What do you think?"

"It's a great dress," Kristen said slowly, "but I don't think it's me." Though she couldn't deny that the dress was flattering, she wasn't that bold.

"Are you sure? You look amazing in it!"

"I'm afraid so. But I would love to take the pink dress."

"What about for the second night? How about the black one?"

"The scar, remember?"

"Are you worried about Greg seeing it, or the rest of the world?"

"He's already seen it. I made sure he knew about my heart condition."

"Sorry if I'm overstepping, but . . . are you worried about *you* seeing it?" Chelsea asked quietly.

Feeling acutely self-conscious, Kristen bit her bottom lip. "I don't understand what you mean."

"It's just that Anderson sometimes acts like other people only see his scars, but I barely notice them anymore. And most people who do gaze at them a moment or say some-thing are only curious. They ask if they're from the army or firefighting. They are concerned about him getting hurt, not pointing out that he has imperfections. He's the only one who's bothered."

Mallory frowned. "I'm with Chels. You talk about your scar like it's some dark secret, like an STD or something. But you were born with a heart condition, right?"

"Well, yeah. What's your point?"

"It's not your fault that you've got a heart that needs a little bit of extra love and attention. Why treat it like a mis-take to be covered up?"

"I get it, but there's knowing that . . . and wearing my scar loud and proud."

"I don't guess it helps if I tell you that one of the reasons I fell in love with Anderson was because of his scars?"

"That's different. I mean, he earned those scars fighting fires, right?"

"No, they're from a bomb in Afghanistan."

"In either case, those scars are symbols of his bravery."

"Not to him, though. A lot of the time, he sees them as flaws."

"Kristen, your scar is a symbol of all you've been through, too," Kaylee said. "I don't think there's a thing about it that should make you feel ashamed or embar-rassed."

"I hear you." Looking at each of them in turn, Kristen gave a small smile. "Thanks for the pep talk. It really did help. A lot."

"So, you'll take the black dress?" asked Kaylee.

"Yes."

While the three women gave each other high fives, Kris-ten giggled, but some of the excitement she'd been feeling had dimmed.

She understood where her friends were coming from, but they didn't know the whole truth. It wasn't just the physical scar on her body that was holding her back, it was also what the scar represented: The fact that her heart condition meant giving up her vision of her future. It meant never having children.

Once Greg knew the whole truth of it, it might even be what kept him from wanting anything to do with her.

Chapter 25

Greg had to admit it. The Broadmoor was amazing. Nestled in the foothills of Colorado Springs, the renowned five-star resort boasted a lake, a wilderness resort, six restaurants, eight bars and lounges, an eighteen-hole golf course, and a luxury spa. There was also a swimming pool, tennis courts, lots of shops—even a pair of swans swimming in the lake.

The walls were covered in priceless artwork and every person on staff was polite, eager to be of assistance, and constantly busy. Greg had never considered himself a fancy-hotel guy—a decent tent and a campfire in the middle of the woods suited him just fine. But after checking in and watching Kristen take a dozen pictures of the lobby alone, he figured he could get real used to hanging out there.

As long as someone else was footing the bill, of course.

By the time they'd been escorted to their suite—which included a private balcony—Greg was thoroughly impressed. He was also fighting back a wave of disappointment. His mom would have gotten such a kick out of the place. She probably would have already FaceTimed his sisters.

The Broadmoor was just the sort of fancy-pants place his mother used to dream about visiting. *Visiting* being the operative word, since they never could've afforded to even get lunch at a place like this. Five-star resort meant five-star prices; a hamburger cost twenty dollars! Going to a drive-thru with seven kids was expensive enough.

Though he understood his mom's reasons, he was still disappointed that she'd canceled on him. He would've loved to drive up to the entrance and watch the valet help her out of the car. Her smile would've lit up the place.

And his mother, sweet lady that she was, would've charmed them all by the time they'd been there four hours.

"Hey, is something wrong?" Kristen asked.

"No. I was, well, I was thinking about my mom. About how much she would've liked to be here."

Seeing the flicker of disappointment on her face, he quickly backtracked. "I apologize, that was rude. I'm very glad you're here. No, I'm delighted. It's just that, well . . ." Frustrated with himself, he felt like kicking himself upside the head. Why couldn't he just shut up?

Kristen placed a slim hand on his arm. "There's no need to apologize. I completely understand wanting to do something special for her. My mom and I are really close and I'd love to treat her to something like this, too."

"I'm glad you understand. But please don't take what I said the wrong way. I'm truly glad you're here. Thank you for coming. I'm going to do my best to make sure you have a good time."

"Don't worry so much, Greg. It may not seem like it, but I'm easy to please."

"Since you're here with me, I'd say you're very easy to please."

"Well, I do tend to be nice to people who take me to five-star resorts." She led him out onto the balcony. "This place is phenomenal."

"It really is." Gazing down, he saw a family with two

young kids and a dog walking along the lake. He wondered if the kids would ever have any idea how lucky they were to get to be there. Of course, right on the heels of that, he gave himself a reality check. Money didn't buy happiness and he had plenty of blessings of his own. It was past time for him to be focusing on that.

Turning to her, he noticed the way her ponytail hung down her back. Her bare back. She was wearing some kind of halter top that was the sexiest thing he'd ever seen. Almost every time he'd visited Kristen at the nursery, she'd been in shorts and a T-shirt. Those shorts had showed off a fine set of legs, which he'd thought might just be her best asset. Now, gazing at that expanse of glowing, smooth skin, he realized that every single bit of her was gorgeous.

He cleared his throat. "If I haven't said so already, I'm looking forward to spending more time with you this weekend."

"You have told me, and I feel the same way. I'm glad I said yes when you asked."

"You look amazing, by the way."

Her eyes lit up, like the compliment really pleased her. "Do you think so? I borrowed half my clothes from my girlfriends."

"Including this top?" It was a turquoise color and made of some kind of shimmery knit. The front had a high neck, which made her bare back even more of a surprise.

"Yes. I never would've bought it, but Mallory promised me that it was classy and comfortable, therefore perfect for here. She was right."

"It looks perfect on you."

"Thank you." She smiled again. "I'm so glad my girlfriends helped me out. When I started packing, I realized that most of my wardrobe consists of T-shirts and jeans. Obviously, I need to get out more."

"I'll be happy to take care of that for you."

"No, wait! I didn't mean that I wanted you to take me on more trips."

"Maybe I want to do that."

Her voice softened. "Maybe I'd like that, too."

"Good." Another burst of awareness hit him hard. Kristen had gotten under his skin. There was something about her that he not only really liked, but that he found himself needing. Maybe it was her positivity? Maybe it was simply the way she made him feel, like all of his burdens weren't quite so insurmountable. Whatever the reason, moments like this made him want to hold her close and figure out a way to make sure that he didn't mess things up between them.

"Are you ready to explore?"

"Yes." She was smiling like they were at an amusement park.

"Where do you want to go first?"

She pointed down to the path around the lake. "Do you mind if we go down there? I want to take some pictures of the swans." She rested a hand on his sleeve. "Oh my gosh, Greg. Do you think the swans ever fly away?"

"I couldn't tell you." She looked so concerned, he did his best to hide his smile.

"Let's go take pictures of them, just in case they're not there later."

"Whatever you want, honey."

Looking adorably embarrassed, she placed her hand on his arm. "I guess I'm acting like a kid, huh?"

"No, you're acting enthusiastic. And don't apologize for that. I love your energy."

Picking up her bag, she said, "How about after we walk on the lake, we go get lunch?"

"That sounds perfect."

Just as they were about to walk out of the room, one of the resort's managers knocked. "Mr. Tebo, we just wanted to make sure everything met your expectations."

"It's surpassed them."

"It's our pleasure to have you and your guest here. We appreciate your service in the fire department."

"Thank you, but it's my honor to be a firefighter."

"We also recently learned you were in the army?"

Greg nodded. "Yes."

He handed Kristen a gift certificate. "We hope you will enjoy dinner tonight on us."

She smiled brightly. "Thank you so much." After the manager bowed slightly, she turned back to Greg. "It's amazing, but I think our day just got even better."

He laughed. "Let's go see those swans."

Greg liked to think of himself as a guy's guy. Though he'd grown up with his sisters, he was usually more at ease with other men. Beyond a few very casual relationships with women over the years, he was used to spending most of his time with other men—or women who had the same profession he did.

All that meant that while he wasn't opposed to escorting a woman around the lake, it wasn't his usual idea of fun. He'd been game to make Kristen happy, but he'd started to wonder if he was going to be antsy, thinking that he'd rather be playing golf or hiking in the mountains.

He'd been wrong.

Kristen's excitement over everything at the resort was infectious. She chatted with other guests, watched a pair of mallard ducks land in the center of the lake, and took a dozen pictures of the swans. In addition, she noticed the variety of flowers and bushes, rattling off their names like certain guys could identify vehicles at a car show.

She also made him feel special. Not because they were at the fancy destination, but because of what he'd done. Kristen was proud of his job and the fact that he'd served in the army. Through her eyes, he began to see his choices not as reasons he couldn't afford to come to classy places like this on his own but as sacrifices to be proud of.

It was a different way of looking at his career. Maybe it was prideful, but Greg found himself standing a little taller and feeling more confident. For too long, he'd almost looked down on his career choices instead of embracing them. He knew it was because his brothers and sisters all seemed to have more money. He hadn't even realized that he'd felt that way, either.

*H*ours after their arrival, Kristen was still very, very glad that she'd told Greg yes when he'd asked her to join him. As much as she wanted to spend time with him—not to mention get to stay at the celebrated resort—she'd repeatedly cautioned herself not to set her expectations too high. She liked Greg, but spending a few hours with him on a date was very different from spending a whole weekend with him. What if they ran out of things to talk about? What if they found out they didn't like any of the same movies?

She'd worried not only about what to wear but about how much she'd have to spend out of her own pocket. Now she realized that if she'd gotten to the hotel with just a five-dollar bill in her wallet, she would've gone home with it, too. Not only was the hotel pulling out all the stops and treating them like royalty, Greg seemed determined to spoil her as well.

Here they were, sitting on the patio overlooking the lake and having cocktails before dinner, and Greg hadn't even blinked when practically every beverage option was at least fifteen dollars.

She was sipping her glass of wine, enjoying the fireplace that had just been lit, and having a great time people watching. But every time she glanced his way, Greg seemed to be looking at her.

"Greg, what's going on?"

"Hmm? Oh, nothing."

"I don't have something on my face, do I?" She lifted a hand and brushed back her hair.

He caught her hand in his. "Don't worry, Kristen. You look lovely."

"I'm not fishing for compliments. I just don't understand why you keep looking at me."

"Fish all you want. I'd just rather look at you than everyone else."

She smiled. "You have all the lines."

"I really don't. While I have dated a lot, I've never dated the same woman for longer than a couple of weeks."

"Not even when you were in the army?" She totally thought he'd had a girl back home waiting for him.

"Especially not then."

"How come?"

"Dating in the military can be tricky. First of all, the rules make it difficult for officers and enlisted soldiers to date."

"But aren't there women you meet at bars and stuff?"

"That's more of a one-night-stand kind of scene. That's not me."

"I see."

"And . . . now I'm completely embarrassed. Kristen, I was actually just thinking about how your ex was a fool."

"Thank you. I've thought a lot about it and I've decided that Clark actually did me a favor. I learned that he wasn't exactly the strongest guy in the world—and by that I don't mean weight lifting. He . . . he had no fortitude."

"Is that right?"

She wasn't sure if he was teasing her or not but decided to keep going anyway. "Clark had a list of things he wanted in a wife and in life, and he couldn't accept even one deviation. I'm not going to lie—I really was upset and hurt when he broke things off, but when my head cleared, I realized that even if my heart was fine, I didn't want to be married to a man who couldn't handle adversity or disappointment."

She waved a hand. "I could be wrong, but I've always thought that life is kind of a roller coaster. There're always going to be dips and twists—and half the time the worst things happen when they're completely unexpected."

"I can see your point."

"Do you, really?" She'd half expected him to look at her in a slightly condescending way, like she was naive.

"As a firefighter, I come across all kinds of people. Some victims fall apart completely. Others are strong as can be while their lives are burning down around them." His expression turned even more serious. "And that's true even though no one ever expects their house to catch on fire or to be involved in a motor vehicle accident."

"I imagine not." She took a sip of her wine. "I sure didn't expect the nursery to catch fire—or to start dating one of the men who saved my life."

He smiled softly. "When Anderson called me over to assist, I didn't expect to see you, acting all tough and feisty."

She laughed. "I was a pill. I'm surprised Anderson didn't try to knock me out."

"I think he might have been tempted, but I was charmed." Reaching for her hands, he added, "I still am."

He couldn't have said anything more perfect. And his words were accompanied by the sweetest expression. Kristen knew that her heart was finally open again. She might be afraid and wary of what Greg would say when she finally told him that she couldn't have kids . . . but she knew she was falling in love with him.

A couple of hours later, after they'd eaten and had a nightcap in one of the lounges, they walked back to their building on one of the dimly lit paths. The stars were out and the scent of jasmine and roses lingered in the air. When he paused, she looked up at him in surprise.

"I can't wait another second," he murmured before pulling her into his arms and kissing her gently.

Just as eager for his touch, she wrapped her arms around his neck and pressed close. And then there was nothing else to say. Greg was warm and solid and gorgeous and could kiss like a dream. Each kiss was slow and thorough and deep.

She honestly didn't know if they'd stood there kissing for ten seconds or ten minutes, but when approaching laughter pulled them apart, she had to catch her breath.

Greg looked caught off guard, too. For a moment he just gazed at her. Then he smiled. "We should probably go up to our room now."

"Probably so."

He took her hand and led her inside. When the elevator arrived, an elderly couple hurried to get on.

Greg held the door for them and asked what floor.

"Five, please," the woman said. Turning to Kristen, she added, "Isn't this just the most magical place?"

Kristen smiled up at Greg. "It really is. It's perfect."

When he ran his hand down her spine, finally settling at the small of her back, she knew he felt the same way. About the resort and their night together.

Things between them were going so well. At last, she might have finally found the right man for her.

Chapter 26

$\mathcal{K}$ risten wasn't sure why she'd put on makeup that morning. All she seemed to be doing was sweat.

It had been a long day at work—and it was only noon. While it was rarely superhot or humid in Woodland Park, both elements were in full force. Each made a day spent at the garden center a little harder; together they made it almost unbearable.

Needing a moment, Kristen went up to her air-conditioned apartment. After washing her face, she grabbed a glass of water and took a few gulps.

And realized that it was the first time she'd taken a water break all morning. No wonder she didn't feel too well.

Walking to the mirror in her bathroom, she pulled her hair from her face and tried to get excited to go back downstairs. It felt like an impossible task, though. It was four days since her weekend with Greg at The Broadmoor and she missed how relaxing it was.

Greg had been everything. Sweet, romantic, attentive, sexy. Each day they took long walks and explored the resort, swam in the pool, and dined by candlelight. They'd also talked so much.

He told her a dozen funny stories about growing up with so many sisters and she in turn told him how she'd become so interested in plants and gardening. Every time they talked, she learned something new about Greg . . . and became even more fascinated by him.

True to his word, they'd kept things easy. The most they'd done was make out for a few minutes before retreating to their separate beds.

As soon as they got back, Greg went on shift, had only twenty-four hours off, then went back for another forty-eight. She'd been fine with that since she knew she'd be working nonstop.

But now she wished they'd found a way to see each other, even for just an hour or two. She could've brought him a sandwich or an ice cream or something. She really missed him.

The truth was, she was falling for Greg Tebo. And . . . looking at her reflection again, she acknowledged another truth: her face looked fat.

Okay, not fat, exactly, but it looked puffy, like she was retaining fluid. And that meant trouble. The right thing to do was call Dr. Gonzales's office, make an appointment for as soon as possible to get checked out, and rest for the afternoon.

So, her brain was working just fine and she knew what she should do . . . she just didn't want to do it.

Maybe it was because she was so tired.

Which was another warning sign she needed to pay close attention to. If she was back home, her mother would have her at the doctor ASAP or on the way to the ER "just to check things out." At the very least, she'd have Kristen lie down with an oxygen tube attached to her nose.

"Your mother might be a nut, but she'd be right, girl," Kristen said out loud. "You need to tell everyone in the shop that you can't work the rest of the day."

The problem was that Jen was out and Marty was a good guy but didn't exactly think on his feet. After checking the time, she figured she could get away with another twenty minutes of rest, so she went to her bedroom, lay down on the bed, and turned on her oxygen.

But the digital gauge didn't budge. Feeling the tank, she groaned. She'd let it get empty.

With a burst of dismay, she realized that she hadn't been home to get the tank switched out because she'd gone away with Greg—and had taken her emergency supply with her.

It had been difficult to confess to Greg that she sometimes had to sleep with oxygen. But he'd been nothing but understanding.

Actually, he'd been amazing the entire trip. She didn't know a single other couple who had been dating the way they had been but still hadn't had sex.

Now she wished she'd thought about that a little bit. Greg was gorgeous and no doubt used to women doing all sorts of things to retain his interest. Why didn't he press her to sleep with him?

Maybe he'd already decided that she wasn't whom he wanted for the long term?

You need to settle down, she told herself. *The way he kissed you had nothing to do with friendship. It was intense.*

She sighed, which brought up a cough. And then another one. Yet another sign that she needed to get some help. Picking up her phone, she ran her thumb across the contacts, looking for Dr. Gonzales's number.

The knock on the door came just as she was about to connect.

Swinging the door open, she saw Marty. "Is everything okay?" she asked.

"No— Yes. We've got a problem." Looking even more agitated, he stuffed his hands in his pockets. "We don't have any of that fancy mulch that everyone likes so much."

"Which means?"

"Which means that Donna Claybourne is freaking out."

"Oh crap."

"Yeah. Can you come downstairs and talk to her? I've tried to take her number so I can call her to let her know when it comes in, but she's not having any of it. She's saying we promised her it would be here today and we reneged."

"All because of a bunch of wood chips," she tried to joke. The woman's attitude really was ridiculous.

Marty didn't crack a smile. "Kristen, Mrs. Claybourne is raising a stink and won't budge."

"I'll be right there."

"Thanks." He turned around and shot down the stairs like the whole place was about to collapse.

Marty was a dedicated employee, but she would appreciate him even more if he would take more initiative and manage more things on his own. Pushing off all hope of either calling the doctor or ordering more oxygen, Kristen walked down the stairs, needing to stop halfway to catch her breath. Uh-oh. She was really struggling.

The moment she stepped into the showroom, she saw that Donna Claybourne did look fit to be tied. Kristen wasn't too worried, though. The woman was picky, but usually reasonable.

"Hey, Donna," she said. "I heard you've got a mulch issue?"

The moment she saw Kristen, Donna's expression eased. "We sure do. Marty said that it's not here because of supply chain issues, but I really do need it, Kristen. We're hosting a family reunion in a week—and if my flower beds look terrible, I'm going to hear about it for years."

"That sounds awful," Kristen sympathized.

"If you met my sister-in-law you'd know I'm not exaggerating. Can you work some magic?"

"I could try another supplier, but that might be more trouble than it's worth. You could end up with two shipments."

"I don't want two shipments." She gestured to the phone

on the counter. "Can't you just call the company and tell them that your very good customer needs her order immediately?"

"I could, but that's not going to make a difference. If they had the mulch in stock, they would have sent it here. We sell a lot of it to a lot of people. I'm afraid you're going to have to give me a day or two to figure something else out."

"I'm sorry, but that just isn't good enough." She folded her arms across her chest. "I know how people work, dear. If supply is limited, then it goes to the squeaky wheel. That's me. And it needs to be you, too."

Donna was pointing to the phone. She expected Kristen to call the supplier and cajole and gripe right then and there.

She was all about customer service, but enough was enough. "I'm not going to call them right now. They don't have the mulch today. I'll call them in the morning and then get back to you, but I doubt my call will do any good. Everyone is in the business of making money. No one deliberately sits on an order as large as the one we've placed."

The woman frowned. "That's not good enough."

"I'm afraid it has to be."

"If you don't make this right, I'm going to ask you to cancel the order and I'll take my business elsewhere."

Donna's mini tirade was bringing in an audience. Whether it was the heat, the argument, or because she'd neglected herself for too long, Kristen felt the room begin to spin.

Donna and her words of irritation faded in and out. Then, with black dots clouding her vision and a jolt of dizziness, she collapsed, gasping for air.

"Someone call 911!" Marty yelled as he knelt down beside her.

"We are!" someone called out.

As her world turned black, Kristen found herself looking on the bright side. Maybe, at the very least, she'd get to see Greg again.

Chapter 27

$\mathcal{T}$he fire chief's codes and announcements were coming fast and furious. Pulling on his new gear specifically designed for brush fires, Greg processed the information coming through his radio as best he could; the words *neighborhood*, *evacuation*, and *tankers* leapt out like red flags.

This was going to be a bad one.

"Tebo, you're with me in the tanker," Captain DeWitt said as the first engine pulled out.

Greg turned to the large tanker truck designed to hold a thousand gallons of water. "Want me to drive, Cap?" Usually DeWitt liked to drive, but the radio was squawking so much, Greg figured the captain would want to be able to concentrate on the information and not the roads.

"Roger that."

Greg quickly climbed in and started the engine. Less than a minute later, they were tearing down the road toward the grass fire that had just erupted near the northernmost section of the county. He kept his attention on the road—and the vehicles whose drivers were either oblivious or simply idiots who refused to pull off to the side.

When one guy in particular stayed passively in their lane, Greg blared the louder-than-a-chainsaw horn, which worked. Finally able to proceed, they tore through the intersection.

"Roger that," Cap said into his mic. "We're four minutes out." Then he spoke to Greg. "Gun it, Tebo. That dang fire just jumped again."

When he pulled up, Greg parked where the captain directed. Without waiting another second, he began pulling hoses on the first engine that arrived.

"Hook up line four to the tanker," the captain called out.

"Yes, Cap." Immediately, he pulled the free hose to the tanker and connected it. Time seemed to slow as his training kicked in. He monitored the water output, assessed the area, then joined Mark and Sam on the line.

"Glad you could make it," Sam said.

"Wouldn't miss it, Cat." He widened his stance as he aimed his nozzle where Mark directed.

Scanning the area, he was dismayed to see that the flames had spread in just the seven minutes that they'd been there, aided, no doubt, by the gusts of wind.

As a team from another house arrived, Captain DeWitt radioed him. "Back to the tank, Tebo. Your replacement will be there in two."

"Roger that." After giving a mock salute to Mark and Sam, he handed over his hose to the approaching firefighter and hustled back to the tanker.

Soon, he shut off his head to everything but what his captain and his fellow firefighters needed. Some guys didn't like manning the tanker—they'd rather be on the front lines. That wasn't him. He'd learned a lot on the job, most notably that there was no insignificant role when fighting fires. All the cogs had to work individually in order for the machine as a whole to function.

For the next hour, he monitored the water level in the tanker and kept the chief updated.

And then, just when he was going to have to suggest pulling in water from a nearby pond, the fire was contained.

Low, cautious cheers rang out. It wasn't finished, but the fear that had hung over them settled. There was nothing worse than an out-of-control fire.

An hour later the only signs of the fire were clouds of smoke and the blackened ground.

"You're good, Tebo," Captain DeWitt radioed. "Disconnect the hoses and pull out the tanker."

"Understood."

Mark helped him put in the last of the hoses. "I've never been so glad to have this new gear," he said. "So much cooler."

"We're lucky." Partly with the profits from the calendar, the Woodland Park Auxiliary and the city council had raised money to give them grass-fire gear to wear.

The lighter uniforms were made of more breathable fabric designed to allow the firefighters to bend and move with more ease, since grass firefighting was lower to the ground than, say, buildings or even forest fires.

"We *are* lucky," Mark agreed. "Someone from Cripple Creek told me that they're going to try to do a calendar, too. Word is out that ours is bringing in big bucks."

Greg couldn't resist smiling. "Yeah?"

"Yeah. I feel bad for not participating. I should've sucked it up and did what you did, Greg. Thanks for stepping up."

"It was nothing. I'll see you back at the station."

"Yeah, okay, buddy."

After making sure that Cap was going back with the chief and no one else needed a ride, Greg pulled out and headed back to the station. Beyond a group of little boys on bikes who waved to him, the trip was uneventful. He was glad about that. He felt a little off. He wasn't sure if it was the adrenaline dump, the fact that he was tired, or even something as mundane as he was used to being in the thick of things, but he knew something wasn't right.

When he got back to the firehouse, he beckoned Mick over to help him wash the truck. He jumped right in, which Greg was glad to see. In no time, the vehicle was sparkling clean—just as the other vehicles streamed in.

"What do we do now?" asked Mick.

"Clean more fire trucks," Greg replied.

He frowned. "Don't they have to clean their own truck?"

"It doesn't work that way. Everyone helps where they can. That's how this place keeps running."

Anderson shot Greg a look. It was obvious that he'd overheard. "Sergeant Velasquez would be real proud of you, Tebo," he said, referring to an officer they knew during their first deployment. The guy was several inches under six feet, but he was a mountain of a man to everyone in their unit.

Greg greatly admired Velasquez. He never handed off anything that he could do himself, and he was extremely fond of giving everyone—officer or not—a piece of his mind if he thought they were slacking.

Greg hadn't realized it, but he'd just been that guy to Mick.

When all the trucks were in good shape and ready for the next emergency, he took a shower. The cool water felt good on his skin, but it didn't wash away the nagging sense of something bad on the horizon.

Still feeling strange, he told Mark he was going to get some shut-eye.

He'd barely lain down when the nightmare came. He was back in Iraq, in a village square playing hacky sack with some kids. Next thing he knew, a vehicle rolled up and exploded a few yards away.

"With me!" he screamed as he leapt on top of the boys and rolled them under another vehicle.

In his waking hours he'd replayed the next minutes in his head over and over. The boys' screams of terror. The heat pouring up from the ground. The sense of bewilderment and panic that he couldn't seem to brush off as another IED exploded.

By the grace of God, the only injuries the boys had sustained were a couple of bruises from his tackle. All he'd gotten was a good little gash from a piece of metal on the back of his calf.

But in this dream, everything went wrong. The bomb was closer, the boys died, and he'd been helpless.

"Greg. Greg!"

He sat up with a cry to find himself facing Sam and Mark. He was sweating and breathing heavily, as though he'd just run uphill.

Though a part of his mind knew where he was, he couldn't keep himself from grabbing at Mark's shirt. "The boys. The kids. Are they okay?"

Samantha frowned but Mark leaned forward and grabbed his forearms. "They're okay, T."

"You sure?"

"Yeah," Mark replied in his usual calm, steady voice. "We're not in the sandbox, buddy. We're in Colorado. We're in Colorado, and the boys are okay." Continuing to stare at him intently, he whispered, "They were okay. Remember?"

"Yeah." He let go of Mark. Little by little, everything came back into focus. He was at the station, not in Iraq. He was sleeping in one of the compartments, not in a tent. He was okay.

And he'd yelled loud enough to bring Sam and Mark over.

Shame filled him. "Sorry about that."

Samantha tapped his foot. "No problem. I'm just glad you're all right." She exited.

Mark stayed in place, a look of concern still staining his features. "Greg, how many of these are you having?"

He didn't even pretend not to know what Mark was talking about. "A couple."

"How often? Once a week? More than that?"

"Once a week." He looked away. "Thereabouts."

"You need to talk to someone."

"There's nothing to say. It's not like I can take sleeping pills or anything. I can't afford to be groggy on the job."

"You're right. But you can talk about it to a therapist."

"Come on, Mark. You know I don't want to do that."

Mark's gaze didn't waver. "Maybe you won't have a choice. A therapist will help you talk everything out."

"I can handle it."

Mark pursed his lips, then spoke again. "Buddy, think about Kristen. What if something happens between you two and you get serious? What are you going to do when you're sleeping next to her every night?" He lowered his voice. "Are you going to warn her that if you start freaking out and screaming to be sure she doesn't touch you, in case you think you're back in the desert and fighting off insurgents?"

Greg opened his mouth to retort, but closed it again, fast. The guy had a point. He'd barely slept at the resort with Kristen. She'd been worried about needing oxygen and thought he was being so understanding about it.

In truth, he'd been more worried about his own issues. He just wasn't brave enough to tell her about them.

Mark was right. There was a good chance he'd eventually have one of these dreams around Kristen—or whomever he ended up marrying. What would he tell her about them?

Was he just planning on sleeping separately forever if they went down the path he thought was in their future? Did he really want his wife to be afraid of him acting out in his nightmares? No way.

"Fine. I'll see someone."

Mark didn't move. "Promise? Because I'm going to be asking you about it."

"I promise." He had more at stake than his pride now.

Or maybe he always did but he was finally realizing it.

After Mark left, he lay back down, trying to get his bearings, when Kristen called.

Realizing that he needed to hear her voice, he picked up immediately.

"Hey, I was just—"

"Greg, I'm sorry, this is Kaylee. I'm a friend of Kristen's."

"Yeah. We've met."

"Right. Well, listen, I just wanted to let you know that Kristen's in the hospital."

He was on his feet. "Which one?"

"Pikes Peak."

"What happened? Is she admitted?"

"Yes. She's been here for about six hours now."

"Why didn't anyone call me earlier?" he blurted.

"We all heard about the big fire. Kristen didn't want me to call you, but I started thinking that you'd probably want to know. She was just taken for some tests, so I kidnapped her phone and decided to reach out."

"You're right. I absolutely want to know."

Kaylee exhaled. "Whew. I was hoping I did the right thing."

He glanced at the time. "I'm on shift but I get off in six hours. Will she still be there?"

"I'm afraid so. Her blood pressure and her lungs are both acting wonky. Kristen's putting up a brave front, but I'm worried, Greg."

"I'll be there as soon as I can."

After pulling on his shoes, he stripped the bed and took the time to make it again. With the way things were going, someone else was going to need to rest sooner rather than later.

His momma's favorite cliché had never felt more appropriate. When it rained, it really did pour.

Chapter 28

$\mathcal{K}$ risten was tethered to a hospital bed yet again. She had monitors stuck to her chest and an IV in her hand. Until a couple of hours ago, she'd even had an oxygen tube—which she unfortunately knew was called a nasal cannula—in her nostril.

Machines beeped constantly, while the nurses kept taking her blood pressure and poking her with needles—and naturally she was back in a hospital gown, too.

Nothing was unfamiliar but every part of it was unwanted.

And so, even though her brain was telling her to get a grip and be thankful for such good care, she was crying.

Oh, she wasn't bawling or creating a commotion. It was more like there was a constant, continuous stream of unhappiness that didn't seem to have an end in sight. Not to mention frustration with her surroundings, her testy, overworked nurse, and her parents, who couldn't stop calling, texting, and emailing.

She'd given up wiping her face with tissues, and now used them only whenever she had to blow her nose. Instead, she'd taken to swiping her eyes and cheeks with her hand, the neck of her hospital gown, or even the scratchy sheet.

Because of this, her face was blotchy, her eyes were red, and she looked even worse than she usually did in her hospital gown.

So when Greg poked his head in after knocking twice, she felt like nothing so much as throwing up.

"Hey, sweetheart, you decent?"

Greg was wearing faded jeans, a black T-shirt, and a tender smile. In short, he was gorgeous, perfect, and whole—while she was unkempt, teary-eyed, and broken. In short, she was not decent at all.

She hiccupped. "What are you doing here?"

"Well now, I think it's pretty obvious," he drawled as he stepped inside the room. Closing the door behind him, he added, "I came here to check on you."

She hiccupped again as more tears fell. Because that was the kind of woman she was now: a helpless, crying, ugly one.

Greg's expression had turned decidedly wary, and he stayed where he was. "Kristen, may I come on over to your side?"

His voice was now less West Virginia twang and more concerned army guy doing threat assessment.

And that's when she realized that he wasn't going to take a single step closer until she gave him permission. He'd closed the door so passersby couldn't see her but was still giving her space.

No, he was doing more than that. He was allowing her to make a decision.

That was usually the last thing she got when she was hospitalized. All her desires were overruled by people who were sure they knew better. And, since she was usually attached to more tubes and needles than she could easily remove, she was forced to do what they wanted.

Given that every orderly, intern, nurse, doctor, or janitor

felt free to walk right in, wake her up, touch her and prod her and write private notes about her in their precious charts . . . his sensitivity made the tears fall even harder.

Her hiccups turned into a coughing fit that hurt like hell.

Observing her tears, Greg strode to her side. Next thing she knew, he was rubbing her back and scanning the machines she was hooked up to.

"All right, honey. Let's take this nice and slow, yeah? Breathe in." When she did as he asked, he bent down slightly to look in her eyes. "There you go. That's better. Do it again."

Kristen inhaled as much as she dared. Taking a breath that was too deep led either to a coughing fit or a stitch of pain deep in her lungs. She closed her eyes and exhaled, concentrating on the way his hand was rubbing her back. What was it about his hand that soothed her in a way nothing else could? Was it because his touch was warmer? More confident? Like his firefighter training had given him a secret skill she hadn't even been aware was necessary?

Was it simply because he was Greg?

"One more time," he ordered.

She blinked and did as he asked. And realized that for the first time in about an hour her eyes weren't leaking.

"They stopped," she murmured to herself.

But of course, he heard her, too. He dropped his hand as he dropped to the chair next to the bed. "What stopped?"

"My tears." Ouch! Why did she have to bring up the fact that she'd been crying?

But since her pride had already gone out the window, she added, "I think something's wrong with my eyes. They keep watering. I can't seem to get them to stop."

His eyebrows rose. "Last I checked, people cry when they're in pain or sad."

Greg leaned back and propped a foot on the opposite knee. Just like they were sitting on the patio at Granger's having a Coke. "There's happy tears, too, but I've always been of the opinion that those don't come around as often as one might think. What do you think?"

She blinked. "About happy tears?"

"Yeah."

"Um . . . well, I suppose I haven't cried all that often because I was happy. It's been more of a sad kind of thing."

He smiled. "That's been the case with me, too." Looking more concerned, he added, "I'm sorry you're feeling so bad and sad, honey."

"Me, too." She licked her bottom lip, which felt far too dry. "Thanks for coming over. You didn't have to, though. I heard about the big fire. Were you there?"

"I was, but it's out now."

She looked him over. His eyes looked tired, but she didn't notice any new cuts or bruises. Or a burn. "Greg, are you okay? Did you get hurt?"

"No."

"What about everyone else?"

"Don't worry." When she obviously wanted more of a report, he added, "I heard a guy from Cripple Creek got a little singed, but everyone else is good."

"I'm glad."

"Me, too, though if one of us has to be stuck in here, I'd rather it be me. You've been in more than your share of hospital beds."

"I'd rather you be okay."

"Mmm." Shifting, he ran a finger down her arm. "Since we're making confessions and all, I might as well tell you that it would've been nice to hear from you instead of Kaylee."

"Yeah, well." She looked away. "I knew you were busy. I didn't want to make a big deal about it."

His eyes grew concerned. "How about you tell me what happened today?"

"I was just off today. I was feeling a little light-headed and having trouble breathing. Then, when I got stressed out with one of my customers, everything went even farther south."

"And?"

"And I passed out."

"Honey."

His tone was so sweet it felt like a warm hug in the middle of January. It also made her want to share even more. "I'm so mad at myself. Even though I knew better, I didn't take my health seriously." Looking down at the IV attached to her hand, she sighed. "Even though I knew I should call the doctor or call someone for help, I lied to myself." Finally looking his way, she added, "Greg, I did so many things wrong and now I'm paying the price."

He picked up her phone and wagged it at her. "Next time call me, okay?"

She didn't feel like she could promise him that. Clark had always acted like he was inconvenienced if she was having a bad episode. What if Greg started to think she wasn't worth the trouble, like Clark had? "I'll do my best."

"What is that supposed to mean?"

He was going to make her spell it out. "It means, you already know that I have a wonky heart. I don't want to subject you to . . . to this. Again." She waved a hand over herself. "I look terrible."

His expression, which had been all soft and sweet, turned stony. "For some reason it seems like we're not communicating real well."

"I'm sorry?"

"I came to see you because I was worried about you. Do you understand that?"

"Yes, of course."

"Just so everything is crystal clear, I want to remind you that I'm a fireman. I'm well aware that people don't look their best during an emergency. I first met you at one such emergency."

"I haven't forgotten."

"Kristen, what I'm trying to say is I don't want, expect, or need you to look your best all the time. In addition, even though I don't care how you look, to me you're always beautiful. But none of that matters. I'm concerned about how you feel."

"I understand."

"Do you? Because I don't know if this is about you being insecure or if it's about me. Like, do you think I'm the kind of man who only cares about looks?" He raised his voice. "Is that what you think of me? That I'm shallow?"

"Of course not. That's not what I meant."

"Then what?"

"Greg, why are we fighting?" Frustrated, Kristen felt the tears begin again.

He stared at her for a long moment, then cursed under his breath as he got to his feet and pulled her into his arms. "I'm sorry. I'm so sorry. You feel like crap and I'm telling you what to do." He kissed her temple. "For the record, you're so pretty that even in here you look gorgeous."

She closed her eyes and leaned into him. "Can we forget I said anything?"

"Nope. We're going to remember what a jerk I've been. So next time we're in this position I'll behave better." He lowered his voice. "My momma would be having a cow right about now. She'd be calling me ten times a fool."

"She'd call you that bad of a name, huh?"

He leaned back so she could see his eyes. They were filled with amusement. "She'd actually have a whole lot more to say, I'm just trying to keep this conversation G-rated."

She laughed, relieved to have the conversation take a lighter turn, and just then the door opened again.

Greg looked over his shoulder, muttered something again, and sat back down.

Kristen smiled at the newcomer. "Hey, Dr. Gonzales."

"Kristen. Looks like my timing couldn't be worse."

"No, it's actually perfect. This is Greg Tebo. He's my, uh, friend."

"Hopefully he's a good one."

Greg stood up and held out his hand. "I am. I was just trying to help her feel better."

"I see."

Kristen was pretty sure her cheeks were bright red. "This poor guy has gotten an eye- and earful from me this afternoon. I'm afraid I've been crying all day."

Dr. Gonzales eyed her more carefully. "Why is that? Are you in pain?"

"No. I don't know."

"Come now, Kristen. We've been through this. Talk to me."

She wasn't sure what was wrong. But she really wasn't in any hurry to act weak in front of Greg. Darting a look in his direction, she wondered how she was going to sufficiently explain herself without seeming weak and helpless.

"I'm going to wait out in the hall," Greg said.

"You don't mind?"

"No, sweetheart. I don't mind at all."

She smiled at him gratefully. Then, unable to help herself, she added, "Promise to stay near? I mean, will you come back in when Dr. Gonzales leaves?"

"Yep. I'm not going anywhere."

When the door closed behind Greg, Dr. Gonzales lifted her wrist to feel her pulse. "That man's a keeper."

"I think so, too."

Still holding her wrist, he looked at the monitor, then punched a couple of buttons to read her chart. Next, he put the stethoscope to his ears and listened to her heart and lungs.

She did as he asked, breathing, coughing, shifting so he could listen to her lungs from the back as well.

At last, he helped her lean back against the pillows and helped rearrange the covers over her.

"What do you think?" she asked.

"I think your heart is doing better." He wrote a couple of notes in her chart. "I'm going to let you leave tomorrow morning."

"That's great news."

"I'm pleased you've recovered so well."

"I wonder what's wrong with my eyes, then. I shouldn't be crying so much, right?"

He smiled softly. "Dear, it's my medical opinion that you've got a common ailment that's causing those tears."

"What?"

"I believe you're in love."

She was so startled, she started laughing. "Come on."

"I'm serious. All the signs are there." Playfully, he wagged a finger at her. "And take it from me, I know what I'm talking about. I deal with hearts all day long."

He was being silly but he'd certainly helped her feel better. "You really are the best doctor in the world."

"You come see me in the office in two weeks. But I'm warning you now that I'm not going to be as nice if you aren't following my orders."

"Understood."

"Good. I'm going to send your man in now."

When Greg came in, he looked worried—and slightly confused. "Your doctor just shook my hand and said that it was good to meet me. Do you think that's weird?"

"Not at all. He knows you're special to me."

Sitting back down beside her, his gaze warmed. "He does, huh? I wonder how he knew that."

Not even caring that her face was likely turning pink, she said, "I think it's pretty obvious to everyone that you mean a lot to me, Greg. A whole lot."

"I feel the same way about you." He leaned over and pressed his lips to hers. "I'm glad we got everything sorted and out in the open."

"Me, too." She reached for his hand and smiled.

When he sat back down, his brown eyes were so full of love they took her breath away. He was everything she'd ever wanted.

She just wished that she was the woman he'd always wanted. When he found out the whole truth about her health, she feared she was going to lose him.

Just like Clark.

Chapter 29

$\mathcal{N}$ ow that she'd made the decision to become a fire-fighter, Jen's life had gotten even busier. The first thing she'd done after speaking to the chief was talk to Emme and Bill and Brittany about everything she was going to need to do. The fire chief and Samantha had recommended some night classes to help her learn all the material in the manual. The chief had also handed her a pamphlet outlining the basic physical qualifications she was going to need in order to pass the physical exams.

Both Bill and Emme suggested that she work no more than fifteen or twenty hours at Werner's Garden Center. So, she'd also had to speak to Kristen there.

In the middle of all of that, Bill had come over to help her talk with their mom about her plans. Emme had volunteered to come, too, but the three of them had decided that their mother would take Jen's news about firefighting—and moving in with Bill and Brittany—better if all three of them weren't there.

They were wrong. Their mother had cried, argued, and yelled at Jen, calling her all sorts of names. Jen had ended up going into her room and packing as much as she could into two suitcases. Devastated by how upset their mother had been, she'd cried the whole way to Bill's.

When they got to his house, Bill hugged her tight. After they filled Emme in, she promised to check on Mom daily.

It rattled her, but within a week, she was starting to be at peace with her choices, especially since she'd also been talking to Ryan about it all.

At the moment, however, Jen was beginning to wonder if she'd upended her whole life for nothing. From the moment she'd arrived at the firehouse at seven that morning, Jen felt like she'd been doing everything wrong.

Maybe because she had been.

Brittany had insisted Jen do the driving from their house to the fire station. Along the way, she'd had to do a tricky left-hand turn and had gotten rattled. By the time she'd finally turned, the car behind her was honking angrily.

At Brittany's suggestion, she turned into a church parking lot to get herself under control, and then to get back behind the wheel again.

All of which meant Jen had walked into the station five minutes late, which had been noted.

And then she hadn't remembered how Dave Oringer wanted her to fold the towels in the laundry area. Or the answer to his questions about grass fires. Or what to do first when someone was choking.

She'd ended up feeling like the worst candidate they'd ever had.

Dave hadn't been shy in making it clear that he felt the same way. "I don't want her going on any calls today," he announced the moment the captain had ended the day's meeting and gone back to his office.

"It's standard for recruits to ride along," Mark said.

"You can have her, then. I don't want her with me."

Sam frowned. "She won't be doing anything. All she's allowed to do is observe."

"I know. I still don't want her."

"Why?" Mark asked, all while Jen was standing there, feeling invisible.

Dave shrugged. "Does it matter?"

"Uh, yeah." Sam looked at Chip and Mark. "Do all of you feel the same way?"

"No," Chip said. He smiled sympathetically at Jen. "She's young but she tries hard. Besides, we all have to start somewhere, right?" He winked at Jen. "Plus, you helped me with all those dinner dishes the other night. That was awesome."

Jen smiled at him before looking away.

"Oringer, I'm sorry, but I don't agree with you, either," Mark added. "Yesterday she ran a nine-minute mile. She's on the right track."

"There's more to this job than running a mile," Dave said.

"I know." Mark folded his arms over his chest. "But Chip's right. The girl is working hard and getting better every day." He grinned at her. "She's getting stronger, too."

Jen cast him a grateful smile.

"So, it looks like that's three out of four of us who are okay with Jennifer," Sam said. "What's the problem, Dave?" Sam asked.

Dave shot Jen another look, causing her to practically shrink in front of him. "I don't need to have a reason, Carter. I'm driving the rig, so I'm making the call. When the bell rings, the girl is staying."

Though Chip and Mark didn't look happy, they remained silent.

Sam did not. "Dave, you're being ridiculous. You know she's not going to get in the way or put anyone in harm's way. What's the problem? Do you not want another woman on the squad?"

"Things happen, and I don't wanna have to worry about

some girl either making a mistake or getting caught in the fray."

"I'd understand if it was like last year, when we were out fighting that brush fire for days. But we both know the likelihood of that reoccurring is slim."

"It doesn't matter. I've made the call." He glared at Jen. "No hard feelings, kid. Right?"

Jen nodded, though she felt stupid about it because of course she did have hard feelings. How could she not? It took effort, but she didn't let her lip tremble. No way was she going to give everyone a reason to say she couldn't handle criticism.

Dave raised an eyebrow at Sam before walking outside to the bays.

"I'm sorry about Oringer," Sam said. "He must have woken up on the wrong side of the bed or something."

That was unlikely, since it was obvious that she'd done things he didn't like. Or he just didn't like *her*.

But she wasn't going to say that out loud. "Yeah," she mumbled.

Chip placed a hand on her arm. "Jen, listen, I'm sorry about that, but don't let him get you down. Don't take him personally, okay? I know he's being a jerk, but I don't think it's you. It's probably just something going on at home. You learn real quick that as much as you try to keep home stuff at home and work stuff here, one or the other bleeds through. It's inevitable."

Jen nodded again. "I'm going to practice pulling hoses. Is that okay?"

"Yep. Go for it."

"I'll be out in a minute," Sam said.

After Sam walked inside, Jen released her breath. She walked to the oldest truck. It was rarely used, so her practicing wouldn't interfere if the bells rang.

A good fire department candidate could pull fifty to a

hundred feet of hose in about a minute. She liked to think she was strong, but she was vertically challenged, which meant that she had to use a different set of arm muscles to pull the first section of hose down.

Most everyone else in the fire department was nice and seemed to have her back.

Even some of the scary guys, like Mark Oldum, had given her a hand when she was trying to scale the wall in the obstacle course. Others had been more standoffish but warmed up when they realized she was tougher than she looked. Yesterday, Mick had invited Jen to sit with him at lunch.

So, it seemed like she was making strides. With everyone but Dave. There was no doubt about it. Dave didn't like her. He left her his dishes to wash, he got on her if she ever was just sitting, telling her to clean or do the laundry or to go back out to the bays and ask how she could help.

But the way he'd just made his opinion about her known—and the way no one but Sam had come right out and said he was wrong—hurt. Going up on the first metal step of the truck, she grabbed a nozzle with one hand and a loop with the other. Holding them securely, she hopped down and started walking, but immediately hit a snag.

Her frustration grew as she realized that barely a foot had released. She yanked again, but it felt like the hose was purposely trying to make her life difficult. Or someone hadn't put it in properly and it was now—as Greg liked to call it—a spaghetti nightmare.

Had she rolled it up wrong?

Tears filled her eyes. Which, of course, made her even more frustrated and upset with herself. She shook her head and dug deep. She had survived her father dying and her mother going off the rails. She could handle a knotted-up hose.

She tugged again. It didn't budge.

Knowing there was nothing to do but lift the entire hose

out and reroll it, she hopped back on the step. Unfortunately, she couldn't seem to grasp the hose properly.

She felt like stomping her foot. Why couldn't she do this? Why did her arms hurt so much? Was it all just because she was too short? If that was the case, she was never going to be able to pull the hoses well enough to be a firefighter. If she couldn't do this, she wasn't going to be able to do all the really difficult things, like carry someone out of a burning building or fight a forest fire for hours or even days at a time.

She'd been an idiot to think she could.

Maybe it really was all too much. Learning how to yield on left turns. Her father's death. Her mother's drinking and depression. Graduating. Falling in love with Ryan—all while realizing he was about to be living on a campus over an hour away. He was moving on, and she didn't blame him one bit.

Despite her best efforts, the tears started to fall. And then it was like a dam breaking. She started crying hard, then harder, until she was sitting on the cement floor of the garage bays and crying like she hadn't since she learned her father had died.

"Hey. Hey, now."

Startled, Jen glanced up. And then felt even worse, which she hadn't thought was possible. Greg Tebo had found her. Which, unfortunately, had just made everything even worse. She swiped a hand over her face and attempted to scramble to her feet. "Sorry."

He stilled her with a hand. "Settle down, Jen. I'm not upset and you shouldn't be embarrassed. Sit back down."

She did as he asked, mainly because she didn't know what to do if she did stand up. Where would she go?

To her surprise, he sat down beside her and rested his arms on his knees. "Mark told me about Dave. I would've been surprised if you *didn't* start crying."

"I don't know what's wrong with me."

"No offense, but it's kind of obvious what is." When she raised an eyebrow, he continued. "You just graduated high school, you've got a part-time job that's sometimes stressful, your boss was in the hospital, and now one of the guys here is acting like an idiot."

"You can't say that!"

"Sure I can. I mean, it's true, right?"

"Kind of."

"You're trying something new that isn't easy for anyone and your whole body hurts. And I know this because mine hurt when I was training to pass my physical—and I'd been in the freaking army!"

"Really?"

"Absolutely."

"I am sore," she admitted.

He lowered his voice. "Plus, not to overstep, but Kristen let it slip that there's a chance you might be dealing with some crappy stuff at home. Yeah?"

"I didn't know she remembered me telling her."

"Kristen cares about you. She told me that your mom isn't doing well. And no, we weren't sitting around gossiping about you. Kristen was sharing with me how guilty she felt because you had to do so much at the garden center."

"She shouldn't feel guilty. Kristen can't help getting sick."

"No, she sure can't," Greg replied. "But Kristen might have told me about you for a reason." When Jen met his eyes again, he continued in a soft tone. "Kristen knew I would understand some of what you were going through, because my dad died, too."

"Has he been gone a long time?"

"About ten years."

"I'm sorry."

He shrugged. "Me, too. I still miss him."

Jen knew she could either brush off this moment or take a chance and let down her guard a little bit more. "Did your mother fall apart after your dad died?"

"No. At least, I don't think she did."

"Oh."

"But things were a little different for her. I've got a slew of brothers and sisters. She had her hands full with all of us."

"If you have sisters, I guess you're used to girls crying from time to time?"

"Yep, though if you ever tell one of them that, I'll deny it. They like to remind me that they're smarter—and stronger—than I ever was."

She smiled. "I find that hard to believe." He was way over six feet and had muscles on top of muscles.

"They might not be able to bench-press as much weight as me, but they are strong as all get-out." He pressed the center of his chest. "They're strong in here, Jen. Just like Kristen is. And just like you."

"I don't know about that. I just lost it in the middle of a fire station garage because of a stupid hose." She winced. "Sam is going to be so disappointed. She's been standing up for me and now I've just shown her that Dave was right. I shouldn't be here."

"Honey, I don't know why Dave is so determined not to work with you. But I don't think for a moment you shouldn't be here. And, as far as Sam is concerned, she's still fired up about Dave. When she saw you struggling with the hose, she was going to come out here to give you a hand, but I asked her if I could talk to you instead."

"Because of Kristen?"

"Yeah. And because I have little sisters. And because when I went off to boot camp I was sure I was going to sail through it, since I was used to playing sports and being pushed myself. But one day, about three weeks in, I started bawling."

"What happened?"

"A sergeant told me to accept that I was fallible. I wasn't perfect and it was wrong of me to imagine that I was."

"Did it help?"

Greg's eyes lit up. "Honestly?"

She nodded.

"Nope. Not right then, anyway. But it did later." He pulled up his long legs and rested his elbows on his knees. "I'm no Sergeant Velasquez, but maybe *something* I said helped? Or, at the very least . . . maybe you know that you aren't alone here? I've got your six, Jen."

"Thank you."

He stood up and held out a hand to help her up. "Now, what's gotten you and these hoses in such a tizzy?"

"They're tangled in a spaghetti nightmare. I'm worried I didn't roll them back properly."

"Maybe you did. Maybe you didn't. Just fix them, yeah?"

"Yes. But, um, I also can't seem to pull them out fast enough. I don't know why."

"Speed counts, but making sure the hose is free of kinks matters more. First, show me how to roll them properly."

"Fast?"

"No. Don't worry about the speed. Or anyone else here. Just focus on one thing at a time. Worry about the task you are asked to do. That's it."

Taking a deep breath, she rolled the hoses up carefully like Sam and Greg had shown her the other day.

"Good," he said as he deposited them easily back in the truck. "Now, show me what you've got."

Pulling her gloves back on, she glanced at the clock, mentally preparing herself to go faster than she had so far.

"No, Jen," Greg said in a clear, firm voice. "Stop worrying about the time. Empty your mind of all the negative and only think about what you have to do. All you need to do right now is pull these hoses. That's it. Understand?"

"Yes."

His voice deepened. "What do you have to do, Jen?"

"I need to grab the nozzle with one hand, the loop with the other, put both ends over my shoulders, and pull them down. I need to advance one hundred feet in less than a minute, then—"

"Stop. Don't worry about what happens next or the clock. Just do it right." He looked down at her. "Do you understand?"

He sounded like he was back in the army, which was kind of freaking her out. "Yeah." She looked up at him.

His expression was like stone. "Let's pretend you're speaking to someone in charge, Jennifer. Now, what do you say?"

"*Yes, sir* or *Roger that.*"

"Jennifer, do you want to be a firefighter?"

Again, his voice was hard. "Yes, sir."

"Are you sure?"

"Yes, sir."

"Then stop focusing on obstacles. Do you understand?"

"I do."

"Good. Now go."

She pulled up on the step, grabbed the loop with her left hand and the nozzle with the right, jumped down, positioned each over a shoulder, and started walking as fast as she could.

"There you go. Good job. How many feet is that hose?"

"One hundred."

"Good. Pull down the next. Go."

"Yes, sir." She jumped up the step and did it again.

When the hose was laid flat, she said, "A hundred feet is out, sir."

"What's the next step?"

"Um, call out to the engineer to hook up to the water source?"

"Are you ready to do that?"

Remembering what she'd read in the manual, she shook her head. "No, sir. I need to check for kinks."

"Correct. Do it."

Sam and Chip had explained to her how important it

was to make sure the hoses had no kinks. Kinks would slow the water and possibly prevent enough water from coming out to extinguish the fire. She carefully eyed the hose, found a kink, and righted it. "It's good."

"Hustle to the nozzle, then. Remember the position?"

"Yes, sir, I do." She picked up the hose.

"What's the next step?"

"I say *Charge the line*."

"Say it, then."

"Charge the line."

Greg shook his head. "No one's going to hear that. Say it like you mean it, Jennifer. Say it like you want to be here."

"Charge the line!"

"There you go." He sounded so kind, she turned to face him. He was smiling. Then, started clapping.

And then she heard more people clapping.

Everyone was there. Even the captain. Even Dave.

"Good job, Jennifer!" Captain DeWitt called out.

"Thank you, sir. Um, Greg helped a lot."

"That's good. That's what we're all supposed to do. We're a team here."

"Yes, sir."

"Good. Now, roll up the hose and do it again."

"Yes, sir, I will."

When everyone started to go back inside, she gazed up at Greg. "Thanks for your help."

"You're welcome." He patted her shoulder before turning around and walking inside.

Instead of feeling abandoned, Jen felt empowered. She could do this. She could get through it. She could get through a lot of things, she realized. All she had to do was take it one step at a time.

Chapter 30

*Y*ou did good with Jen," Anderson told Greg as they ran with Mark up a hill near Anderson and Chelsea's house.

"Whatever you told her seemed to be exactly what she needed to hear," Mark agreed.

Greg didn't want praise for helping a seventeen-year-old kid with a lot on her plate. "I didn't do all that much. The girl just needed a break and a little help focusing. Poor thing."

"Sam said something about Dave was the least of what she's going through," Mark said. "Is that right?"

"I think so. She's working a ton, working out a ton, dealing with a mother who's got her own problems, and all the other crap that comes with being her age." He paused, then added, "Kristen told me she's got a new boyfriend, too, and he's about to leave for college down in Pueblo. I'm sure she's thinking about that, too."

"I thought Dave was a little out of line," Anderson said. "I know it's the norm to give recruits some grief, but it was too personal." As they turned down Burdette, he added, "I was tempted to say something to him. I didn't, but I wanted to."

"I thought the same thing," Greg said. "But I didn't, either. I was worried that he would think I was on him because of my dating Kristen and Kristen is Jen's boss." As they started up the next hill, he took a deep breath. "I wish I had, though. Constantly picking on new recruits doesn't help them or us."

"I did speak with him," said Mark when they started down.

"Oh yeah?" Anderson asked. "How did that go?"

Mark chuckled. "Not too good in the beginning. At first Dave reacted like I was out of line. Maybe I was. But when I told him that she'd been sitting on the ground crying after trying to untangle those hoses, he looked pretty upset."

"Did you get any answers, Mark?" Anderson asked. "Why does he feel like Jen's doing such a bad job? We've had other volunteers and candidates before. She's actually better than most. I've never heard her talk back once."

"Turns out that Dave supervised another kid fresh out of high school back when he was working in Jefferson County. The kid had promise but wouldn't listen. Like, ever. One day when they were called out, the captain insisted Dave take the guy along."

"Uh-oh," Greg said.

"Yep, you guessed it. The kid messed up."

"What happened?" Anderson asked.

"He got injured . . . and almost injured one of the victims at the scene."

Greg winced. "That's tough."

"Yeah. But worse, about a week later, when the actions came up for review, his captain reprimanded him. It was like he'd completely forgotten that he had forced Oringer to take the kid along."

"That was convenient for the captain," Greg said.

"Yeah." As they slowed down to a jog, Mark added, "So,

it's not Jen as much as who she reminds him of. He doesn't want to be responsible for her getting hurt."

"Yeah, he's covering himself," said Greg.

Mark shrugged. "Yeah. And who can blame him? We know that stuff went on in the army, too. You were a good cap, Greg, but not every officer was fair."

Anderson glanced at Greg. "Sorry, but part of me thinks that girl needs to get a thicker skin. I mean, Dave isn't gonna be the worst person she'll ever deal with."

"I agree, but that's not the issue right now," Greg countered. "We're supposed to be supportive and teach her. We can't teach her anything if she's afraid of messing up. Plus, we have to think about Sam, too."

Mark nodded. "That's why I went to talk to Dave. I didn't want Sam to think that she was out on a limb on her own."

They were almost back at Anderson's house. Mark wiped a band of sweat off his face with the bottom of his T-shirt. "So . . . moving on . . . I guess things with Jen's boss are going well?"

Greg nodded. "I think so. But her ex did a number on her. He dumped her just a couple of hours before the wedding rehearsal at the church."

"What?" Anderson looked incredulous. "Who does that?"

"I couldn't tell you." Taking a breath, he added, "As you can imagine, she's got some trust issues."

"What are you going to do?"

"Nothing. As you know, making promises and breaking them isn't my style. I've told her that we'll take everything as slowly as she wants to."

"I'd do the same."

Greg smiled at him. "We're experts at waiting."

"You mean hurry-up-and-waiting," Anderson joked.

"Yep." Thinking about how sweet Kristen was, he said, "Plus, I don't want to be anything like her jerk of an ex. I get the feeling that he put her down a lot. It sounds like he kept finding fault with her, then finding more."

Mark frowned. "I hate guys like that."

"Yeah. Me, too."

"How's her health now?" Anderson asked.

"Better." He smiled. "I got to meet her cardiologist and heard him give her a stern talking-to about taking care of herself."

"So you have ammunition." Mark grinned.

"Yeah. A little bit. Of course, I just hope Kristen has learned her lesson about taking breaks, staying hydrated, and not overdoing things."

Anderson whistled low. "Something tells me that she wouldn't appreciate you saying that she needed to learn her lesson."

"She wouldn't appreciate it at all." Greg frowned. "I'm not looking to be controlling, but Kristen doesn't realize how it feels to see someone you care about struggling to breathe! Standing on the sidelines, not being able to do anything to help her, isn't fun. Like, not at all."

"What are you going to do if she doesn't change?" Mark asked.

The question hit a nerve—especially because he didn't have an answer. Greg scowled. "Why are you asking?"

His buddy looked uncomfortable, but he didn't back down. "Hey, not everyone changes just because someone asks them to."

They'd reached the top of the final hill and stopped, breathing heavily. Anderson was bent over his right leg, stretching it.

Giving Anderson a few minutes, Greg studied Mark. "It sounds like you have experience with someone who didn't want to change."

Mark's expression said he was still haunted by it. "I do. But we're focusing on you and Kristen."

Now that he'd calmed down a bit, Greg gave Mark's

question some consideration. "To answer your question . . . I don't know what I'm going to do if Kristen doesn't want to make those changes. There's a part of me that wonders if there's more going on with her health than she's telling me."

"Ask her."

"I have, and she's been pretty open." He rubbed the back of his neck. "I don't know. I guess it's just a feeling I have. All I do know is that if I can't trust her to take care of herself, I'm going to feel like I have to be the one to do it."

"And?" Anderson asked.

"And . . . I don't know if I want to take on that responsibility." Thinking of all the fresh-faced, too-sure-of-themselves second lieutenants he used to be in charge of, he said, "I already did enough of that in the army."

"We *all* did enough of that in the army," Mark said.

Anderson stretched his arms above his head. "For what it's worth, I think Kristen might surprise you. People do change. I sure did. I bet you guys grew up as much as I did in the army."

Greg nodded. He agreed with Anderson to an extent. People did change their priorities, their careers, and maybe even what they wanted in a partner.

"I don't know, Doc. I mean, yeah, we have different jobs than when we were in the army, but do you view the world differently than you used to? I mean, you might react smarter, but did you change at your core?"

They had now reached Anderson's driveway, and when neither of his buddies answered right away, he decided to push.

Greg glanced at Anderson. Really looked at the scars. "Did getting those scars change who you are on the inside?"

Anderson frowned but didn't look offended by the question. Only reflective. "Not the scars, no, but the army made me value simple things more. It made me regret how cocky I'd been in high school and ashamed of how much I used to take for granted. The army gave me a bigger appreciation for Woodland Park and Chelsea and my family. Depending on you guys and everyone in our unit made me realize that I was only one person, and therefore weaker alone than in a group together. But do I think I fundamentally changed? No, I do not."

"Mark?"

Mark shook his head. "I've always been a little too intense and like a sheepdog trying to shepherd everyone around me. I've always been that way and still am."

"It made you a good sergeant."

"Yeah, but not always the best boyfriend. Although I have learned to keep my mouth shut, I'm still always sure I'm right."

"The problem is that you *are* usually right," Anderson joked.

"Not always. I've made some mistakes. But if you asked me to never analyze a situation or try to find a way to solve a seemingly unworkable problem? It would be next to impossible for me. It's how I got through school and the military. It's a part of who I am."

"I feel the same way about most of my character traits," said Greg. "I'm still a little too confident. I still sometimes say too much when I should shut up and listen. I still fight off tears when I see kids hurting. I still have that same drive I did when I was twelve or thirteen and wanted to be someone my father could be proud of." He trailed off. He didn't know what else to say.

"You need to talk to Kristen, Greg. Tell her what's important to you—and ask her to share more, too. I don't know . . . sometimes I think women who weren't in the service assume that soldiers don't want to ever talk about our feelings."

"Because we don't," quipped Mark.

"Maybe not with a lot of guys, but we've learned to

share a lot with each other." After a pause, Anderson continued. "I'm okay talking about my feelings with Chelsea. Plus, she always helps once she understands what's bothering me. It's made us stronger. Kristen might be thinking that you won't understand her feelings or what she needs."

"You've got a good point."

"I can tell you this—if you two don't have a future together, both of you will be glad to know now."

"I'll call her and see if she wants to come over."

"There you go. For the record, I hope you start talking more. I think that's all you two need. I like Kristen and Chelsea likes her, too."

"Thanks."

Greg continued to turn it over in his head after he got home and showered.

Finally, he accepted that nothing he was thinking was going to make a difference and he needed to reach out to Kristen. He pulled out his phone and gave her a call.

She sounded so happy when she picked up. "Greg, I was just about to call you!"

"Really? What's up?"

"I met the nicest veteran today. He reminded me of you."

He smiled. "Oh yeah? Was he tall, dark, and almost bald?" he teased.

"Well, he *was* almost bald. But, unlike you, I don't think he lost his hair by choice. I think he was near eighty."

"And he reminded you of me?"

"He was so kind and warm. Just a really good man, I could tell. You would've liked him."

"I bet I would have. Thank you for the compliment, by the way."

"You're welcome, but it's true. You're a really good man, Greg."

And that's why he really needed to get things sorted out between them. Not because she gave him sweet compliments, but because she made him feel like he was worth something. She made him feel good just by being herself.

"Come over for dinner."

"Come over for dinner? When?"

"Tonight."

"Tonight?" She chuckled. "I'm sorry. I sound like a parrot."

"I want to see you. I'll grill some salmon. We can have potatoes and a salad."

"That all sounds wonderful. Is it a special occasion?"

"Beyond just wanting to see you? No . . . but I wanted to be with you someplace quiet." He took a deep breath. "Kristen, I think we need to talk."

"Oh?" She sounded wary.

"I mean, I want to discuss some things."

"This sounds serious. Is something wrong? Maybe we should just talk about whatever's on your mind right now."

He was really messing this up. "Kristen, nothing's wrong. I just want to discuss some things." When she didn't say anything for a few seconds, he added, "I promise, I'm not trying to be evasive. I mainly just want to spend some time with you."

"All right. What time?"

He glanced at the clock. It was three. "What time can you get off work?"

"Six."

"Is seven too early?"

"No, I can do that. Would you like me to bring anything?"

"Just yourself. I'll text you my address, okay?"

"Okay."

"See you soon."

"Yes, I'll see you soon. Bye, Greg," she said softly.

"Bye, baby."

When he hung up, he looked around at his living room. And winced. He had four hours to grocery shop and put his place into some semblance of order. It wasn't all that messy, but it looked as bare as his army barracks.

He had to level up and maybe hang a poster or two on his walls if he was going to ask Kristen to open up more.

Chapter 31

"How's the wine, Kristen?" Greg asked from his position in front of the grill. "Is it okay?"

"It's wonderful." She took another sip to show that she liked his selection. And she did. Greg had chosen a pinot noir from Washington State. She was no wine aficionado but even she knew that he'd made a good choice. It was a pretty far cry from the eight-dollar bottles she usually picked up at the liquor store.

She hadn't expected anything other than a six-pack of beer for them to share. She would've been fine with it—or even just soda or water. But the effort he'd made to please her was a nice surprise.

Actually, everything about this evening was a nice surprise—from his phone call to his offer to cook, to the state of his town house. It was as clean and tidy as if he were worried about passing an inspection. A couple of framed movie posters adorned the walls as well as a massive television, which she supposed was the number one requirement of every bachelor pad.

In addition to the television, he had a couch upholstered

in a light-gray suede, a pair of coordinating chairs in black leather, and a square coffee table. His kitchen was nothing special, but he had more pots and pans than she did, and she loved his brightly colored Fiestaware dishes. All in all, it was a comfortable home that really seemed to suit him.

She was taking in every bit of it, because this was the first time she'd come over. Which was strange. They'd spent a lot of time together—and had even shared a hotel room. But being in his personal space felt like it was taking things to the next level. She loved every opportunity to learn more about him.

After taking another sip of the wine, she stood up. "Are you sure you don't need any help? I feel bad that I'm just watching you do everything."

"I've got this, so sit back down." When she did, he smiled at her. "I like to see you relaxing." He closed the lid on the grill. "The fish is going to be done in about five minutes."

"Cheers, then."

He grinned at her and raised his own glass of wine.

Ten minutes later, they were seated at his table with plates filled with fish, potatoes, salad, some steamed vegetables, and some pot stickers that he admitted were from the freezer section at the grocery store.

"Everything is amazing."

"It's nothing special. Like I told you the other day, my mother made sure we knew how to cook *something* so none of us would starve. But with all the hours she worked, she only cooked simple food. Besides, if we waited on her for all our meals, we'd go hungry."

"You make me feel spoiled. I was an only child and doted on."

"Nothing wrong with that."

"I guess not. I do love hearing the stories about your siblings though."

"I'm grateful for them."

His comment seemed simple and straightforward, yet Kristen felt he was holding something back. She wondered if he didn't like the idea of being an only child. Or was she overthinking things?

"Do you want . . . a lot of kids?" she asked hesitantly, thinking she might as well find out.

Something in Greg's expression shifted. Maybe he'd become more guarded? Or had he noticed that *she* was more wary? "I do. I like the way I grew up, with a houseful of noise." His expression softened. "There was always someone to play with or to talk to. Quinn and I shared a room, and there were plenty of nights when we talked long after Mom and Dad told us to turn off the light."

"I stayed up late, too. But I was reading, not talking."

"Nothing wrong with that." He sipped his wine. "Nowadays I can't imagine anyone having seven kids."

She pretended to shiver. "Seven pregnancies is a lot."

He grinned. "You ain't kiddin'. My mom never complained about all those pregnancies, but it must have been exhausting. My oldest sister, Rachel, has four kids. She makes it sound like that's more than enough." Looking at her closely, he added, "Two or three sounds a little easier to manage."

"I agree. It does."

"What about you?"

"Me?"

"Yeah." He looked at her more intently. "Kristen, what do *you* want? Just one or two, or a whole brood?" When she bit her lip, a line formed between his brows. "Do you want kids?"

Here it was. She needed to just tell him. But she was afraid. Afraid to ruin this really nice meal. Afraid to ruin their really nice relationship.

Afraid to see him look at her like she was defective, or worse, with a fixed and stoic expression that would make it obvious he was hiding how he really felt.

"We should probably talk about that."

He shoved his dishes to one side. "Okay."

And . . . still, she procrastinated. "Maybe we should do the dishes first."

He stood up and held out his hand. "I like a clean kitchen as much as the next guy, but I'd rather hear what you have to say."

"Oh, nothing, really. Never mind. It's no big deal." Not to a casually dating couple. Just to her.

"If it's important to you, it's important to me." He waggled his fingers. "Come on, now. Take my hand."

What else could she do? She stood up, reached for his hand, and immediately felt like she wasn't alone in the world any longer. His hand was so rough and strong. Solid. She clung to it before she could stop herself.

Greg curved his fingers around hers as he guided them to the suede couch in the living room.

"This is a gorgeous couch, by the way."

"I don't need a lot, so I try to get stuff I really like."

"Well, I really like this," she teased. "Though it's a bit of a surprise for a guy who's spent most of his working life outdoors. I would've guessed you had a couch in something sturdier."

Greg flashed a smile. "Like camo?"

She chuckled. "Maybe denim? I don't know."

He leaned forward. "Kristen, here's the deal. All my life I've kind of been the action guy. I played sports. I was in the military for years. Now I'm a firefighter. I'm used to doing things and working on teams. I'm not as comfortable with relationships."

"Okay . . ." Her mind was racing. Was he about to break things off? Had she done something wrong? Did she even need to tell him about her heart and how that affected her body?

"Unlike you, who's had a fiancé, I've never had a serious girlfriend. The women I dated were sweet and I liked them, but we never got anywhere close to where you and I are now. Where I hope we are."

He pursed his lips, then burst out, "What I'm trying to tell you is that I don't have a lot of experience talking about my feelings. But I am used to reading people. I'm real good at that. And I think you're hiding something."

"Greg—"

"Hang on. I don't mean to interrupt, but if what you're hiding is absolutely none of my business, then so be it. But if you, like me, want to take things further, then I'd like to know what you haven't been saying. I'd feel better."

Well, there it was. He'd just been brave enough to put everything out there. Now she needed to do the same thing. It was time. "Greg, there's no easy way to say this. Lord knows I've tried to think of a better way to do it." She took a deep breath. "I can't have children," she said in a rush.

He frowned. "What do you mean? You can't have children, or you don't want to have them?"

"Can't. You know I was born with a congenital heart defect. Essentially, one of my arteries constricts too much. It carries oxygen to my lungs but it takes a lot of effort. A pregnancy would put too much stress on my heart."

"And most of your other organs, too, right?"

She nodded. "Right."

"This is what you've been keeping from me?"

She nodded again. "I was afraid. This, ah, problem I have, it's the reason Clark broke up with me. I had told him about my heart defect when we got serious, but he was such a jerk that he thought I was exaggerating."

He raised his eyebrows. "He thought you were exaggerating a serious heart condition."

She knew he was incredulous, but she felt even more embarrassed. She should've known better. "Yes. He, well, he made a joke about it one evening and my parents overheard. My dad pulled him aside and told him exactly what's wrong with me and how serious it is. Which was awkward."

"By then you were engaged, right?"

"Yeah." Unable to look at Greg, she averted her eyes. "Our parents were close. I think Clark didn't know how to break things off. But our relationship was strained."

When Greg didn't speak, she felt even worse. "Anyway, uh, eventually Clark said he didn't want to marry someone who was damaged and oh, by the way, might not live all that long."

"What do you mean by not live that long?"

"Well, um, statistically someone with my condition doesn't have the same life expectancy as other people." She swallowed. "So, that's why he broke up with me right before our wedding. He tried to come to terms with it all but couldn't."

"He sounds like a horrible guy, Kristen. There was no reason to wait so long to break things off if that's how he really felt."

Unfortunately, Greg wasn't saying Clark was wrong, only that his timing was. She attempted to swallow, but her mouth felt like it was filled with cotton. "You know the rest. I gave him back his ring and we were through."

"You're better off without him, sweetheart."

"I know. I still struggle with feeling unworthy—and I was afraid to tell you."

He stared at her, his eyes searching her face. "Did you really think I'd see you as damaged, like Clark did?"

"No, but I thought you might want to stop seeing me. And while I wouldn't blame you, I . . . well, I'd be pretty sad about it."

"You're saying you'd understand if I broke up with you because you couldn't carry a baby inside your body?"

Unable to get a read on him, she nodded slowly. "Well, yes."

"Do you *want* to be a mother? What about adoption? Or surrogacy? What about being a foster parent?"

His voice had turned rough, which made her even more

uncomfortable. She couldn't be sure, but it felt like this was a test and every one of her answers needed to be correct. "I've never thought about surrogacy. I like the idea of adoption, but I'm worried about all the stories you hear about waiting years and years." Her voice hitched. "I would love to be a mom."

"Okay, then."

Okay? She studied his face but was disappointed to find it void of all emotion, like he was keeping every thought in his head firmly under lock and key.

After enduring his silence for a few moments, Kristen shifted uncomfortably. "Greg, remember that first thing you said—you know, about discussing feelings?"

"Yeah?"

"Well, it would be really great if you could share some of them right now."

He looked abashed. "Sorry. I'm trying to understand how a man who said he loved you could treat you so badly."

"Is that a reflection on him . . . or me?"

He frowned. "Him, of course."

That was good, but she wasn't feeling all warm and fuzzy. After all, he still hadn't said anything about babies—specifically, how he felt about her not one day carrying his.

He stared at her another long second. "Why did you keep it a secret that you're not able to give birth?"

"I told you."

"You still don't trust me, do you?"

"I do." At least, she *wanted* to trust him.

He sighed. "Kristen, look. I really like you; I think we could have a future. I'm willing to be by your side for just about anything. But if you keep me at arm's length, I'm not going to be by your side, am I? You shouldn't have kept that a secret."

"We're in a new relationship. I'm not going to share everything with you right away. I sure don't expect you to do that with me."

"I don't have anything that I'm keeping secret."

"Nothing?"

"No, not really."

"Nothing about the army or what you did?"

His expression hardened. "That's completely different."

"Is it, though?"

"You're looking for things to fight about. You know I did things that I can't share. I was a soldier, Kristen."

"I'm just saying that you're assuming a lot if you think I'm keeping you at an arm's length just because I didn't tell you something that's painful for me."

"I think we're at a standoff."

She stood up. "No, we're in need of a break. Thank you for dinner but I think it's better that I leave."

He stood up, his dark eyes looking flat and cold. "All right."

He didn't ask her to stay. He didn't try to talk everything out. *Well, that said something, didn't it?* Pure disappointment coursed through her. She'd hoped things would be different. No, she'd hoped Greg would be different.

It looked like she was wrong.

She went to the table by the door where she'd left her purse. "I'll see you later."

He stepped forward. "I'll walk you out."

She was tempted to say that wasn't necessary but nodded instead.

She wondered what was going to happen to them. Would he one day forgive her for keeping her condition from him? Would she be able to forgive him for responding the way he did?

When they reached her car, she pulled out her keys. "I'm not sure what just happened, but I am glad we talked. You were right to force this, Greg. I'm sorry I didn't tell you everything about my heart earlier."

He shoved his hands in his pockets. "Be careful driving home."

Without another word, she got into her car, started the ignition, and pulled out. Drove the short distance home, wondering if everything was all her fault.

And then decided it didn't matter if it was or wasn't. As far as she was concerned, trust had to be earned and given. It was tricky and unwieldy, like a scared animal you have to wrangle and coax and tame.

Chapter 32

$\mathcal{G}$o, go, go!" Greg yelled. No one was listening. Smoke was in the air, so thick that no one could see. And the radio attached to his vest wasn't working properly. He pushed a couple of buttons. Nothing. Just the low buzz of static burning his ears and grating on his patience.

They were all going to die and it was his fault.

"Cap! Captain Tebo!"

"Yes, Corporal?"

"Lieutenant Wallace sent me over to you. What do you want me to do, sir?"

The kid's expression was panicked. His grip on his weapon was fierce. The kid might have been trying to follow orders, but his insides were twisted into nervous knots. "Man up, soldier. We got this."

Just as the kid smiled back at him in relief, an explosion landed not three feet from him.

"Down!" he yelled. But it was also too late.

Especially for Corporal Fuller. He was now in a thousand pieces.

Tears threatened to choke him. He fought hard against

it. Everyone was counting on him to be tough. He was a soldier. An officer.

But the pain still came.

The kid had come to him for reassurance. All Greg had done was smile and tell him lies.

"Tebo!"

"Yes, sir. Fuller's dead. He's dead—he's—"

"Greg. Wake up. You're in Woodland Park. You're okay."

Greg struggled to open his eyes.

"Wake up, buddy. Come on, now. Look at me."

Finally, the voice registered. It was Mark, but they weren't on the battlefield.

Greg realized where he was. In the firehouse. In one of the closet-sized sleeping quarters.

He wasn't in the sandbox.

His chest and face were damp. He grimaced. He'd been sweating heavily. And probably yelling.

Mark was studying him with a concerned expression but remained silent. Like he was afraid to spook him further.

His friend's sympathy somehow made it worse. "Sorry," he mumbled, sitting up. "I guess I was dreaming."

"Yeah, you were." Mark was standing against the wall, giving him space.

Finally, *finally* Greg pulled himself together. "Is everything okay?" It was a stupid question. If there was an emergency, they'd already be on the truck heading out.

"Yeah. It sounded bad, Greg. Where were you this time? Iraq or Afghanistan?"

Mark had been there, too. Worse, Greg had been Mark's captain. His superior officer. How come he couldn't get out of that spin cycle like Mark had? Even Anderson, riddled with scars, had finally found a way. Why was Greg the one still tortured by the past while Anderson and Mark had moved forward? How come he was the one who was so weak?

"Tebo, where were you?" Mark repeated.

He blew out a burst of air. "Iraq."

"What were you dreaming?"

"Nothing." There was no way he was going to start discussing his dreams. "I'm good." He averted his eyes as he got to his feet. "I'll be down in a minute." He swallowed. "Captain DeWitt send you in here?"

"No."

"Then why—"

"We all heard you, Greg." Mark stepped to the door of the cubicle but didn't reach for the handle. "Look, I don't know how to say this in a way that will finally get you to listen, but I'm going to try again. Greg, the only person you're fooling is yourself. You need to go to the VA and talk to someone."

"I will."

"No. Now. Take time off and do it." Mark's expression hardened. "Stop acting like you're invincible. You're as vulnerable as the rest of us."

"How come it's just me? Why aren't you freaking out and yelling like a coward in the middle of a firehouse? Why isn't Anderson?"

"You don't think Anderson had to come to terms with all the scars littering his body?"

Ashamed, Greg looked away. "I know he did."

"Look, there are things that still set me off." For the first time in years, some of Mark's steady countenance seemed to crack. "I'm still dealing with my father's disappointment in me and my girlfriend sending me a Dear John letter, okay? That's the stuff that keeps me up at night. We've all got stuff we can't seem to let go of."

"I didn't know you got a Dear John."

"I know you didn't, because I don't like to talk about my past, either. But just because I haven't shared doesn't mean I'm not still working through it. If you're dreaming of what happened in Iraq, it's because bad stuff happened there. That's what those VA counselors are for. So people like you and me can talk to people who know what it was like."

"Mark, why aren't you dreaming about all the crap that happened in the desert? We saw a lot of the same things."

Mark gazed at him intently. "Who says I never do?" He turned and walked out.

Tebo, you're a real jerk, thought Greg. Okay, he was a lot worse than that, but that was a start. Still frustrated with himself, he rubbed a hand over his face, catching sight of himself in the mirror.

His eyes were bloodshot. There was two days' growth on his cheeks, not because he didn't have time to shave but because he preferred the stubble to the feel of freshly shaved skin against the breathing apparatus. His hair was almost shaved off completely. Practically bald, the way he liked it.

He looked exactly like he had back in the army. Well, there were probably a few more lines around his eyes than there used to be, but other than that, he looked the same.

He looked at his reflection a little more intently. And finally saw what he always tried to ignore. His face was shuttered. There was a film of denial that didn't use to be there.

He might have been able to fool the photographer for the calendar, but he hadn't been fooling Mark or Anderson. Maybe he'd been avoiding his brothers and sisters because they wouldn't have been fooled, either.

He'd been fooling only himself . . . and maybe Kristen.

The truth hit him hard. He'd made sure she knew how much she'd disappointed him by keeping secrets. Like he was some kind of open book.

No, like he had no faults.

The hurt look that had appeared in her eyes before she'd walked out the door flashed in his brain.

And then and there, he recognized the truth. He absolutely had stuff that he hadn't been eager to share. He absolutely did have secrets.

And he knew at long last what he had to do. He was going to ask for some time off, drive over to the VA, and make an appointment in person.

He could hear Mark's voice in his head. *About damn time.*

Chapter 33

Jen was still struggling and Dave still seemed intent on making sure she felt even worse than she already did. She couldn't remember a day when he hadn't belittled her for some reason. Although Sam had told her more than once that Dave didn't mean anything personal, Jen felt differently.

And today? Well, today had been one of the worst days yet. He'd found fault with the way she did push-ups, disputed her answers when Sam quizzed her about the text she'd been studying, and then made her rewash all of the pans in the kitchen.

She couldn't believe it. She'd almost told him what he could do with his criticism, but she'd felt everyone's eyes on her.

She glanced at the clock; all she had to do was get through twenty more minutes and then she could go home and collapse.

Taking one last look at the tanker, she decided that it was as clean as it was going to get and started packing up the cleaning supplies.

"Where are you going?"

Picking up the rags she'd used to wipe down the truck, she straightened. "I'm done."

"I still see streaks. It's not good enough."

She knew he was just trying to rile her up. "Sorry. I have to go anyway."

"You're going to leave it like this?"

She'd had enough. "Like what? That tanker truck is really clean. I've polished the chrome twice."

"I don't like your attitude. Just good enough isn't good enough here. We save lives. You aren't going to be able to get away with doing things halfway."

"First of all, this is a tanker truck, not a human being. Secondly, I've done everything you've asked me to do, even when it was obvious that you were just making stuff up to mess with me."

"What did you say?"

Jen couldn't take it anymore. "What is your problem? Is it just me or all women or people my age? I get doing grunt work, but the way you treat me goes beyond that. Why do you hate me so much?"

Belatedly, she realized that Chip and Mark were standing inside the door and were listening. Great. She was probably going to get let go, but she needed some answers.

"I don't hate you."

"It sure seems like you do."

"What are you going to do? Go tell on me to Samantha? To the captain? Oh, I know, complain about me to your brother?"

Mark stepped forward. "Seriously, Dave. Since I said my piece to you days ago, you haven't let up for a minute."

"Don't you see it?"

Mark's eyebrows lifted. "See what?"

"See that something's going to happen to her. She's too young. She's going to get hurt and it'll be on us."

And just like that, all of the animosity and anger she'd been holding on to slid away.

Jen felt herself relax.

"You really are worried sick about Jen getting hurt, aren't you?" Greg asked.

"Well, yeah. Aren't you? And you, Mark?"

"Of course, but I'm just as concerned about helping her get hired on."

"Why?"

"This girl is scrappy," Greg said. "Sure, she doesn't know a lot, but I didn't know much, either—and I came out of the military."

"I just don't like her being here. We shouldn't have to be responsible if something happens."

"This is about when you were in Denver, isn't it?" Mark asked. "The young recruit who got injured and you almost lost that mom and her son."

"He didn't just get injured. His leg was so badly burned he still isn't the same. I should've known better than to let him get in the thick of things."

"I think your problem with Jen is more about you than her performance or her inexperience," Greg said. "I think you've been carrying that pain around with you all this time."

"Like you'd know anything about that."

"Actually, I would," Greg said. "You all know about the nightmares I've been dealing with . . . but there's more to it." He cleared his throat. "Sometimes, even the sirens set me off. Sometimes, I don't know if I'm going to be able to do my job." He looked down at his feet. "Thanks to Mark, I started going to a therapist again for my PTSD.

"It was suggested that I continue to see someone after I got out of the service, but I ignored that advice. I didn't want everyone to realize how weak I was."

"What are you talking about, Tebo?" Sam said softly. "No one would ever consider you weak."

"I know. It was a mistake. It was a real mistake to pretend I don't have any crap that I'm covering up." He gave

Jen's shoulder a shake. "Just like it's wrong of you to be so worried about our little Mighty Mouse that you can't give her a chance to prove herself."

Dave frowned. "And you really think this Mighty Mouse is going to be able to do that one day?"

"Watch me," Jen said with as much confidence as she could muster. No one had actually said that she was going to become a firefighter one day, but they'd given her something better than assurances. They'd given her their belief that it was possible.

"Come on in, Oringer. We'll have a talk," Captain De-Witt said.

"Yes, sir." Dave took a step forward, then turned and looked at Jen. "All this time I was saying 'no offense,' I knew it was offending you. But . . . I promise, it really wasn't about you. I apologize. I shouldn't have been such a jerk."

A shiver coursed through her. "Thank you."

When he disappeared, Greg said, "You okay?"

"Yeah. Well, I mean, except for one thing."

"What?"

"Mighty Mouse?"

He grinned. "Sorry, but it fits. You are a little thing and you are strong."

"Hmm."

"Hey, you don't get to choose your nickname; your nickname chooses you," Mark said. "I promise, it could be worse."

"Yeah. I guess it could."

"You out of here now?"

She nodded. "Are you sure I'm not in trouble? I feel bad for Dave but I wasn't going to take his crap indefinitely."

"You took it long enough." Greg rubbed his hand over his cheek. "I probably should've stepped in earlier . . . I just didn't want to make his attitude worse."

"I understand." Weighing her words carefully, she

added, "I didn't expect becoming a firefighter would be easy and I don't know if I have what it takes to succeed."

"You do," Mark said.

She smiled at him. "I hope you're right. And . . . well, every day I'm here I want it more. I don't want everyone to take it easy on me. I want to be good enough to feel like I am good enough."

"Well said, Mouse. If you keep believing that, you're going to be just fine."

When Ryan picked her up a couple of minutes later, he smiled. "Something about you seems different. What happened?"

"There was a big showdown between Dave and me . . . and the whole squad."

"No way."

"It was intense, but I think things are going to be better from here on out."

"I hope so," he said as he turned the car toward his house. "My mom is still counting on you eating supper with us tonight. Are you still good with that?"

"Of course."

"I have to warn you, it's tuna casserole night."

"Your mom already texted me about that."

"Yeah?" He looked wary but hopeful.

"Yeah." She smiled, thinking about how many things were better now—with him, and with her family, too.

To Jen's relief, her moving out seemed to be exactly what their mom had needed. She'd returned to grief counseling and acted ready to start living again.

Ryan had moved down to Pueblo and was living in a dorm and working out with the team. He'd been experiencing his own share of hazing from the upperclassmen, but it wasn't anything he couldn't handle. Luckily, because he was so close, he was able to come home every Monday to have supper and spend the night. She'd started joining his family for supper and then hanging out with him until he took her back to her brother's late at night.

She and Mrs. Halstead had gotten close. So close that Ryan sometimes joked that his mom looked forward to seeing Jen more than him on Monday nights.

"I told your mom that I love her tuna casserole," she told Ryan.

"No one loves that."

"I do."

He parked his truck in the driveway. "You're sweet, Jen. I . . . I'm really glad we started going out."

"Me, too."

Unfastening his seat belt, he leaned over and kissed her. "I missed you."

"I missed you, too."

"Things will get easier when football season is over."

"By that time, I'll be able to drive down to see you."

His expression was soft as he brushed her hair back from her face. "You will . . . and you might even be an official probie by then."

"One step at a time, right?"

Kissing her again, he nodded. "Right."

Just as Ryan put his arms around her, the front door of his house opened. "We better get going," said Jen. "Your family is waiting."

Ryan sighed, but he didn't look upset. Actually, he kind of looked like she felt inside. At peace. Like things were perfect.

Chapter 34

$\mathcal{K}$ risten had come very close to firing Marty. His leaving a hose running for five hours was not only going to give her a whopper of a water bill but probably a hefty fine from the city.

Of course, accidents happened, which meant that she needed to give Marty some grace. No one was perfect, least of all her. However, now that Jen was working only two days a week, Kristen needed employees she could rely on. She didn't know if Marty was one of those. Though he'd been with her the longest, he was also forgetful and nervous. There seemed to be one mishap after another whenever he was around.

She was beginning to think that she needed to draw a line between what she owed a longtime employee and what she owed herself—and her customers.

She stewed about what to do as she raked the gravel in the paths around the cacti and succulents at the back of the lot. She'd designed the display to help homeowners who were looking to conserve water. Unfortunately, only commercial customers seemed interested in zero-water land-scaping.

Now the area served mostly as her getaway. It was private, quiet, and she could look busy while she decompressed. Boy, she needed that! Sure, she was hiding, but it was better than snapping at Marty.

"At last!" a familiar voice called out from the other end of the lot. "Marty assured me you were back here, but I was starting not to believe him."

Turning, she was stunned to see Greg. He looked like he always did. Tan, fit, gorgeous, and casual. Today he was wearing a plain gray T-shirt that molded to his torso like it had been designed especially for him, and those darn snug-fitting faded jeans.

Kristen's mouth went dry.

She couldn't believe he was here. He'd been so upset with her the last time they'd been together. Then he'd texted her that he was taking some time off and would likely be out of touch for two weeks.

Kristen had guessed that had been his way of breaking things off with her.

She'd been sure of it when she hadn't gotten a single phone call or text in seventeen days.

Not that she'd been counting.

So, the fact that he was here made no sense. Nothing had changed. She still couldn't get pregnant and she had still kept it a secret from him. Those were two strikes against her.

Leaning on the rake, she continued to watch him ap-proach. His hair was as short as ever but he was unacharac-teristically clean-shaven. He looked good. Very sexy. Very . . . Mr. March.

She wished she hadn't noticed.

Kristen debated what to do. She knew he wasn't the type of man to make a scene at her workplace, so she wasn't worried about that.

For a second, she considered going on the offensive and forcefully asking what he wanted . . . but there was something in his expression that was too—was it *happy*?—to ignore.

Besides, no matter what her pride was screaming, the rest of her was so excited to see Greg that she didn't want anything to disturb this moment. She had missed him so much.

In the end, she decided to be cautious. If he'd come to fight again, she was going to shut it down. But maybe, just maybe, he was there to say something good.

Or maybe, if nothing else, she would enjoy seeing him again before they officially ended things.

And so she matched her tone to his positive expression. "You caught me," she joked as she carefully leaned the rake against the side of the metal shed. "I come out here when I need a minute to get myself together. Believe it or not, this isn't a very popular section of the garden center."

"I can believe it." He frowned at a large sequoia cactus. "It's so stark compared to all the trees and flowers you have everywhere else."

"I like to say that there's something for everyone," she quipped. "But, um, be careful of that saguaro. Those needles are no fun to pull out."

He gave the cactus a wide berth. "Having to dodge giant cactuses to talk to you seems very appropriate."

"That would be cacti. And I don't know why you'd say that."

"Because right now the situation between us is pretty prickly."

His voice sounded rough.

Kristen wondered if it was from a fire he'd fought recently—or if he was as filled with emotion as she was. "At least you're not calling *me* prickly," she joked. "Because that would be bad."

She mentally wrinkled her nose. This conversation felt

like a caricature of the conversation that they should be having. The one where he apologized, she explained herself better, and they ultimately decided to either reconcile . . . or end things for good.

By the time he reached her side, she knew she had to put everything out in the open. As much as she wanted things to be like they used to be between them, she needed to guard her heart. "What do you want, Greg?"

"I want to talk to you."

"About what?" she replied.

"You know what. About the conversation we had. About the things you said and how I reacted. About how I feel about you."

His words were everything she wanted to hear, but so painful. Did she want to once again see the disappointment in his eyes when they talked about the way she'd kept secrets from him? No. No, she did not. "I'd rather not discuss this now."

"Are you sure? No one's around."

"I need to go back to the store. Marty's all alone."

"I see."

Well, *she* didn't see. "Greg, why are you here? Why didn't you just call?"

"I can't say what I need to say over the phone."

She sighed. "Greg, nothing's changed. I still can't have a baby and I still can't change the past."

"Maybe I don't want you to change."

Yes! That traitorous, wishful part of her wanted to jump up and down. But another part didn't appreciate him acting so high-handed. He had a lot of gall to stroll into her shop—looking gorgeous—and act like he had every right to interrupt her day!

Especially since she was doing something as important as raking gravel, she reminded herself sarcastically.

"I don't know, Greg," she said at last.

His light-brown eyes warmed. "That's not a no, right?"

"It's also not a yes."

He folded his arms across his chest. "Kristen, what do I have to promise in order to get you to talk with me?"

His drawl was thicker, sexier. That voice, combined with his looks and the warm, sweet way he was currently gazing at her was almost impossible to resist.

That was the crux of it, wasn't it? Even after the way they'd left things, and seventeen days of silence, she still wanted him.

She didn't want retribution. She wanted a resolution. "You don't have to promise anything, Greg. We can talk."

"When?"

She glanced at her watch. "The shop closes in an hour. Will you come back with me to the front? If Marty has everything under control, we can go up to my apartment now."

He seemed to hesitate. "You sure? I want to talk to you, but I can wait until tonight."

"I'm sure."

When she reached for the rake, he held out his hand. "I can carry that for you."

"It's just a rake. I've got it, Greg."

His mouth pursed but he didn't argue.

When they got back, the shop was as quiet as she'd hoped. Marty was standing behind the counter, looking at his phone. He looked up with a guilty expression and said, "Hey. I was just about to tell you that I'm going to start cleaning up."

"That sounds good."

Looking from her to Greg, he added, "Is everything okay?"

"Everything's fine. Greg and I were just catching up. We're going to chat a little bit in my apartment. You go ahead and get started. I'll come down in a little bit and double-check everything. Okay?"

"Sounds good. See you in two days." Marty darted a

quick look at Greg, then blurted, "Kristen, I really am sorry about the hose."

Thinking how irritated she'd been with him—and how glad she was that she'd taken a break—she smiled at Marty. "I should be the one to apologize. I shouldn't have gotten so upset. Everything is fine. Enjoy your days off."

"Thanks, Kristen."

Turning to Greg, she said, "Well, I guess we can go on up." When she paused at the foot of the stairs, he said, "You lead the way. I'll follow."

As she led the way up to her apartment, Kristen realized that Greg had been talking about something more than just a staircase.

Chapter 35

$\mathcal{G}$reg was nervous. It wasn't a feeling he was all that familiar with. Regret, guilt, frustration—he dealt with those all the time. But he hadn't felt so nervous since the first time he'd led his unit into enemy territory.

As he slowly followed Kristen up the stairs to her apartment, the memory hit him hard.

The day the major issued those orders, he'd followed them immediately. But when his sergeant asked where some of the soldiers should go . . . he froze. He'd stood there like a fool, afraid to send one of the soldiers under his care into harm's way.

That was when his sergeant, Mark Oldum, knew he was in over his head. "Do your job, Lieutenant!" he'd practically yelled in Greg's ear.

And that was how he felt now. He was in over his head, scared of saying the wrong thing, and almost as worried about leaving something out.

But he knew what he had to do.

He stood to the side while Kristen unlocked the door and turned on the light.

"Come on in," she said, then frowned as she scanned the room. "Sorry for the mess. I guess I should've cleaned this morning."

He couldn't deny that it looked like someone had tossed half her clothes on the floor and furniture before sprinkling a week's worth of mail on top of it.

Greg smiled.

"I don't care what the place looks like. All I want to do is talk to you."

Kristen nodded distractedly, looked down at her clothes, and frowned. "This is rude of me, I know, but I've been working outside in the heat all day. Would you mind if I took a very quick shower?"

"Of course not." He gestured to the kitchen. "What do you want to drink? I'll pour you something cold while you do that."

She got that deer-in-the-headlights look. "There's no need for that. The kitchen . . . I think there are dishes . . ."

He wanted to laugh. And hug her. And, yes, kiss her until the state of her kitchen was the last thing on her mind.

"I don't care, honey. What do you want to drink?"

"Uh . . . there's some lemonade. Would you mind getting me a glass of that?"

"Not at all."

She edged to her bedroom. "Get yourself something, too."

"I will. Go on, now."

Kristen turned and disappeared into the bedroom, softly closing the door behind her.

Figuring he had at least ten minutes, he walked to the sink, where there was a pretty good pile of dishes. After pouring Kristen a glass of lemonade and filling his own with water, he turned on the faucet and set to washing and rinsing.

Taking comfort in the mundane chore, he practiced what he was going to say, trying out different apologies and ways to admit that he, too, harbored secrets that he was reluctant to share.

She came to the doorway just as he was drying the last of the dishes.

"Greg, what are you doing?"

"Nothing."

"Mm-hmm. I wish you wouldn't have done that *nothing*."

"Yeah, well . . ." He picked up her glass, turned to her, and felt his mouth go dry.

There she was, dressed in a pair of crisp white shorts and a blue linen blouse, smelling of fresh soap. Her feet were bare, her tan was golden, and her legs were perfect.

Kristen was as beautiful as ever. As sweet and fresh as the day he saw her in the hospital and was captivated by her pretty blue eyes, her girl-next-door looks . . . and her independent spirit.

"Where do you want to sit?" he asked. "Kitchen or living room?"

Her eyes darted to the small bistro table in the corner of the kitchen. It was littered with newspapers, a box of cereal, and what looked like a bag from a fast-food restaurant. "In the living room," she replied.

"Go sit down. I'll bring over our drinks."

She didn't move. "Greg, you don't need to wait on me."

"I'm not. I'm trying to help you." When she looked like she was going to protest again, he added, "It's only lemonade."

"You're right." After she picked up a pile of clothes and tossed them through the doorway onto her bedroom floor, she sat down on the couch. She accepted the drink from him and took a fortifying sip.

Greg sipped from his own as he sat down next to her.

When she put down her glass, he knew he couldn't put it off any longer. It was time. "Kristen, I need to apologize."

"You already did that."

"Not enough."

"I appreciate that, but I'm not a person who needs multiple apologies. I believed you the first time."

She might not have needed to hear the words, but he sure needed to say them. "Sweetheart, not only did I overreact about your secret, I did something worse. I've been keeping secrets of my own. I suffer from PTSD."

Eyes wide, she leaned forward. Obviously, Kristen was waiting for him to drop the other shoe.

It almost made him feel like laughing. He'd just confessed his big secret and it didn't even faze her.

This wasn't going the way he'd imagined!

So he started to explain. Probably as much for himself as for her. "I have nightmares and sometimes loud, sudden noises set me off. I think it all stems from when my unit was in the middle of an insurgent attack. I caused a corporal's death."

Sympathy filled her gaze. "Oh, Greg. I'm sorry."

"Yeah." Taking a fortifying breath, he continued, his voice thick with emotion. "I froze under fire. If I'd been a better officer, the corporal would have gone home to his family." Too ashamed to meet her eyes, he averted his face. "That day has haunted me for years."

"What happened to you?"

"I pretended I was okay."

"No." Resting her hand on his arm, she added, "I mean, during that attack. What happened to you?"

He could practically hear the bombs firing in the distance and feel the heat from the landscape burning into his skin. "Nothing."

"Greg. What were you doing?"

"I was trying to get the rest of my unit to safety. It was chaos. I was running next to my sergeant and yelling into my radio for a chopper and dragging a wounded private . . ." His voice drifted off. How had he forgotten about pulling Private Tomilson?

"So you did all you could, but you weren't perfect."

"No. No, I was not."

"What happened to the private you were dragging to safety?"

"He had to go into surgery but he made it out. He's okay." Again, Greg mentally shook his head. He'd been so focused on Corporal Fuller, he'd blocked the memory of freckle-faced Tomilson. Even the fact that Tomilson had invited Greg to his wedding.

"I'm sorry you've been dealing with PTSD," Kristen said softly. "I've heard that those episodes can be very painful."

Knowing that he had to come completely clean, he added, "When we were at The Broadmoor, I was afraid to sleep. I was afraid I'd have a nightmare and scare you half to death."

"I wish you would've trusted me enough to tell me about your nightmares."

"Me, too."

"Do you think you're going to be okay?"

He nodded. "I started going to counseling again and it's helped a lot. But it's hard, you know?" He exhaled. "That's why I told you that I would be out of touch for a while."

"I thought you wanted space from me."

Kristen looked so upset, he wished yet again that he'd done things differently. "It wasn't that. Not at all, sweetheart. I should've told you what I was doing, but . . ."

"But you were afraid," she finished.

There was nothing he could do but keep laying it out there. "I was afraid you'd decide I wasn't good enough for you."

"You felt the way I felt about telling you I couldn't give birth to your child."

"Yes. I'm so sorry that I faulted you for worrying about the same thing."

Gazing into his eyes, she bit down on her bottom lip. "Now that everything is out in the open . . . what do you want to do next?"

"Kristen, I'm just going to say it. I love you. I love you enough to be honest with you and finally be honest with myself. I love you enough to come over here and beg you to let me try to explain. And, I love you enough to wait for as long as you need me to wait until you feel the same way."

"You're not going to have to wait to hear me say the words. I love you, too."

"That's it?"

She smiled. "I don't need to be right or wrong. I just want to be happy. And I'm happy with you."

He could hardly believe his ears. He'd been sure she would reject him. Or, at the very least, make him grovel a bit before letting him back into her life. He reached for her hands. "Listen, about our future. I need you to know that I want you, kids or no kids."

"I want kids, Greg. I would love to have a family with you. A big, noisy house with lots of kids and dogs and messes and chaos."

He lifted one of her hands and kissed her knuckles. "Then we'll figure out how to make that happen. We can do whatever you want."

She smiled brightly. "I always hoped to adopt. If you'd be open to that one day?"

"Any day."

"Maybe just, ah, not seven times."

He laughed as he pulled her into his arms. "Like you just said. Being happy is enough. And being happy means being together, so that is enough."

"It's more than enough," she said as she pressed her lips to his.

That was all the incentive he needed to show her just how much he cared. How much he treasured her. Both the woman she was and the future they were going to have together.

Chapter 36

The next morning, Kristen was up with the sun. Knowing the day was going to be another hot one, she fixed herself a large iced coffee and went out for a walk around Memorial Park. She was determined to walk thirty minutes a day. It would help her heart and her soul. For too long she'd put everything she had into her shop, but the recent events in her life had demonstrated that working all the time wasn't good for her health—physical or mental.

After stretching a bit, she picked up her drink and walked the path around the small lake at the edge of the park. From there she'd walk by the senior center, the library, and the elementary school. It was an easy walk and it also allowed her to see quite a few other people doing the same thing.

To her surprise, she saw Greg, Anderson, and Chelsea out walking, too. "What are you three doing out my way?"

Greg put his arm around her and kissed her brow. "Looking for you, obviously," he teased.

Chelsea chuckled. "Actually, the guys just finished a run with Mark," she explained. "I was able to convince two out of the three of them to join me for a walk over to Jo's Ko-laches."

"Mark is about to go on duty," Anderson explained.

"Why don't you join us?" Greg asked. "Do you have time?"

"For Jo's? Absolutely."

They paired off, Chelsea and Anderson walking side by side while Kristen and Greg followed them. Kristen couldn't help but release a little sigh of happiness. This was the perfect morning. The air was a crisp sixty-seven, the sun was out, and the sky was once again a perfect Colorado blue. Even better was the fact that she felt good and was walking beside one of the most handsome men in Woodland Park. Who just happened to be her boyfriend.

"What's made you so smiley?" Greg asked. "Is it the company or the pretty day?"

"It's probably everything. We finally talked, it's a beautiful day, and seeing y'all is a great surprise. I didn't know you went running around here in the mornings."

"We usually don't. But we decided on a longer run today. Anderson is off."

"And Mark goes on this morning?"

"Yep. I have a meeting with my counselor at ten, then I'll report in after."

"That's nice of Captain DeWitt to allow that."

"I agree. Everyone is being really good about it. I'm lucky."

Just as they were about to step inside Jo's, they saw Jen and Ryan, who had clearly been running hard. When Jen saw them, she practically skidded to a stop.

"Hey, Kristen!" she said.

Kristen smiled. "Hi. This must be everyone's morning to get outside. I ran into Greg, our friends Anderson and Chelsea, and now you two!"

"It's the best time to run," Jen said. "I'm trying to increase my endurance and Ryan's helping me."

"She's doing great," he said.

"Do you two want to join us for a kolache?" Kristen asked. "My treat."

Jen exchanged glances with Ryan before shaking her head. "Thanks, but no thanks. I don't think I could eat anything right now."

"I have to head on back to school," Ryan said. "Thanks, though."

"Okay. I'll see you this afternoon, Jen," Kristen said.

"I'll be there." She smiled shyly at Greg before she and Ryan continued down the sidewalk.

Inside, Anderson waved them over. "I ordered a dozen kolaches, so get whatever you want to drink and then come join us."

"Do you want a coffee?" asked Greg.

Kristen held up her plastic cup. "I'm still good. I'll save you a spot." When she slid into the booth, Chelsea was already eating a fruit-filled kolache and sipping coffee.

"Sorry, I couldn't wait," she said. "I was starving."

"Where's your kiddo?"

"Jack spent the night over at Camille and Frank's house," Anderson said. Camille was Chelsea's friend and former neighbor. "They're puppy-sitting one of their kids' new dogs."

Chelsea smiled at her husband. "I don't know who was more excited about the sleepover: Jack, Camille, or the puppy."

"Jack is currently dog-crazy," said Anderson.

"All little boys are, aren't they?" Greg asked as he joined them.

"Probably," said Anderson as he passed the box of breakfast treats around.

Savoring the first bite of her choice, Kristen relaxed against the booth, happy to listen to the other three chat about boys and puppies and the weather.

She commented every so often, but mainly she was just

enjoying the moment. A mere twenty-four hours ago she'd been afraid that she and Greg weren't ever going to patch things up. A year ago, Chelsea and Anderson were struggling with their own issues, or so she heard through the grapevine. Now, the four of them were together—and the guys were even working with Jen at the station. She seemed to be blossoming under their direction.

"Kristen?" Chelsea prodded her arm. "Did you hear me?"

"I'm sorry?"

"I asked if you wanted to meet for another walk tomorrow morning."

"Oh! Thanks, I'd like that. I'm afraid I got distracted thinking how everything has worked out with everyone. Even Jen and her boyfriend, Ryan."

Greg curved an arm around her shoulder. "I'm glad about that, too."

"Now all we have to do is find someone for Mark," Chelsea mused.

"Sorry, sweetheart, but I think you should leave that idea alone," Anderson said. "Mark is in no hurry to start dating."

"Why?"

"He hasn't said much about it, but I think he was really serious about a girl when we were in the army and then it ended badly," Greg said. "It's pretty much put him off serious relationships forever."

Kristen exchanged a look with Chelsea. Though no words were spoken, Kristen knew Chelsea was thinking the same thing she was: that anything was possible with the right person.

"Oh no," Anderson groaned. "I know that look. Don't start matchmaking for Mark."

"I'm not going to do anything crazy," Chelsea protested. "But if I meet someone who might be right for Mark, I'm not going to pass up the opportunity."

"Please. Pass it up," Greg said. "Mark was really hurt."

"I understand," Kristen said. She couldn't help but smile, though. After all, hadn't she been sure falling in love again was going to be impossible? But then she met Greg.

Thirty minutes later, when Greg was walking her back to her car, he said, "You're not going to listen to our advice about Mark, are you?"

"I am. But I have to agree with Chelsea. If there's an opportunity for him to find happiness, I'm not going to turn a blind eye to it. I can't help it." She looked up at him, worried that he was going to argue. But instead of looking irritated, he looked amused. "You're not mad?" she asked.

"Nope." Pulling her against the side of her car, he kissed her. "If we can find each other and fall in love, anything is possible."

Wrapping her arms around his neck, Kristen hugged him tight. They probably had a little ways to go until everything between them was perfect, but that was okay.

They had all the time they needed for that. Besides, they were living proof that perfection was overrated.

Epilogue

The sound came an hour before dawn. Beside him, Kristen jumped. "Greg?"

"I'm here," he soothed. "Go back to sleep."

"What time is it?" she murmured.

"Time for you to go back to sleep."

His wife opened one eye. "Are you sure?"

"Always. Stop asking me questions, honey. I've got this." He bent over, kissed her brow, then turned off the monitor his mother had assured him he wouldn't need.

Greg thought his momma was right about that, but he'd never say that to his wife. Kristen loved to fall asleep listening to Johnny's baby noises.

Throwing on a T-shirt, he walked down the hall to Johnny's room just as their eight-week-old baby boy let out another cry. "Hey now, none of that is needed. I'm right here," he whispered as he cradled the nine-pound bundle against his chest.

Johnny squeaked again and kicked his legs.

"It's okay, buddy." He laid him down on the changing table, thanked the Lord that the diaper was simply wet, and then got to work getting his son settled comfortably again in his onesie.

Minutes later, Greg carried him down to the kitchen and set a bottle under the Keurig-like dispenser. A few months ago he'd had no idea that formula machines existed! Minutes later he was sitting on the couch feeding their son.

One of Johnny's hands was on the bottle. His other was touching Greg's hand. Seeing that tiny hand against his own never ceased to make his heart melt.

"You're a lot of work, buddy. It's a good thing we love you so much," he murmured as Johnny looked back at him with bright-blue eyes.

As the baby continued to drink greedily, Greg reflected once again how their son had come into their lives. After just a two-month-long engagement, they'd had a loud and casual ceremony in one of the downtown hotels in Colorado Springs. All of Greg's family was there, along with Kristen's Texas relatives and all of their friends, even including a couple of Greg's army buddies who were able to make the trip.

As soon as he and Kristen returned from their honeymoon, they'd begun the adoption process with two different agencies. Everyone had warned them that they could be waiting for years for a baby, so he and Kristen had wanted to fill out all the paperwork as soon as possible.

Then they'd settled in to wait. They enjoyed their work—and being newlyweds—and Kristen got about halfway through decorating the town house.

Then the craziest thing happened. His brother Copeland's ex-girlfriend was pregnant and decided to put the baby up for adoption. She reached out to Copeland because she'd heard through the grapevine that Copeland's big brother Greg was trying to adopt. It turned out that she didn't like Copeland much but had always thought Greg was great.

They'd gotten the call and had flown to West Virginia a week later. They named Johnny after Greg's dad.

And now, here Johnny was, nestled in Greg's arms and claiming Greg's heart every time he looked his daddy's way.

"Is he okay, honey?"

He should've known Kristen wouldn't be able to go back to sleep. "Yep. The two of us are just chatting about life in the middle of the night. You should be sleeping, though."

"I know. I would just rather be with my two guys."

"Come sit down with us, then."

She cuddled next to him on the couch, tucking her legs under a blanket. To his surprise, she didn't take Johnny. Instead, his wife appeared content to sit and watch Greg feed him his bottle.

"Do you ever think about how amazing and strange life is?" she asked after a few minutes passed.

"What do you mean?"

"I never would've come to Colorado if I hadn't had such a bad heart. I only chose Woodland Park because of Dr. Gonzales and the dry weather. Honestly, I don't think I would've ever left Texas if Clark hadn't jilted me."

"You mean if Clark hadn't been such a royal jerk."

"Well, yes." She chuckled. "And as for you? Well, you only came to Woodland Park because you were friends with Anderson and he was from here."

He nodded. "You and I still wouldn't have met unless you had a fire."

"And if I hadn't thrown such a fit that Anderson had to ask you to give him a hand so he could call the doctor."

"This is true." Pleased that Johnny had finished his bottle, Greg rested him against his chest and patted his back.

Kristen continued. "For so much of my life, I wished I was different than I was. I wished I was whole and undamaged and perfect. But everything 'wrong' was actually what made me better."

"I've been thinking something similar. I tried to hide what I thought were flaws. But learning to accept my weaknesses has made me stronger, not weaker."

"So, we've both moved forward."

"We have. We've stumbled and tripped and even fallen a time or two, but we didn't quit, did we?" He smiled. "I think I'll take my bumps and bruises."

"And babies," she added.

"Yes, sweetheart. And babies." As Kristen leaned against him, Greg moved Johnny to his other arm. Seconds later, both the baby and his wife were asleep. Both resting against him. Both trusting him to look out for them.

He felt a sense of peace deep inside of him. Knew that his father was likely looking down from heaven and smiling.

Greg wasn't perfect, but he figured he must have done something right to earn this moment.

It was so beautiful, he closed his eyes and gave thanks.

Acknowledgments

I felt as if I was "moving forward" as much as the characters when I worked on this novel! I'm so grateful to have had the chance to write this Woodland Park Firefighters series, not only because the stories were close to my heart, but also because the actual writing of them pushed me in a variety of ways.

I have many folks to thank for their help and kindness on this journey. First is my editor, Tracy Bernstein. Tracy, thank you for your careful eye, attention to detail, determination, and your belief in these novels. I'm continually amazed by your many talents!

Next, I owe a great deal of thanks to Jennifer Lynes and copyeditor Randie Lipkin. These ladies improved each page. I'm so thankful for their skills and patience with me! I'm also so grateful for the time and talents of the cover designers, marketing departments, and publicists at Berkley. The entire team made these books something of which to be proud.

In addition, I owe so much to Lynne, who takes the time to do a first reading of every book, my online FB group members who volunteer to read and blog my novels, Nicole Resciniti for being the superagent that she is, and my husband Tom, who takes care of pretty much everything—even when I'm not on deadline.

Finally, as with every book, I'm grateful to God for gifting me with the ability to tell a story. I feel like I have the best job in the world. It's a blessing, indeed.

Ready to find
your next great read?

Let us help.

Visit prh.com/nextread